"What exactly do you want, Lance?"

"Well, first I want to set things right between us," he said, his voice throbbing with a sincerity that she knew was as false as his smile. "But if you'll look at it objectively, you'll have to admit that I did you a favor, getting out of your life. I'm still pretty much the same gadabout I always was.

"But I have changed in one way—call it a late developing sense of responsibility. Which is why I'd like to see my son, maybe even take him on an outing now and then—"

"No! Never!" In her agitation, Christy's voice had risen, echoing through the hall. "Now get out! And don't come back!"

CUSTODY

Irma Walker

BALLANTINE BOOKS • NEW YORK

For Mary Jocius, a good friend who's always there when she's needed.

Chapter 1

*T*o *Christy Havens, one of the best times of the day was* coming home after work.

As she drove along the broad highway that led east from Puget City, following the graceful curve of the bay, she found herself relaxing, although the afternoon traffic, as always, was very heavy, even after she turned south, away from the bay.

The building boom that had struck Washington State in the 1970s had wrought changes in all outlying areas of Puget City, and she passed one development after another, some of them sporting blocks of condominiums and apartment buildings, others row upon row of tract homes.

Her final turn was onto Old Orchard Road, a newly widened blacktop that had once been a single-lane country road that led through miles of apples groves and small farms. The newly constructed houses in this valley were custom-built and more widely spaced than in the tracts, but the housing sprawl was still apparent here. Only a few of the old farms still remained, small verdant oases among the clusters of expensive homes.

As Christy slowed to allow a construction company truck, its huge sand-colored cement mixer revolving in the rear, to pass, the old doubts stirred. Had she and Miles made a mistake, buying in an area where the cheapest of the new homes going up around them was several cuts above their own modernized farmhouse? They had felt so lucky, finding a place they could afford within a reasonable commuting distance of both the university where Miles taught and her job in downtown Puget City, but they hadn't considered the effect on their son, Tad, who was now ten. Did it trouble him that his parents were so much less prosperous than those of the other children at his school?

Well, it was a little late for second thoughts, Christy reminded herself, trying to be philosophical. And besides— she loved the old house. Coming home to it, even after seven years of living there, was always a relief, something she looked forward to every workday.

It wasn't that she didn't love her job, she reflected as she drove past the huge pseudo-Tudor that belonged to their next-door neighbor and then turned into the driveway beside the old frame house that Miles and she had bought the first year of their marriage.

Or maybe *love* wasn't the proper word to express how she felt about selling computer software to businessmen. *Like* was more accurate than love, come to think of it. What she really found satisfying was knowing that she was good at her job—and that she had one of the best sales records at Computers Now, Inc.

But love it? No, certainly not in the same way that

Miles, her husband, loved his work as a professor of English literature at Puget City University. The fact that she thought of the way she earned her living as a job while she automatically called what Miles did "his work" pointed out the difference.

She felt a stab of envy, but she put it aside as unworthy and got out of her car, a four-year-old Pinto. She had more pressing things to worry about right now than whether she had chosen the right career. Coming home this particular day was not the unadulterated pleasure it usually was—not with her mother's dark-blue Chrysler sedan parked in the driveway and the knowledge that she had a whole evening of Jessica's company ahead of her.

Jessica's visits were something to be handled with as much diplomacy and patience as possible—and a prayer or two that *this* time her mother would stay off Miles's back, and also that she wouldn't spoil Tad too much by bringing him more expensive presents than a ten-year-old boy needed. That just encouraged Tad's already too acquisitive nature.

As Christy stood beside her car, staring up at the tall frame house, she felt a slackening of the tension that the sight of her mother's car had evoked.

In a neighborhood of expensive homes, most of them no more than five years old, the old farmhouse she and Miles had bought was too old to be fashionable, yet not old enough to have the charm of a Victorian.

It was also defective in other ways: a cranky furnace that was long past its prime, an inconvenient arrangement of its rooms, antiquated plumbing, and too few closets, not to mention a mortgage that was a struggle to meet even on two salaries. So why was it that she always felt so—so safe and secure within those walls—as if she needed some protection from the outside world?

For a brief moment, an old bitterness, a remnant of her disastrous first marriage, brushed her mind, but she quickly rejected it. This was not the time to brood about the past—not with Jessica waiting inside with her usual list of complaints and grievances and glancing little remarks that always seemed to point out Christy's judgmental deficiencies.

But she lingered anyway before she went inside, long enough to admire the huge oak trees that shaded the wide yard, their leaves a rich May green, and then to examine a loose board in the porch flooring and the paint that was flaking off a wooden railing. The spring rains had taken their toll again—which meant another paint job, another round of repairs. . . .

Sighing, she let herself into the house. In the big entrance hall that always held a mustiness, no matter how often it was aired, she paused long enough to hang up her jacket and scarf before she turned into the living room. Her mother was seated in one of the room's two love seats, a woman's magazine lying open across her knees. The hammered bronze ashtray beside her chair had already collected several cigarette butts—which meant she had been there for at least an hour.

As usual, Jessica was dressed as if she were going out to dinner at one of Puget City's fancier restaurants. Her oyster-white suit was impeccably tailored; her tiny feet, of which she was inordinately proud, were encased in expensive Italian shoes with four-inch heels. Tiny diamonds sparkled in her earlobes.

For a moment, Christy's mind played a trick on her and she felt detached, as if she were an outsider seeing them both, the mother and the daughter, for the first time.

Ever since she could remember, people had remarked how little she resembled her mother, who had been Puget City's prettiest eighteen-year-old the year of her debut. The implication in these remarks had been a source of hurt to Christy when she was a gawky teenager, but now, after seven years of marriage to Miles, she had finally come to appreciate that while she wasn't petite and doll-pretty like her mother, she did have her own claim to attractiveness.

Or at least, she amended, in the eyes of one very prejudiced beholder, she passed muster. How often had Miles told her that her long legs were elegant, that her russet hair reminded him of the fall leaves of one of his beloved New England sugar maples, that a man could drown in her now-blue/now-green eyes? And why, even though he spoke as if he were teasing, was she sure that he meant every word when he added that she was the sexiest woman in the world?

"So there you are." Jessica's voice held the characteristic huskiness of a nonstop smoker. "What on earth have you been doing, Christine? I'm sure I heard your car pull up at least five minutes ago."

"I was looking at the front porch." As Christy came into the room and kissed her mother's cheek, the familiar scent of Jessica's perfume engulfed her and she felt a wave of affection for her sometimes prickly parent. "It's going to need a new coat of paint before long."

"Well, if you insist on living in this old barn, you have to expect problems." Jessica's eyes moved over the room. Although spacious, it was sparsely furnished with mismatched tables, a low chest of drawers, lamps made from pottery jars, and the pair of love seats.

Christy had found the love seats, well-worn but comfortable, through a newspaper ad, which was how she'd furnished most of the house. She was quite content with her choices—except when her mother was there to point out their deficiencies.

Suddenly impatient with herself because, once again, she'd regressed and allowed herself to feel the old desire to please her mother at the cost of her own taste, her own preferences, she stared at Jessica with appraising eyes, deliberately allowing herself to note the too-taut facial skin that was a dead giveaway to two face-lifts in the past six years. Although Jessica was fashionably thin, there was a haggardness around her eyes that negated the youthfulness of her figure. So why, Christy wondered, did she still feel as if she were in some kind of competition with Jessica, one she, Christy, didn't have a ghost of a chance of winning?

And why, when she knew there was no way on earth she could ever win her mother's complete approval, outside of divorcing Miles and marrying some fabulously wealthy man, did she still allow Jessica to get under her skin?

She realized that Jessica was staring back at her, a pucker between her finely plucked eyebrows. To forestall the lecture she knew was impending, she said hastily, "How about some coffee—or would you rather have tea?"

"Tea, please." Jessica retrieved a small paper sack from the cushion beside her and handed it to Jessica. "I was browsing around that new gourmet food place in Old Puget City, and I saw these tins of English tea—I remembered how you like Earl Grey, so I got this for you."

Christy looked at the tin of tea with genuine pleasure. Although she seldom bought English tea, because it was too expensive for everyday use, Earl Grey was her favorite. Impulsively, she bent and kissed Jessica's perfumed cheek again. "You're a love," she said.

"You don't always think that," Jessica grumbled, but Christy knew her mother was pleased. "Where is Tad? I made it a point to come early, because I brought him a new game and I thought we could figure out the rules before you got home. You did tell him that I'd be staying overnight, didn't you?"

"Of course—and he's delighted. But since I wasn't sure what time you'd be arriving, I didn't dare change his after-school schedule. He'll be home from Mrs. Wright's at the usual time—I always try to be here when he gets home nights, Mother.''

''Well, I certainly approve of that. In fact, I wish you didn't have to work at all. And as a computer salesperson, of all things. Honestly, it's so—so tacky. If you insist on working, why didn't you choose something like—well, like interior decorating? Or do something with your painting— it's a shame to neglect a talent, you know.''

''I work because we need the money. We're still paying off those hospital and funeral bills that Miles's mother left, you know, and our health insurance didn't cover all the expenses from my own stay in the hospital last year,'' Christy said, with more patience than she felt, since Jessica knew very well why she worked. ''And I chose computers because—because it's such a growing field.''

And also because it was the most practical thing I could think of at a time when I desperately needed some stability in my life. . . .

''Even if it wasn't necessary for me to work,'' Christy went on, ''I think I'd do it anyway. I'm good at my job, and besides, I enjoy dealing with people—and I'm not really interested in playing golf or bridge parties.''

''Well, of course you have to do what you think best,'' Jessica said, sighing. ''But the women in our family have never worked—it just wasn't done.''

''The times they are a-changin', Mother,'' Christy said lightly.

She didn't bother to point out that the fortunes of the Ames family had changed, too—and for the worse—since the days when Jessica had been the pampered only child of George and Irene Ames, once pillars of Puget City society.

The only reason Jessica could live reasonably well without working was because of a divorce settlement from her second husband, a wealthy real estate broker. That he had settled so generously was not through altruism, but because of Jessica's shrewdness. She had been prudent enough, before she would agree to marry him, to get a favorable marriage agreement drawn up by the best lawyer she could afford. And from her standpoint, it had been a wise move, since the marriage had barely survived its seventh anniversary.

"Some things never change—such as good breeding," Jessica said reprovingly. "If you hadn't been so—so hasty about getting that annulment from Lance, you and Tad would be living on Winthrop Island right now instead of here in this barny old house. You'd still be a Winthrop— and a leading hostess in Northern Washington society. Honestly, when I think of what you threw away simply because of your possessiveness and unreasonable expectations—"

"What I threw away was an indifferent and unfaithful husband!" Despite herself, Christy's voice trembled, and it was anger at her own weakness that provoked her next words. "And why do you persist in pretending that I had a choice, Jessica? Lance was the one who asked for that annulment—he wanted no part of me *or* his son. So why don't we drop the whole subject before we both say something we regret?"

At Jessica's offended stare, she took a deep breath, then added, her tone conciliatory, "I'll go fix us that tea—and I'd better put out some cookies, too. Tad will be home any minute, and he'll be ravenous, as usual. There's a new *Glamour* on the coffee table you can look at. I'll be back in a few minutes."

She hurried from the room, not waiting for an answer— and already ashamed of her outburst. She, of all people, knew that Jessica's little barbs were like gnats; they might sting for a moment, but they were harmless and quickly forgotten. So why had she allowed her mother to get under her skin? Now Jessica would be sulky for the rest of her visit—and a sulky Jessica was not the greatest houseguest in the world.

In the big old-fashioned kitchen with its cheery provincial wallpaper—and its twenty-year-old range and refrigerator—Christy put on the kettle and then stood by the window, staring out at the backyard and its profusion of flowering shrubs and neat squares of spring flowers—scarlet and yellow tulips, velvet-leaved violets, and pansies.

But she wasn't really seeing the flowers or the lush lawn Miles was so proud of. Nor was she thinking of Jessica, or even of Lance, her first husband. No, it was the thought of Lance's father, Neville Winthrop, that caused her to frown.

In the past month, her former father-in-law had called her three times, asking permission to see his grandson. The first two calls had come at the house in the afternoons— but yesterday morning, for the first time, he had called her at work. She'd been out of touch with Neville for ten years—how could he know not only where she lived, but where she worked? And why, after all that time, did he suddenly want to see Tad? He had made it so plain, that day ten years ago, that he didn't consider Tad to be his grandson. And he'd never shown the slightest interest in him before this past month. So why now?

Christy winced, realizing that if Jessica found out about Neville Winthrop's sudden interest in his grandson, about his offer to set up a college fund for Tad in return for visitation rights, she would add her own two-cents worth and exacerbate an already miserable situation.

A door slammed, and Tad's whistle preceded him into the kitchen. Christy turned, smiling, and as always, her heart swelled with pleasure as she greeted her son. His hug was uninhibited, almost vigorous enough to knock her off her feet. From the father he'd never seen, Tad had inherited a natural athletic ability, along with Lance's tightly curled hair, the color of old gold, and his darkly fringed eyes, so surprising a blue against his olive skin. He had inherited something else from Lance, too—that devastating charisma that made him a natural-born leader, not only with other kids, but with adults—even his teachers.

So much for environment over heredity, Christy thought with an inward smile.

Well, she had a lot to be grateful for. Tad, although still a little small for his age, was robustly healthy, his only illness a bout of mumps when he was five. And Tad was lucky in another way, too. Few boys had a natural father, much less a stepfather, as caring as Miles.

"What's for dinner, Mom?" Tad said, looking around the kitchen.

"Stroganoff—and noodles," she said promptly. "One of your grandmother's favorite meals."

"Hey, that's right. Grandma Jessica is spending the night, isn't she? When will she be here?"

"She already is—in the living room. Why don't you take her tea in while I start dinner?"

"Okay," he said agreeably. "Maybe I should take her some cookies, too," he added, his tone offhand. "You know, in case she's hungry?"

"And maybe you might be persuaded to help her scarf them down? What did you have to eat at Mrs. Wright's?"

"Just some cherry pie. It was only a little piece," he said.

"Uh-huh. Tad the bottomless pit. Okay—but leave your grandmother at least one." At his quick grin, she gave him another hug. "So how was school today?"

The grin slipped off Tad's face. "Okay, I guess," he said, shrugging.

Christy regarded him thoughtfully, but before she could probe any further, the kettle sputtered, signaling that the water had begun to boil. She poured the bubbling water over the tea in the stoneware pot, then arranged a few chocolate-chip cookies on a plate. The cookies came from a box, but—well, she didn't have time these days to do much baking. And if Jessica said anything about it, she just might retaliate and point out that it was grandmothers who traditionally provided homemade cookies to their offspring, not the other way around.

Carrying the loaded tray carefully, Tad went out of the kitchen, whistling. The whistling was something new, one of the sudden passions that Tad acquired from time to time. Which meant that it would be just as quickly discarded when he had mastered those trills and double notes to his satisfaction, Christy thought, and again the old fear stirred.

She shook her head, repudiating her worrisome thoughts, and started dinner preparations. As she browned chopped onions and the bite-sized pieces of beef that had been marinating in the refrigerator all day, she reflected that with Tad here, Jessica would be in a good mood. Maybe, just maybe, they could get through this visit without any fireworks.

She put the browned meat on to simmer and returned to the living room. For a few moments, she stood in the doorway, watching the two of them. As Jessica talked with Tad, asking him questions about school, about his playmates and his baseball, another of Tad's passions, her voice was softer, certainly without its usual critical edge. The truth was that in Jessica's eyes, her grandson could do no wrong—and didn't Tad take advantage of *that*, Christy thought with a sigh.

Tad looked up and saw her standing in the doorway. The smile that lit up his small face was so sweet and guileless that her breath caught for a moment.

Okay, so include her with the adults who were susceptible to Tad's charm—the charm that was so natural to him, so unconscious at this point in his life. But she did recognize her son's faults, too. He could be indolent and easily bored—and he had a materialistic nature that bordered on greediness.

On the other hand, she reminded herself, Tad also had a healthy conscience, a love for animals—and a sense of humor that she liked to think he had picked up from his stepfather. He wasn't perfect, but why the devil should she expect perfection from the offspring of two such *imperfect* parents as herself and Lance?

"Okay, young man," she said, noting that the cookies had been reduced to a few crumbs. "Off you go to your room. It's homework time."

"Aw, Mom—Grandma Jessica brought me a neat new game. We have to figure out the rules and stuff before we can play it. Do I have to do my homework now?"

"You have to, you have to," she said lightly. "Otherwise, you'll be trying to do it late Sunday evening when you're bone-tired. You'll have plenty of time for games after dinner."

Looking sulky, Tad started for the door, but he remembered his manners and turned back to give Jessica a wet kiss on the cheek.

"Thanks for the game, Grandma," he said before he went off. A moment later, they heard his feet clattering on the stairs.

"Surely, for one evening, his homework could wait," Jessica said, her voice fretful. "After all, I don't get to see him nearly as often as I'd like. I can't remember the last time you three came into the city to see me—and you're always so busy that I hesitate to come out here too often. I have the feeling sometimes that I'm in the way."

Christy felt a pang of guilt. Jessica was right—they hadn't been in to visit her lately, but it wasn't anything deliberate. It was just that their jobs, the house, the routine of day-to-day living, seemed to eat up all their spare time.

"I'm sorry, Mother—we'll just have to make more time for each other in the future. We do manage to do something together as a family every weekend—and you know you're always welcome to come along on our Sunday excursions to the zoo or the park. But Miles and I have a strict rule about Tad's homework. He has a tendency to put it off if we don't watch him. And besides, you can visit with him all you want this evening after dinner." She smiled at her mother. "But I'm warning you—he's a whiz at games. I wouldn't advise you to make any side bets with him."

Her attempt at lightness earned her a brief smile. "Well, just don't push the boy too hard and expect too much from him. That doesn't work, you know."

Christy nodded agreeably. "You're right, I'm sure." In an attempt to change the subject, she added, "Why don't you come in the kitchen with me while I fix dinner? I want to hear what you've been up to lately—"

"No, I think I'll drive over to the shopping center and pick up a few things I need," Jessica said. "I'd just get in your way, anyway—you know I'm no good in a kitchen." She hesitated; her smile was so patently false now that Christy braced herself even before Jessica added, her voice a little too honeyed, "You'll never in this world guess who called me yesterday, Christy."

"I can't imagine—Nancy Reagan?"

Jessica gave her an annoyed look. "Really—if you don't want to hear this, just say so."

And if I said so, would you really drop it, Jessica?

"Sorry. Just my little joke," Christy murmured. "Who called you yesterday, Jessica?"

"Well, this will knock you over—it was Neville Winthrop."

A coldness started up in Christy's chest. Somehow, she kept her face impassive, but only at the cost of a sick churning in the pit of her stomach. "Fancy that," she managed. "What did he want—your advice on investments?"

This time, Jessica ignored her attempt at humor. "He sounded—well, rather pathetic, I thought. You know, as if he were feeling really depressed. I understand he's been trying to talk you into allowing him to see Tad, Christy— and that you've refused."

And I understand now why you called to announce a sudden overnight visit, Jessica. . . .

"Yes, I *have* heard from him—several times," Christy said. "Since he failed to get my permission to see Tad, I guess he decided to use different tactics, such as persuading you to intervene. I'm glad you're sensible enough to realize it would never work."

Briefly, Jessica's determined smile wavered, but she recovered quickly. "I don't understand why you're being so difficult about this. After all, Neville *is* the boy's grandfather. It isn't like you to be so—so vindictive, Christy. Don't you think it's about time you let bygones be bygones?"

"That isn't the reason why I refused his offer. Until a month ago, Neville completely ignored his grandson. And that's the way I want things to continue. This sudden interest in Tad—I'm not sure what's behind it, but I have every reason to be suspicious. Neville is—well, I'll just say that you don't know the whole story, Jessica. There were some things that happened that—"

She stopped, realizing that she was treading on shaky ground. It would be impossible, too humiliating, to tell Jessica the whole truth about her marriage to Lance, about the lies that had devastated her so.

"—that are too painful to talk about," she went on, "but I will tell you that when Lance and I broke up, Neville made it plain that he had no interest in Tad and never would have. So please—let me handle this in my own way.''

''I just don't understand you.'' Jessica's voice was aggrieved. ''Neville assures me that he's apologized to you for his behavior. And he explained that it was all a big misunderstanding, that he's very sorry now he was so—so quick to jump to conclusions.''

''Yes, well, I don't happen to believe—''

''And I understand that you've returned the presents he sent Tad—including an expensive riding horse. You do know that Tad was heartbroken about that, don't you? He told me about it while you were in the kitchen. Of course, he believes it was a mistake, that the horse was delivered to the wrong house, but you know how crazy he is about animals—''

''I know that he isn't ready for the responsibility of a pet, especially a horse. When he's a little older, maybe next year, we intend to get him a puppy, but a horse is out of the question. For one thing, this area isn't zoned for large animals, even if we had a barn or stable to keep one in. I suppose Neville was misled by our address—Old Orchard Road. I'm sure the last time he was out this way, it was all farm land. So we'd have to board it out—and the cost would be prohibitive.''

''Well, Neville told me he'd offered to pay for the maintenance of the horse, and I'm sure that would include stable fees—and anyway, what about the other gifts he's sent Tad? Why on earth did you return *them*?''

''The last thing Tad should have is a lot of expensive toys. He has everything he needs now—and a good home with Miles and me tops the list. I don't want him to end up like—like his father, a parasite who spends his life rushing from one excitement to the next. If I open the door even a crack, then I'll be admitting the same kind of materialism into Tad's life that I've been trying so hard to protect him from. And I'd like to change the subject, if you don't mind—''

"But I do mind! Someone has to make you see what a mistake it would be to shut Neville out of your son's life. Do you think Tad is going to thank you when he finds out—and he will, mark my word!—that you turned down a trust fund that could someday send him to Yale or Harvard instead of a second-rate place like Puget City University? What is he going to think of your decision then?''

Christy stared at her fixedly. "What did Neville promise you, Jessica?'' she asked abruptly. "A Mediterranean cruise on his yacht this summer? Or was he crass enough to offer you money?''

An unlovely flush covered Jessica's throat. For a moment, her eyes wavered, but she rallied quickly and returned to the attack. "Well, if you want to turn this into a verbal brawl, there are a few things I could say, too, you know,'' she said, tossing her head. "I'm wondering about your real motive for refusing to let Neville see his grandson. There couldn't be a little bit of revenge in all this, could there?''

"Why don't we just drop the whole subject?'' Christy said wearily. "After all, until Neville started this campaign of his, I hadn't thought of—of the Winthrops for ages. Which is just the way I like it.''

"You can't even say Lance's name out loud, can you?'' Jessica's eyes were shrewd. "Tell me the truth, Christy— don't you sometimes compare Miles with Lance?''

Christy felt a thrill of anger. She took a deep breath, fighting back the angry words that rushed to her lips. "All the time—and then I thank God that I'm married to someone like Miles,'' she said. "Lance Winthrop means nothing to me—and the last thing in the world I want is to discuss him with you, with anyone. That's all in the past—and best forgotten.''

"Are you sure? I wonder—"

"The subject is closed, Mother," Christy said.

Jessica rose to her feet and brushed a cookie crumb off her lap. "I can see that you don't want my advice—as usual. So I'll just leave you and get on with my shopping."

She picked up her purse, and started for the door. But being Jessica, she had to have the last word.

"There's one more thing I feel I'm obligated to say— for your own good. If you persist in this—this vendetta you have against the Winthrops, the day will come when you'll regret it, Christine."

She flounced out, leaving behind the spice-and-floral odor of her perfume. Christy felt angry at herself for allowing Jessica's words to pierce the protective shell she wore during her mother's visits. She stood for a long time, staring at the empty doorway. She had intended to slip upstairs to have a private talk with Tad and find out if, as she suspected, something had gone wrong at school that day, but she knew that she needed a little time alone to get her nerves settled. She went into the kitchen to finish dinner preparations.

She was standing at the sink, shredding carrots for salad, when the front doorbell rang. She muttered a "dammit" under her breath, dried her hands on a dishcloth, and went to answer the door.

Through the fine net curtain on the glass door panels, she saw the outline of a man's shoulders. Another salesman—well, she'd get rid of him in short order—

But when she opened the door, her breath escaped her in a long, whistling sigh. Maybe it was because she and Jessica had been talking about him, but for one shocked moment, she thought the man standing there, looking so confident, so sure of his welcome, was a hallucination, an aberration of her mind.

Then he smiled, a beguiling smile that reflected a lifetime of winning people over, of being the center of attention wherever he went, and she knew that he was all too real.

After ten years of ignoring their existence, Lance Winthrop had finally come to see Christy—and his son.

Chapter 2

It seemed odd to Christy, who had changed so much herself, that ten years had left so little mark on Lance.

The late afternoon sun highlighted the golden glints in his hair, and he flashed the same smile he'd worn the evening she'd met him—and also on the day he'd asked for his freedom. Time could have stood still for ten years, for all its effect on Lance's incredible good looks.

A columnist for a New York paper had once called Lance "Society's Golden Boy" and had gushed about his devastatingly blue eyes and his hair the color of an old Roman coin. The description was still valid, Christy thought now; only she, who had suffered so much pain at this man's hands, knew that appearances were deceptive, that under that golden exterior was a core of pure brass.

As Lance's smile deepened, her defenses rose and she

looked at him with stony eyes, taking care to hide her shock. Not for anything would she allow Lance to guess how painful, how traumatic, the breakup of their marriage had been until, she'd laboriously, day by day, put the pieces of her shattered life back together.

"Yes?" she said, raising one eyebrow, as if he really were the door-to-door salesman she'd expected.

"Don't tell me you don't recognize me, Christy-girl," he said easily. "How quickly they forget," he added, and she remembered that the throwaway line, the lazy use of currently popular clichés spoken ironically, had been one of his conversational gambits.

"It would be difficult to forget you, Lance. What is it you want?"

"Right now, I'd like you to invite me inside so we could have a friendly talk. We have a lot of gaps in our histories to fill in."

His voice had deepened and taken on a coaxing tone. For a moment, Christy's mind slipped a cog, and she was back in Bermuda on their honeymoon, back to that hazy, unreal time when all that had mattered to her was this man's smile, his deep, rich voice, his touch. How young— how stupidly naive and young she had been at eighteen, not to have seen through him, not to have guessed that everything he'd said was a lie. . . .

Unconsciously, her face must have hardened, because Lance's expression subtly changed. "Come now—let's be civilized about this, Christy. We have some important things to talk about—such as our son."

Alarm bells rang inside Christy, so strongly that for a moment she was speechless. Instinctively, she retreated backward, and Lance must have taken this for an invitation, because he followed her into the dark entrance hall.

Realizing that she had missed her chance to slam the door in Lance's face, Christy stood there, her body rigid, staring at him, letting him see her scorn. A muscle in Lance's jawline twitched. For a moment, he looked uncomfortable, as if it really mattered that she loathed the sight of him.

He looked away first—up the stairs, so solid and umcompromisingly plain, that led to the second floor, then at a watercolor of Puget Sound that she'd done herself—during those long-ago days before she'd given up such frivolous things.

"It's very good. Is the artist someone I should know?" he asked; he was smiling again.

"What exactly do you want, Lance?" she said, ignoring his question.

"Well, first I want to set things right between us," he said, his voice throbbing with a sincerity that she knew was as false as his smile. "We parted so stupidly—I know now that I was a real bastard, that I handled the whole thing wrong. My only excuse is that I was—well, call it mesmerized by Alissa. She got under my skin and I couldn't seem to think of anything except—"

"Except her money? Her father's millions? Yes, that *would* be mesmerizing to you."

He looked at her with hurt eyes. "After all this time, you still bear a grudge? But that's such a waste of energy. The past is the past. I know I treated you abominably, but you must remember that I was a lot younger then. I've changed,—I'm not the same man I was nine years ago."

"Ten years," she corrected—and then could have bitten off her tongue.

"You've changed, too," he said. "You were always beautiful, but maturity has—well, you're a real knock-out now. Your hair is magnificent, and you've finally learned to handle that elegant body of yours. You used to walk like a newborn colt—now you move like a dancer. I noticed it when you got out of your car a while ago and went into the house.''

When she got out of her car? Had he been watching the house, spying on her? If so, why had he waited until now to ring the doorbell? Had he seen Jessica's arrival earlier and waited for her to leave?

"What exactly do you want?" she asked again. "If this is some kind of delayed-action guilt—"

"It's not delayed. Even at the time we split up, I regretted the way I had to—the way I treated you. But if you'll look at it objectively, you'll have to admit that I did you a favor, getting out of your life. We were never right for each other. You're the settling-down kind, and I'm still the same gadabout I always was. But I have changed in one way—call me a late bloomer when it comes to a sense of responsibility. Which is why I'd like to see the kid, get to know him, maybe even take him on an outing now and then—"

"No way is that ever going to happen! You gave up that privilege ten years ago—and I have the papers you signed to prove it." In her agitation, Christy's voice had risen, echoing through the hall. "Now, get out, Lance—and don't come back. If you do, if you try to talk to Tad without my permission, I'll call the police and have you arrested!"

"But I'm the boy's father," Lance said, sounding so wounded, so reasoning, that she wanted to vomit. "Surely, I have the right to—"

"You have no rights where Tad is concerned. You signed them away. In fact, there's no evidence that you even are his father. If you'll check, you'll find that his birth certificate lists his father as *unknown*. I went to a lot of trouble to have it changed. And Miles adopted him legally after we were married. All Tad knows is that he has a biological father somewhere—and that the man deserted me before he was born. He accepts that—he thinks of Miles as his real father."

"Why didn't you take the easy way out and just tell him that I was dead?" Lance asked. His mouth twitched slightly, and for the first time, she noticed the tiny lines beside his mouth, the deeper one between his eyebrows.

"Because I was sick of lies and deception."

To her surprise, color stained Lance's cheekbones. Her stare seemed to embarrass him further, because he cleared his throat and looked away.

"Okay," he said finally. "I deserve that. I acted like a heel. And believe me, I've had some tough moments, trying to rationalize away the things I did to you. But give me credit for a few decent instincts. I do feel some responsibility toward my son. I admit it's come a little late, but I really have changed. At least let me see the boy—and why do you call him Tad? Isn't his name Steven?"

Christy brushed his questions aside with a scornful gesture. "I won't have you coming into Tad's life and getting him confused. Kids his age are very impressionable. When you drop out again—as you eventually would when you got bored with playing the father—it would just upset him. What he doesn't need is divided loyalties—"

"Is *that* what you're afraid of? That I'd try to come between you and the kid? Hell, all I'm asking is to meet him—you can introduce me as an old friend of the family's if you like. Then if we hit it off, maybe you'll allow me to do a few things for him, such as taking him to the zoo in Puget City once in a while. He'll benefit from it, Christy. And I promise not to interfere with his life."

"His father and I take him to the zoo—quite often," she snapped. She stared at him with cold eyes. From the distance of time, she realized how transparent he was— why hadn't she seen through him eleven years ago and saved herself all that misery, that pain? Was she so much wiser now—or had Lance himself changed? Was his charm, his charisma, wearing a bit thin?

"Where is your wife?" she asked suddenly. "What does Alissa think about this sudden interest in your son?"

Lance ran his fingers through his hair, ruffling his curls, a boyish gesture she remembered. At one time, that gesture could melt her very bones. Now it only exacerbated her anger, because it reminded her of the naivete that had made her such a perfect victim.

"We've busted up—it just didn't work out," he said. "I guess it's like that old Cole Porter song. It was too hot not to cool down. And when it did, there was nothing left." He took a step toward her, his eyes intent. "You don't know how many times I've kicked myself for letting you get away, exchanging what we had for—"

"What we had? What we had was zilch, nothing, based on one big fat lie," she retorted. "You may have forgotten, but I remember how rotten it was, being married to you—"

He was so close now that she could feel his breath on her face. She caught a familiar scent—of mint, of shaving lotion—and her stomach churned, leaving her feeling weak.

"Are you sure? You don't remember anything at all that was good about our marriage?" he said softly.

She looked him straight in the eye, refusing to give way before his slow advance. The loathing she felt must have been all too apparent, because again his face flushed, and Lance was the one who backed away.

"I think I've made myself very clear," she said. "Now get out! My husband will be home any minute. He's extremely protective of me. It might be very uncomfortable for you if he finds you here."

For a moment, she was sure he meant to argue with her, but he fooled her. He shrugged, gave her a good-natured smile, and then said, "Well, I gave it the old college try. Maybe that will count for something."

He smiled again—white teeth flashing against tanned skin—and added, "You're making a mistake, taking the hard line, you know. Not only will you be depriving your—depriving Tad of a father, but also of a very wealthy grandfather. It's something you should think about, Christy-girl. It's possible you're not being fair to the kid."

Then he was gone. As she watched him go, she remembered that he'd always walked like no one else—high on the balls of his feet, as if the wind were perpetually at his back, pushing him along.

And his last remark about depriving Tad of a wealthy grandfather? *Typical Lance*, she thought.

"Who was that, Mom?" It was Tad; he was standing at the foot of the stairs, staring after Lance.

"Nothing to concern yourself with, Tad." Christy forced a smile, hoping he hadn't noticed how shaky her voice sounded. "This house seems to draw salesman like—like flies." *Not exactly a lie . . . the house did seem to attract a parade of door-to-door salesmen.* "How is the homework coming? All finished?"

"Yeah. I didn't have too much today." Tad's voice was absent. "Say, about that guy. He took my picture when I came home from Mrs. Wright's—or at least I think he did. Of course, it could've been the house he was aiming his camera at. Does he know me from somewhere?"

"No, he doesn't know you," she said around a sudden coldness. "You say he took your picture?"

"Uh-huh. I asked what he was doing in our yard, and he said he was interested in old houses. He was real friendly—he looks familiar, too. You sure I've never seen him before?"

"I'm sure."

And he looks familiar because you see his face every time you look in the mirror. . . .

Tad still looked doubtful, and to head off any more

questions, she added quickly, "We didn't get much chance to talk when you came in from school. How did you make out on that history quiz?"

The animation drained out of Tad's face. "I got a B plus," he said listlessly.

Puzzled by his lack of enthusiasm—history was not his best subject and a B plus was more than an acceptable grade—Christy pushed her own worries to the back of her mind and probed gently. "Hey, that's neat! How did Cappy do?" Cappy was Tad's best friend—and also his most ardent rival.

"He got a C," Tad said, a gloomy satisfaction in his voice.

"Uh-huh. It just may be that you'll win that bet the two of you made, after all. What was it? That the one who got the lowest grades on his next report card would do the winner's yard chores for a month? Right now, it looks like Cappy will be working for you this summer."

Tad's face lengthened. "He'll have to do it this fall. Did you forget? Cap and most of the other guys are going off to Camp Blue Ox, soon as school ends." He gave her a pleading look. "Mom—I know you and Dad said I couldn't go to camp this year, but . . . well, that's all anybody talks about at school lately. Even Sammy Swit's parents changed their minds and said he could go, and you know what tightwads they are. It's gonna be a real blast—"

Christy sighed. So *that* was what had been bugging Tad lately. It had been a hard decision, deciding against sending him to Camp Blue Ox this year. Had they been wrong? If only it wasn't such an expensive camp. . . . Maybe they could tighten their belts a little more, cut back somewhere else, or even borrow the money from the credit union or—no! She and Miles had thrashed all this out, weighing the pros and cons, and they had decided that the expense simply wasn't justified. Like everything else these days, the tuition of Camp Blue Ox had gone sky-high, and there were too many other bills pending this year, too many places where their money should go.

"Your father and I explained why we can't afford to send you to camp this summer," she said. "You know about your grandmother's hospital and funeral expenses—and my hospital bills, too. We thought you understood."

She waited for some response from Tad; when it didn't come, she added, "I know it's not easy, going to a school where most of your friends' parents have more money than we do. Did I ever tell you that it was pretty much the same for me? Your grandmother and I lived in a condominium in a very old, very wealthy neighborhood, and all my friends were—well, they had a lot more material things than I did. So I do understand what it's like. But I learned to live with it—and so will you. And you have so much that's more important—like a father who spends so much time with you. Wouldn't you rather have Dad home instead of always off on business trips like Cappy's father is? How often do your friends' fathers take your gang on camping trips the way your Dad does?"

"Yeah—all the guys think Dad's real neat," Tad said listlessly.

"We'll still have a lot of fun this summer, Tad. There's a lot of things we can do—like taking a bay cruise and camping out, and maybe we can rent a cabin at the beach for a few days."

"That'll be great," Tad said, but he looked dispirited as he wandered off toward the kitchen.

For once Christy didn't call after him to stay out of the cookie jar. She leaned against the newel post, her eyes closed, feeling limp, her thoughts churning. Miles would have to talk to Tad and explain again why they'd had to cancel his usual two weeks at summer camp. And what on earth was she going to do about Lance? What did his visit, this sudden interest in his son, mean? Did it have anything to do with Neville's phone calls? But no, that couldn't be. According to the gossip columns, Lance was estranged from his father, had been since his marriage to Alissa Concord—

An old memory surfaced, one she had suppressed for a decade: Lance and Alissa lying together, their naked bodies entwined, asleep in each other's arms. . . . Another memory assaulted her, then another, all so painful that she gasped aloud and clasped her hands tightly at her chest. When she realized she must look like the heroine in an old-fashioned melodrama, she dropped her hands to her side, turned swiftly, and ran upstairs to change out of her office clothes and into something more comfortable.

But when she was in the bedroom she shared with Miles, she gave a helpless look around, forgetting why she'd come there.

Knowing she would get no peace until she dispelled the flood of memories, she flung herself down on the large brass bed she was so proud of and buried her face in Miles's pillow. The odor of the hair lotion he used to keep his thick, unruly hair under control was comforting, and she gradually relaxed, hugging the pillow, only to discover that this was a mistake, because suddenly the flood gates of the past opened and memories overwhelmed her, carrying her back to those brief months that had been both the most ecstatic and also the most terrible time of her life.

Chapter 3

When Christy was eighteen she'd overheard one of her mother's friends call her a "late bloomer." At that time of her life, when she was taking her first uncertain steps into adulthood, the phrase troubled her. She wasn't sure if the woman had meant it as a compliment or a criticism. It was the same uncertainty about herself that made Lance's courtship so traumatic—and effective.

Since the Winthrops were the closest thing Puget City had to royalty, she had heard about Lance and his exploits long before she met him. All the girls at Mrs. Cummings's School were fascinated by Lance Winthrop's extraordinary good looks, his playboy reputation, and the stories of his daring feats on the racetracks of Europe and the ski slopes at Aspen—and his sexual adventures in the bedrooms of the international set.

His love affairs were legend, and there were few of Christy's girlfriends who didn't secretly dream of someday, attracting Lance's attention during one of his rare, whirlwind visits to his father's estate, an island in the Sound a few miles north of Puget City. On rare occasions he attended local parties and dances, and then the gossip ran riot, especially if he centered his attention on one girl.

An affair with Lance was always brief, but it was rumored to be an experience the girl never forgot. For that short time, Lance ignored all other women, concentrating his attention on the one of his choice. When it was over, he seldom came back for an encore, but the girl was said to remember the precious moments forever.

Christy, already unsure of herself, was certain that such an experience would devastate her, but she was careful not to voice her views aloud. For one thing, she wasn't really a part of any of the cliques at Mrs. Cummings's School. Only because of her friendship with one of the wealthier girls at the school was she sometimes invited to the larger private parties or to a dance at Puget City Country Club, where the membership fees were too expensive for Jessica's budget.

That her mother had to scrape hard to pay her tuition at the expensive private school was a source of guilt to Christy. Every time Jessica moaned about the expense, Christy studied harder, trying to justify the sacrifice, even though her mother seemed indifferent to her high grades. The prestige of having her daughter attend the fashionable school and hobnob with daughters of wealthy local families was the real reason why Jessica kept her at Mrs. Cummings's School. If Christy were to fulfill her hopes and make an advantageous marriage, Jessica herself would be able to return to Puget City society.

So Christy had been an unsure girl of eighteen, a recent graduate of Mrs. Cummings's School, and a late bloomer when she first met Lance. She had been invited to a postgraduation dance at the country club by one of her friends, and Jessica had made a big fuss about it, buying her a gown that was much too expensive and sophisticated. She felt so ill at ease that she'd been in misery most of the evening, even though she'd been surprisingly popular, a phenomenon so new that she hadn't yet come to terms with it.

When one of her dancing partners, the brother of a schoolmate, left her near the terrace doors after a round, she slipped outside, seeking the dark and privacy of the garden. She curled up on a bench in a hidden spot among the trees and eventually, the peace of the garden quieted her jangled nerves. She was almost ready to go back inside when a man's voice came out of the darkness. "So there you are, Christy. Too stuffy inside, was it?"

She recognized Lance's voice even though the light was so dim she couldn't make out his face. Earlier, she had been standing near the door when he came in with a crowd of people his own age. He was telling them a yarn about a skiing trip he'd just returned from, and she told herself it was too much, a man who looked like that having such a sexy voice, too. She also envied his poise; he was completely at ease as he stared around the ballroom, his smile confident. His gaze lingered on Christy for longer than seemed natural, and she had felt the color rise to her cheeks—and knew when his smile deepened that he'd noted her blush and was amused by it.

In the powder room, she listened silently while several of her friends speculated about Lance's unexpected appearance, wondering if he would single out one girl to dance with that night. From their secret smiles, she'd suspected that every girl there, whether engaged or not, had hopes of being the lucky one.

So what was he doing out here in the garden? And how was it that he knew her name?

"What's the matter—did I startle you?" His voice held a subtle amusement, as if again he had sensed her confusion.

Christy took a deep breath, knowing she had to say something. "You did rather—I guess I was woolgathering."

To her surprise, her voice sounded normal, if a little breathless, and when Lance laughed, she felt a spiraling thrill that seemed to start in her abdomen and end up in her chest.

He sat down on the stone bench beside her. As if he could see in the dark, he found her hand with unerring ease and pressed it gently. "I'm Lance Winthrop, a guest of one of the club's members—and perfectly harmless. And your hands are very cold, Christy. You've been sitting out here too long by yourself."

"How did you know my name?" she asked.

"Because I asked a friend, 'Who is that beautiful girl with the russet hair and the stars in her eyes who's dancing with that clod with three left feet?' He told me your name was Christy Owens, that you had just graduated from Mrs. Cummings's School for Young Ladies, but I'm sure I heard that part wrong. No one would name a school that."

Incredibly, she giggled—she who so seldom even smiled. His hand tightened around hers, and suddenly she felt giddy—and wildly excited.

For a long time, they talked. He teased her, charmed her, and she found herself answering his questions with an ease she'd never felt with any other man, even boys her own age, telling him about her father, who had died when she was five, leaving behind an impeccable social position and no money; about her stepfather, who'd had plenty of money, but who had talked out of the corner of his mouth and insulted all of Jessica's friends.

Lance listened with flattering attentiveness as she told

him that she was planning to major in art that fall at Puget City University in preparation for a career as a commercial artist. She didn't even notice how little he said about himself or his own future plans.

When one of her friends finally came looking for her and they went back inside, Lance's hand was clasped firmly around her arm, a proprietory gesture that immediately had everyone buzzing. For the rest of the evening, he danced with her, ignoring the people he'd come with. His eyes never left her face, and while a small sane voice inside Christy warned her that when the evening was over, she would never see him again, for these hours she gloried in his attention, in the envy she saw in the eyes of her friends, in their escorts' speculative stares.

He didn't ask her if she had come with another man. Whether he had no qualms about moving in on someone else's date or whether he had already determined that she was unescorted, an extra woman with her group of friends, she never knew. But when the band began to put away their instruments, it was Lance who took her home, leading her to his low-slung car and seating her with a solicitude that made her feel pampered and very desirable.

If he had tried to make love to her that first evening, he probably would have met with resistance, at least a token one, more because of her shyness than anything else. But he didn't suggest any stops on the way home, and when they reached the condo where she lived with Jessica, he kissed her gently, then told her she'd better run inside before he forgot his scruples and ravished her on the spot—which was a very public spot indeed, since he was in a no-parking zone.

He found her key in her evening bag, and pressed it into her hand, a gesture that seemed gallant and so thoughtful that it didn't occur to her until months later that a man who had seduction down to a fine art would know all the tricks for making a woman feel cherished.

In a daze, Christy floated up the front steps and let herself into the house. Jessica, who always waited up, was dozing in her chair in the chic living room with its off-white furnishings. Christy had learned to color the descriptions of her social evenings to satisfy Jessica's high expectations, but tonight she was careful not to mention Lance's name—or tell her mother that she'd danced with him most of the evening.

Instead, she murmured that she'd had a wonderful time, but that it had been so stuffy at the club that now she had a headache and thought she'd better take a couple of aspirins and get to bed. But she lay awake, too excited to sleep, reliving every minute of the evening—and wondering how she could possibly bear it if she never saw Lance again.

And why hadn't he tried to seduce her? Was it because he hadn't found her desirable? Or was it her age, the fact that she was so damned gauche and unsophisticated?

"Oh, Lance—I'd change for you," she whispered into her pillow. "I'd learn how to say clever things that would make everybody laugh, how to dress and walk and talk like the women you're used to. Just give me a chance. . . ."

The next morning, as she came downstairs, feeling logy and headachy because she'd slept hardly at all, the doorbell rang, and when she answered it, a florist's box was delivered into her trembling hands. The flowers were a spring bouquet—baby's breath and yellow rosebuds and tiny, perfect daffodils—and the card said simply, *"Let me come into your life, Christy. Have dinner with me tonight. I'll be there at seven."*

He hadn't signed it, but then, he didn't have to. As she carried the box upstairs to her room, as she buried her nose in the fragrant flowers, she knew—every sinew and bone and muscle in her body knew—that Lance had sent them.

Even then, she didn't tell her girl friends when they called to find out what had happened after she'd left the club with Lance, nor did she tell Jessica, who left the house early that evening to attend her weekly bridge party.

It took Christy a long time to decide how to wear her hair and to choose a dress. In the end, she wore one of the narrow shifts that were popular that year and arranged her hair in a simple, timeless style—pulled back from her face and fastened with a tortoiseshell clasp.

But when she looked in the mirror, she saw that nature had taken care of the problem of how much makeup to wear. Her eyes sparkled with excitement, and she didn't need to add blusher to her cheeks. She applied a darker lipstick than she usually wore and borrowed some of Jessica's perfume, a heavier scent than her own floral cologne, and when the doorbell rang and she went downstairs to admit Lance, she held onto the banister tightly because of the feeling that she was floating a foot above ground.

From the beginning the evening was pure enchantment. What Lance said and what she replied, where they went and what they ate—if they ate at all—and what the orchestra played when they danced was all a dream. The only thing that registered was Lance's eyes, which lingered on her face as if she were the only person in the room. Even while he was ordering dinner, his hand covered hers tightly as if he were afraid she might run away.

Later, while they were dancing, he murmured in her ear, "Let's get out of here. I have to talk to you, Christy-girl, have to kiss you." And she went along willingly, letting him lead her from the supper club, as entranced as if he were the Pied Piper and she one of the doomed children.

He took her to a fishing lodge he'd borrowed from a friend, and although at some point the cabin must have registered on her mind, because later she remembered that it was furnished in rustic oak and peasant prints, it was Lance—his smile, his touch, his voice—that filled her world, blotting out everything else.

They drank wine in front of a roaring fire, not talking now, just staring into each other's eyes. The rest of the world seemed to have disappeared into a shimmering mist.

Christy had never before been so aware of her own body. Her skin seemed incredibly sensitive to the slightest stir of air in the room, while at the same time she seemed immune first to the chill in the cabin, and then, after Lance had started the fire, to the heat from the hearth. Her hair, floating around her shoulders, crackled when she moved her head, and her body seemed to be permeated with an electric energy, even while she felt a strange lassitude in her limbs that made it hard to move, even to raise her wineglass to her lips.

There was fire and ice in her veins, too. Fire, when she read the message in Lance's eyes. Ice, at the knowledge that this man she was so crazy about might walk out of her life tomorrow, having chalked up another girl on his score-card of conquests.

But the fire was stronger than the ice, and when Lance leaned forward to kiss her, she settled against him as if her bones had suddenly turned to water. The pressure of his lips increased so subtly that it was almost with bemusement that she realized she was getting her first French kiss. His breath was minty, tasting of the wine he'd just drunk, and his hands, when they moved along her arms, were so skillful that she felt no alarm or embarrassment, not even when he bared her breasts and then fondled and kissed them lingeringly—oh, so very lingeringly, so knowingly!

All the time Lance was undressing her, his voice whispered words of desire, of admiration, in her ear, and his breath, stirring the tiny hairs around her face, was strangely erotic. With infinite patience, he initiated her to sex, gentling her as if she were a wild colt when she pulled away with shock as she felt, for the first time, the hardness of a man's full arousal between her naked thighs. With his hands, his lips and tongue—and his rich, throbbing voice—he penetrated her defenses, one by one, and when at last he invaded the final citadel, she was consumed with such an earthshaking storm of sensation that she felt as if her soul had been separated from her body.

Later, as they lay exhausted on the couch, he asked her to marry him, and in her gratitude that she wasn't to be one of his one-night stands after all, she didn't ask herself why a man who could have had any woman he wanted would propose so quickly to a nobody like her. Instead, she buried her face in his chest, too deliriously happy to speak, and when he threw back his head in a laugh, she laughed too, dizzy with happiness. It was only a long time later that she wondered who Lance had been laughing at that night—himself, her—or his father.

The next day it was time to tell Jessica, to begin the complicated preparations for a society wedding. "Puget City's wedding of the season," one newspaper rapturously called it. Jessica was ecstatic. For the first time in her life, Christy had done something that made her mother proud of her. Jessica never explained how she raised the money for the expensive wedding, but, being Jessica, she made sure that it was everything tradition demanded of someone who had just snagged Puget City's catch of the decade.

During this time, Lance spent every evening with Christy. They attended parties, went out to dinner in company— sometimes with her friends, sometimes with his—but afterward they always ended up at the cabin on the Sound. In

Lance's arms, with the fire coloring their nude bodies with its ruddy glow, Christy was confident that she had tamed the playboy, was sure of Lance's love, and believed his whispered assurances that he was a reformed man now that he'd found the girl with whom he wanted to share the rest of his life.

With some part of her mind, she was aware of her friends' incredulity, of their envy, but it was as unimportant as Jessica's occasional bouts of nerves. She met Lance's father and found him intimidating and overbearing; he looked her over as if he were purchasing one of the antique sports cars he collected. He questioned her brusquely— about her health, her background, her education. She knew that she'd passed his test when he gave her a sapphire bracelet, saying that it was time she looked the part of Neville Winthrop's daughter-in-law.

"When you make me a grandfather," he added, "I'll give you a ruby-and-diamond necklace. And if it's a boy— well, the sky's the limit."

Although she didn't want to accept such an expensive gift, she was afraid of offending Lance's father. So she put the bracelet away in her mother's safety deposit box, not wanting the responsibility of having something so valuable in her trinket box.

The sun shone on their wedding day—which, Christy was to think later, pointed up the absurdity of old folklore.

It was on her honeymoon that she suffered her first disillusionment. Lance had chosen a vacation resort in Bermuda that seemed very romantic to Christy, even though Jessica was disappointed and remarked that it seemed a little uninspired for a man of Lance's sophistication and background. So it was a shock when, a few days after their arrival, Lance began to show signs of restlessness.

When he grumbled about the accommodations and complained that Bermuda was dull, she hid her hurt and redoubled her efforts to keep her conversation sparkling, trying to ape the sophisticated women he seemed to admire.

And when he came back to their suite one afternoon with the news that he'd run into some old friends and had accepted an invitation to join them on their yacht for a cruise to Bimini, she was delighted to see his good humor miraculously restored.

But to Christy's despair, she quickly discovered she was susceptible to seasickness. At first, Lance was patient with her, but when her nausea persisted, he became irritable and told her to stop acting like a spoiled child, that motion sickness was all in a person's head. It was their first quarrel, and it left her bewildered and lost, because he seemed so callous and uncaring.

It was then that she noticed how attentive he was to Alissa Concord, one of the other guests. Alissa was a narrow-hipped brunette with sultry eyes who was four years older than Christy in age, a hundred years older in experience. The daughter of a shipping mogul, she was the kind of self-assured, privileged girl who had made Christy feel like an outsider at Mrs. Cummings's School. Whenever she looked at Christy, there was a sly triumph in her almond-shaped eyes; for the first time, Christy wondered how accidental Lance's meeting with his yachting friend had been.

When they docked in Bimini for a few nights' stay before their return to Bermuda, Christy quietly went ashore to seek out a doctor. By now, she had reason to believe that her nausea was caused by something other than mal de mer. When the doctor confirmed her suspicion and told her she was two months pregnant, she knew it must have happened soon after she and Lance first made love, that she had been wrong when she'd assumed that her irregularity had been caused by the stress of the wedding.

She dreaded telling Lance the truth, sure that he would be angry and somehow blame her even though, shortly after they'd become lovers, when she'd suggested that she go on the pill, Lance had been against it.

"The pill still hasn't been proven completely safe to my satisfaction, Christy-girl." He'd smiled at her so winningly that she'd felt warm all over. "Besides, if you get pregnant, it's okay with me. The papa thing could be a blast—and think how grateful the old man would be."

But what if Lance had changed his mind about wanting to be a father? He was so indifferent to her these days, hardly speaking, even in the privacy of their cabin. When he made love to her, it seemed mechanical, almost as if he were performing a necessary task.

That night, in their cabin, she blurted out the truth. To her surprise, Lance threw back his head in a triumphant laugh, and then he was whirling her around the cabin, telling her that she was the greatest little brooder in the world.

Their return to Puget City was precipitous, as so many things in her short marriage had been. They were back in Bermuda, having docked that morning; when she returned to the hotel from a hairdresser's appointment, she found Lance piling clothes into an open piece of luggage.

"Start packing, Christy," he told her briskly. "The old man wants us to come home. We'll be staying with him on Winthrop Island for the next few months."

"I don't understand—why can't we finish our honeymoon?"

"Because the old man wants us to come home."

"Do you do everything your father tells you to do?" she asked in bewilderment.

"He pays the bills," he said, shrugging. "As long as I take his orders, he can be pretty generous. Which is something you should think about."

Christy absorbed this in silence. The question of where Lance got the money he spent so lavishly had never come up before, but she had assumed, as did everybody, that he was wealthy in his own right. Several times, when she'd asked him what his plans were after the honeymoon, he had shrugged and told her not to worry, that everything would fall into place when the time came.

"Then you don't have an income of your own?" she said finally.

"Not a sou. The old man pays for everything—which is why he can turn the screws anytime he wants." There was a brooding look on his face that chilled her. "But my day will come. He can't live forever—although I'm sure he expects to."

"But—you graduated from Harvard. You have a degree in business administration. Why don't you find a job and be independent?"

"Slave forty hours a week in some grubby office? You've got to be kidding!"

"Then why did you bother to go to college? You must have made good grades if you got your degree."

"My allowance was in direct proportion to my grade point average, my naive friend. Fail a course and zip—down went my allowance. So you can be sure I kept my grades decent. And don't look so damned shocked. It's the old man's fault. He raised me to expect the best, and then, out of the blue, he suddenly put out his claws. Right now, he's ordered us to return home. Seems he wants to make sure—"

He broke off and gave her a rueful smile. "Look, I know I haven't been the perfect bridegroom, but you must realize that this is all new to me. I'm really nuts about you—and I promise to behave and settle down. So when Neville asks how things are going between us, tell him what he wants to hear. After all, he *is* paying the bills.''

His smile was so infectious that she forced back her doubts and nodded, tacitly agreeing to his request. But the fact that Lance was totally dependent upon his father dismayed her, and she made up her mind that as soon as the baby was born, she would urge him to get a job, convince him that she was willing to live in a small apartment while he got established, that all she really wanted was him—and the baby.

For the next four months, they settled into life on Winthrop Island, the island that had belonged to the family since the days when Lance's great-grandfather had been one of Washington State's lumber barons.

The island, in a remote part of the Sound, was like a separate little world—or like a prison, Christy often thought. The house was old, as carefully preserved as a museum, with its art treasures, its paintings, its antique furniture, its library of rare books. At first, because Lance was attentive again, solicitous when she was nauseated, a condition that continued well past her fifth month, she tried to be content, not to ask questions or complain.

When the spells gave no sign of stopping, she finally consulted a Puget City physician who specialized in difficult pregnancies. After a thorough examination, he was very blunt.

''You'll have to curtail sexual intercourse immediately— and rest at least four hours a day. No hard physical activity— and try to stay away from mental stress, too. I want to keep a close eye on you, so I'll have my nurse set up your appointments two weeks apart.''

He must have seen her fear, because he patted her arm and told her that she was a strong girl, that chances were good that she would carry the baby full-term.

That evening she repeated the conversation to Lance. He watched her, his eyes unreadable, but with the sixth sense she'd developed where Lance's moods were concerned, she knew that he was disappointed in her, that somehow he blamed her for the physical flaw that made carrying a baby difficult. Although he kissed her and told her to take it easy and follow the doctor's orders, his words had a hollow ring, especially when he added that he'd better move into one of the guest rooms so she could get more rest at night.

For the next month, she seldom saw Lance except at breakfast and dinner. She suspected that he left the island nightly, because his personal motor cruiser was gone every morning when she got up. He would show up in time for breakfast, looking nonchalant and unrepentant, only to disappear into his room for the rest of the day with orders not to be disturbed.

Although he always turned up for dinner with his father and Christy in the mansion's huge formal dining room, he was unusually subdued, and as soon as his father retired for the night, Lance left too, not bothering with explanations. Soon afterward, she would hear the sound of a motor launch and know that he had left the island.

By now, she hated the island and disliked the gruff, uncommunicative man who was her father-in-law. She knew that something was very wrong with her marriage, too, but in her inexperience, her fear of making Lance angry and bringing their estrangement to a head, she didn't know what to do, how to cope with her suspicions.

When she finally sought her mother's advice, she received no sympathy, only the admonishment to grow up, to try to act as if she had some sense for once in her life. Christy knew—Jessica made it very clear—that if she left Lance she couldn't expect to be welcomed back into her mother's life. Since she had no money of her own and was in the seventh month of a very touchy pregnancy, she felt helpless, as if she were adrift in a nightmare.

And, too, she still had some illusions left, and still wanted desperately to make a go of her marriage. Following her doctor's orders to avoid stress, she pretended she didn't notice Lance's neglect and went quietly on with the daily routine that had been prescribed for her.

The hope that somehow the baby would make a difference sustained her. She didn't question Lance, even though by now she knew his weakness for roulette and suspected he was patronizing one of the area's private gambling clubs.

And then, with one of the mercurial changes of mood that she had come to recognize as part of Lance's nature, he came to her bedroom one evening in an exuberant mood.

"Toss a few things in a suitcase—it's time you had a change of scenery, love. We've been invited to go cruising with Corky Lafferty. He's an old buddy of mine from Harvard—sort of a square-peg type, but loaded with money. How does a cruise down to San Francisco grab you?"

At her incredulous stare, he added impatiently, "Look, you can rest just as well on Corky's yacht as you can here. The sea air will be good for you—and since you don't have morning sickness any longer you don't have to worry about nausea. Oh, and something else. Be a love and tell the old man that this is your idea. You're really in tight with him, now that you're going to make him a grandfather."

Christy knew then why she had been included in the invitation. Neville might be indifferent to his son's nightly excursions away from the island, but he would undoubtedly draw the line if Lance left her alone for an extended time when she was so far along in her pregnancy. She started to point out that she was, after all, just two months from term, but before she could speak, Lance put his arms around her and nuzzled her hair with his chin.

"It'll be a gasser—things are just too damned dull here on the island. You want your old man to be happy, don't you?"

So Christy packed some sports clothes, including her new maternity swim suit and a matching beach coat, and when Neville questioned her, she took the brunt of his disapproval and insisted that she needed a change of scenery, using Lance's own words.

"Good girl," Lance told her later. "You're learning how to handle the old boy. Too bad things turned out the way they did or you'd have it made."

When Christy asked what he meant, he only shrugged and changed the subject.

Christy had hoped that the cruise would bring them closer, but from the moment she came aboard and realized that Alissa Concord was one of the other guests, she realized that it wouldn't be that way. The yacht hadn't cleared the breakwaters in the harbor before she had her first bout of seasickness. The nausea was constant, wrecking her determination to be a good sport, and she was forced to spend most her time in the cabin she shared with Lance, her body wracked with frequent spasms of nausea.

When she finally ventured out on deck, feeling weak and dehydrated, she looked so wretched that she knew she was a pall on the other guests. It didn't help that Alissa, incredibly sexy in her string bikini, was constantly in view, sunning herself on deck, stretching her lush body like a lazy cat—and watching Lance with hungry eyes. Although they seldom spoke to each other, the sexual tension between them was almost palpable—at least to Christy.

The third night out, Christy awoke early in the morning with cramps so strong that her whole abdomen writhed with pain. In her fear, she cried out for Lance. He didn't answer her, and when she turned on the light beside her berth, she discovered she was alone in the cabin.

Some instinct, something stronger even than her fear for the baby, took her to Alissa's cabin. In their carelessness—or maybe their arrogance—they had left the door unlocked, and when she opened it and looked inside, they were lying together on the bed. They must have fallen asleep just after making love, because Lance still lay between Alissa's thighs, his hand still cupping one of her breasts.

For a long time, Christy stood in the doorway, staring at their naked bodies, both so lean and sleek and tanned. Her gorge rose, almost choking her, but even then she behaved in a civilized manner. Instead of being sick on the floor of Alissa's cabin, she turned and ran, leaving the door open behind her, and made it into the bathroom of her own cabin before she became violently ill.

While she was still leaning against the washbasin, a wet towel pressed against her face, another cramp twisted through her abdomen and she knew it was time to get help. She stumbled to the nearest cabin and banged on the door. The next hours blended into a nightmare of dark shadows rimmed with red, of cramping pain, of voices and faces showing various degrees of concern. Somewhere toward the end, there was a short trip in the yacht's dinghy, then a long ride in an ambulance. Eventually, she was in the emergency room of a hospital, surrounded by nurses and doctors.

She was aware that Lance had accompanied her, but she kept her eyes closed and pretended not to hear his explanations, his apologies. Then she was being wheeled into the delivery room, and despite her fear, she breathed a sigh of relief, because Lance couldn't follow her in here. The shadows rolled over her again, and now she was only aware of pain, of voices, of something catastrophic happening inside her body, as if it were being wrenched apart.

Later, she awoke in a hospital bed. Her first instinctive act was to place her hands on her abdomen, and when she realized that she was no longer carrying the baby, she cried out in fear. Her panic didn't subside until a nurse, who came bustling in, assured her that she'd been delivered of a perfectly normal six-pound boy. Although she was very weak and would have to stay in bed for several days, the nurse added, there was no reason for alarm. She would be good as new in short order—and able to care for her baby.

But of course she hadn't been as good as new in short order—nor for a long time. During the next three days, although she waited for Lance, he didn't come, didn't visit his son. Whether from shame or indifference, he sent no flowers, no messages. In fact, he could have dropped off the face of the earth.

Christy knew the nurses pitied her because she didn't have any visitors. Not wanting to face Jessica yet, she decided not to notify her about the baby's birth until she was better able to cope with her mother's questions and endless advice. Except when they brought her son to her to nurse, she lay staring at the ceiling, too apathetic to talk to the nurses and the other patient in her room, to read or watch TV, or even to think.

The evening of her third day in the hospital, she finally had a visitor—Neville Winthrop.

He came into the room without knocking, then stood at the foot of the bed, his face granite-hard. ''Well, young woman, you've managed to wreck my plans quite thoroughly, haven't you?''

"I don't understand what you're talking about," she said wearily.

"Don't play the innocent with me. And just in case you're suffering from the delusion that you have some legal claim on me, I've come here to say my piece in person. I'll pay your hospital bills, but after that, as far as I'm concerned, I have no further obligation toward you—or your bastard."

"You must be out of your mind! What are you saying?"

"Did you think you could trick me into supporting the offspring of your lover, girl?" Neville's eyes blazed down at her. "Lance told me how you lied to him, how you convinced him you were a virgin. If I didn't feel like twisting his neck, I'd be sorry for him. Any man so besotted with a woman that he'd let her fob off another man's bastard on him deserves what he gets. Well, you won't get away with it. That baby will never get a penny from me, so don't come around trying to ingratiate yourself. From this moment on, as far as I'm concerned, you've ceased to exist."

He turned on his heel, leaving her speechless with shock.

During the rest of the day, Christy went through hell, moving from bewilderment and disbelief to, finally, some kind of understanding of what must have happened.

For some reason still obscure to her, Lance had convinced Neville that another man had fathered his son. Maybe he hadn't wanted any competition for his father's estate—or maybe he had simply wanted to be rid of her once and for all.

But why, she asked herself for the hundredth time, had Lance married her in the first place? It didn't make sense—and she was too tired, too disillusioned, to figure it out.

One thing she did know—she wasn't going to let Lance's desertion send her into a tailspin. Ever since the moment when she'd discovered Lance in Alissa's bed, a deep anger had been churning, growing inside her. Neville's visit, his cruelty when she was at her most vulnerable, had brought it all to a head. The bitter hurt of Lance's betrayal had jelled into a new hardness, a determination that from this day on, she would direct her own life and no longer be a victim, a target for other people's lies and deceptions.

She didn't try to contact Lance when she was discharged from the hospital. Using one of her credit cards, she rented a car and, with her son beside her in a portable bassinet, returned to her mother's condo in Puget City. She knew she'd need help until she found a job to support herself and the baby.

At first, when she was subjected to her mother's endless recriminations, she often wondered if she wouldn't have been better off living alone in a furnished room somewhere. But all this soon changed, although not because of anything she herself did.

Jessica, who all her life had been so self-centered, had finally succumbed to love for another person. It wasn't Christy—it had never been Christy—but she wasn't jealous. How could she be when it was her own son who had won Jessica's heart?

Tad was a month old when Lance finally turned up. He waited until he saw Jessica leave the house before he finally rang the doorbell. Tad was sleeping in his crib upstairs, and Christy was sitting at the kitchen breakfast bar with a cup of coffee between her elbows, staring into space—something she did a lot of, those days.

Somehow she wasn't surprised to see Lance. She had known that eventually he would turn up, if only to settle the details of their divorce. When he gave her the disarming smile that had once played such havoc with her senses, she stared back at him with bleak eyes and moved aside so he could come in. Although his smile didn't waver, his nervousness was obvious. When he bent his head to kiss her, she flinched violently, and a look of discomfiture crossed his face.

"I guess you think I acted like a heel," he said.

"That's too mild a word for what you are. You're a bastard, Lance. A lying bastard."

Lance looked hurt—as if she were the one at fault. "Look, I can explain how it all happened—the old man must have told you about our deal, didn't he?"

"Yes, but I'd like to hear your version," she said with a craftiness that, like the hard shell around her heart, was new to her.

"Well, for one thing, I didn't intend for anyone to get hurt. I admit just about any girl who fit the old man's qualifications would have done at first, but—hell, after I got to know you, I really dug you, Christy. You're a special girl."

"How special? Being stupid and naive and easy to fool?"

"Hey, it wasn't like that! Okay, the old man turned the screws, told me to find someone—well, *healthy*, *young*, and *malleable* were the words he used. And a virgin. He wanted to make sure that his grandchild was—you know, a Winthrop. At first, I rushed you because you fit the bill, but then I really fell for you. I had every intention of making our marriage work, but I'm just not meant for the long haul—you know what I mean? You're better off without me. You'll come to realize that eventually—"

"I know it now. I wish I'd never met you—but maybe it was good that I did," she said, every word edged with acid. "Because I'll never make the same mistake again. You've cured me of any romantic ideas about men I once had."

"You have every reason to be bitter," he said. "And I want to do the right thing. You and the kid will need money, so I have a proposition for you. You get an annulment and I'll pay all the expenses and settle enough on you to keep you going for a while. You know I don't have my own income, so I can't make it as much as I'd like, but I can rake up enough to pay your expenses until you decide what you want to do—"

"I'm planning to get a divorce, not an annulment," she interrupted.

"Hell, that's no good. Look, I'll put my cards right on the table. It has to be an annulment, because—well, because I plan to get married again."

"To Alissa Concord?"

"Yeah. Nothing against you, Christy. It's just that— well, we got it on right from the start. Alissa and I are two of a kind. We talk the same language, dig the same things—"

"And she does have all that money, doesn't she?"

"Okay, the fact that Alissa has money of her own, that she'll inherit more from her father someday, does have something to do with it. I've never lied about having expensive tastes."

She stared at him fixedly. "And just in case it doesn't work out, you intend to keep your options open, don't you? If you desert me and your son and take off with Alissa, you're afraid Neville would disown you and make your son his heir. So you've convinced him that someone else fathered our baby—and it also gives you an acceptable reason to bow out of our marriage. And that's the real reason you want an annulment. You really are a poor excuse for a human being, Lance."

Briefly, Lance's eyes wavered, but he shrugged and said, "Okay, get it out of your system. Call me names if it makes you feel better. But I'm trying to be honest with you, and the fact remains that I intend to marry Alissa. Unfortunately, she comes from one of those strict Catholic families. No divorces, see?''

"How do you expect me to get an annulment when we have a child?''

"That's no problem. We'll both claim the marriage wasn't consummated—after all, the kid was born just six months after the wedding. If there's any question, you say another man fathered the kid.''

"It doesn't bother you that this would make your son a bastard?''

He smiled crookedly. "Who cares about such things these days?''

"I care. Someday, your son will care.''

"Okay, it isn't perfect but—look, if you divorce me, you'll be admitting the marriage was legal, that the kid is mine, and that gives me some legal claim to him. So what's more important to you—your pride or having complete custody of the kid? If you get the annulment, then I'll sign anything you want, giving up all my legal rights to the kid. And that means you can spit in Neville's eye if he ever comes around, wanting to take over. Which seems to me to be a pretty good bargain.''

Christy was silent as the craftiness that was so at odds with her true nature stirred again. Lance was right—making sure that he could never change his mind and try to get custody of their son was worth any humiliation.

And then there was Neville, a ruthless and powerful man who could hire the best legal minds in the country if he ever decided he wanted his grandson. The fear that he might someday try to get custody of her son, using Lance as his instrument, would be like a sword hanging over her head.

In the end, Christy got the annulment—and Lance signed away all rights to his son. Since then, she'd had no contact with him. So why had he come back into her life again? What did he *really* want—and why did she feel so sure that it was something more than a whim, something that had nothing to do with any latter-day interest in his son?

Chapter 4

Miles Havens *watched with amusement as his student*, Joyce Petersen, continued her diatribe against the irrelevancy of romantic love in the modern world. He was also aware of the deepening glower on Ira Levine's face.

The two of them, both seniors and equally opinionated, had clashed before—and not always with the kind of objective intellectual differences of opinion he tried to foster among his students. Well, he thought wryly, anything that served to turn musty old concepts into terms that would apply to the here-and-now was worth risking a few fireworks. And a good argument was always an effective antidote for spring fever. He was teaching *Romeo and Juliet*, which always inspired arguments about romantic love.

Joyce finished her tirade against the stupidity of women who fell for the seductiveness of romantic love. She ended with a quote—the gal did do her homework!—from *As You Like It*, the one about men dying from time to time and worms eating them, but not for love. Then she sat down with a challenging look toward Ira, as if daring him to top that.

Surreptitiously, Miles glanced at his watch. He could call on Billy Clark, who had raised his hand, but he knew that Billy, who had a crush on Joyce, would only concur with her views in order to score a few points with her. On the other hand, Ira was waving his hand frantically, and there were only a few minutes before the bell. Time would limit the fireworks.

Lay on, Macduff, Miles thought as he nodded to Ira.

"Look, Joyce, you don't understand where Shakespeare is coming from," Ira started out, in the lecturing tone that was guaranteed to frizzle Joyce's already frizzled hair. "Shakespeare had these kids kill themselves rather than go on living without each other, and that may seem pretty stupid four hundred years later, but the idea he was trying to get across is still relevant."

Joyce gave a less than ladylike snort and he glared at her, waving his hand.

"Look around you, for God's sake, if you don't think that kind of love still exists! Every day women give up careers to stay home and take care of some guy and have kids. And men hold down grub jobs they hate so they can support their wives and families. It's just a different facet of the same thing—you know, giving things up for love. So Romeo and Juliet went for broke—maybe working at an eight-to-five job you hate is a kind of death, too."

Joyce spoke without asking to be recognized. "Oh, come *on*, Levine! You aren't trying to tell us you believe in eternal love, are you? With your reputation?"

Levine's lean face took on a wolfish look. "Yeah—I believe in love. There's all kinds. At this point in my life

I'm not ready for the eternal kind. But someday I will be. Are you interested, Joyce? I've got a vacancy right now.''

The class exploded into laughter. Joyce gave him a long, level stare and, when the room was quiet again, she said sweetly, "I'd rather stay home with a good book. And you're waffling, Levine. You're talking about sex—and that's something else. If you're so sold on love, how come you haven't committed yourself to one girl yet?"

"Give me time. Someday, when I'm ready to handle it, the right gal will come along and zap—that'll be it. The real thing, the long haul. Hell, it could even be you." He gave her a mocking smile. " 'Come live with me and be my love, and we will all the pleasures prove. . . .' "

The bell cut through Joyce's answer, and Miles was well satisfied as he gave out the assignment for the weekend. His students would read *Romeo and Juliet* with a little more attention—or so he hoped. Now if he could just keep Levine and Petersen from killing each other before spring semester was over, he'd have it made.

Later, as he was walking across the campus, heading for his car in the faculty parking lot, he thought about his students' reactions to the idea of romantic love. Every year the same subject came up—with a little help from the prof—and every year it took a different direction. Sometimes it was a solid intellectual discussion of changing values and mores, sometimes, like today, it ended up on a more personal level, but always it added zest at the end of the semester, just when even the most devoted student got a little antsy with prefinals tension. Strange how *Romeo and Juliet*, written four hundred years ago, could evoke so many diverse opinions on love.

And since love was a subject pertinent to his own life, he was always tempted to inject his own thoughts. Oh, yes, he could tell them a thing or two about love, these kids who thought they'd written the book on the subject.

Love was a tall, slender woman with hair the color of autumn leaves. Love was a tight budget and an old house on the edge of town that needed constant repairs. And love was being part of a family, too—the three of them spending a quiet day at the beach or taking a day-long hike through the wilderness part of Granite Falls State Park, or sitting in the bleachers at the ballpark. Love was watching Christy with Tad, seeing the glow in her eyes as she bent over the boy's bed to tuck in his covers at night before they went to their own room, to the private world that encompassed only the two of them.

Love was sex, too. The kind that made his loins ache at the most inconvenient times of the day when he thought of Christy lying beside him in their big brass bed. . . .

God, he was a lucky man! How had he gotten so damned lucky—to have what most men dream about and never find? The one—the only—woman he'd ever really wanted, as well as a great kid like Tad. And, as icing on the cake, work that was fulfilling and satisfying. Okay, so the bills stacked up once in a while. Christy never complained about them, never pointed out that he could make three times as much money working in an office in the city.

An auburn-haired girl passed, reminding him that it was on this path under these same Douglas firs that he had first met Christy. She had been hurrying along, heading for her computer class in the Bus Ed building, when she'd stumbled over an exposed root, breaking off her heel.

One look into those lovely eyes and he'd had the kind of revelation that can change the direction of a man's life. He knew he couldn't let her go, couldn't take the chance that he wouldn't be able to find her again. So he abandoned his class that day, and by the time he'd fixed Christy's heel,

he had her name and phone number—and a promise that
she would have dinner with him the next evening.

His own audacity had astonished him. He'd always been
a low-key guy. In fact, his popularity with girl students
surprised him, since he wasn't charismatic, like John Nobles,
who taught history, nor did he try to speak the currently hip language, like Curtis Earle, PCU's fiery-tempered
head coach.

But his classes were always filled, with a long waiting
list to boot, and he had very few dropouts, a rarity for an
English professor these days, with so much attention being
given to technology. Miles knew it wasn't his looks or his
sex appeal that made his classes popular. Christy believed
that it was his enthusiasm for the literature of the past that
drew them. He often suspected that students simply felt
comfortable in his class.

Is that how Christy feels about you, Miles—comfortable?

The question slipped through his defenses out of nowhere,
and because he always tried to be honest with himself, he
didn't banish it back into his subconscious.

*Okay, Miles, there it is—the sinister stranger at the
wedding, the ultimate question: Does Christy love you with
anything near the passion you feel for her?*

The sex between them was great—but did she feel the
same fireworks he did when he touched her, when she
touched him in return? Wasn't there a—a holding back in
her, even during their most intimate moments, a watchful-
ness, a barrier that he never seemed able to penetrate? He
could live with that reserve he sensed in her because he
had to live with it, but—oh, God, what he wouldn't give
to know that she felt the same vibrations he did!

*Come on, Miles. Face up to the truth. It's a little more
than that. You still wonder, even after five years, just why
a girl like Christy would marry a guy like you, don't you?*

That was the crux of the whole thing, wasn't it? Christy

was so—special. No matter what she wore or how tired she was, she always glowed with an inner beauty that tore out a man's heart. While he—well, face it. He was an ordinary-looking dude. Sure, he had his share of girl students who got crushes on him, who stayed behind after class, asking inane questions, even though he discouraged this sort of thing. It was no secret that all reasonably attractive men teachers got that kind of attention.

And that described him to a T—reasonably attractive. Tall enough to look down into Christy's eyes, but legs a little too lanky, body a little too lean. His face was—just a face. Long and angular, with the aquiline nose that reflected his New England ancestry. He'd often been told he had a great smile, and he had a full head of dark-brown hair, still untouched with gray, but he wasn't any Paul Newman.

Or even a Lance Winthrop. . . .

Miles frowned so ferociously that a passing student gave him a startled look. Busy with his own painful thoughts, he barely noticed. After all these years, did he still harbor doubts about Christy's feelings for her first husband? And wasn't *that* some kind of stupidity? He knew that Christy loved him, not Lance, in the very way that Levine had tried to describe love today. She was a passionate woman, and sex played a part in it, but sex wasn't the most important factor in their marriage. That factor was trust—and Christy, who had been wounded so deeply, needed so much to be able to trust again.

So this was something he gave her, something that counted a helluva lot more than a handsome face. She knew he would always be there, taking her part, standing by. He'd give her the moon if he could. Hell, he'd even go to work in some damned stuffy office pushing papers around if she wanted it—and wasn't it lucky that she liked being the wife of an English professor and never seemed to notice the state of their checking account?

He unlocked the door of his seven-year-old Chevy, slid his long legs under the wheel, and half an hour later was pulling up in front of the house on Old Orchard Road. But before he went inside, he paused to consider his mother-in-law's car in the driveway and turned an appraising stare on the old house he and Christy had bought the year they were married.

It always looked shabbier than usual when Jessica was visiting. Was it because of her remarks about musty houses and leaking roofs, or was it Jessica herself, with her brittle talk, her too self-consciously stylish clothes, and her restless, critical eye?

Well, no help for it. Jessica was part of the package— but just once, he'd like to toss her out on her bony arse when she was yammering away at Christy, bombarding her with her spurious advice. Of course, Jessica did have a few redeeming qualities that made her visits endurable. She loved Tad; with him, she was a softer, certainly more like-able, person. How had it happened that somewhere along the way she had developed such unrealistic expectations for Christy? At what point had she decided that Christy was to fulfill her own thwarted social ambitions? Was it some kind of ego transference? If so, she had chosen the wrong person.

When he came into the kitchen, Christy was slicing french bread on the square slab of old marble she used as a cutting board. For a while, he watched her unnoticed, assessing the tiny pucker between her eyebrows. She was wearing a cotton sweatshirt over washed-out jeans, and she looked more like eighteen than twenty-eight as she attacked the loaf of bread with her knife.

One of the things that Jessica criticized often, along with Miles's "pedestrian" job, his lack of ambition, and his other failings, was the difference in their ages. He was thirty-eight, ten years older than Christy, and only eleven years younger than Jessica herself. And sometimes, like now, he felt about eighty. It would age any man, the prospect of spending the next few hours with Jessica—and the ghost of Lance Winthrop.

Oh, Lance's name wouldn't come up during the evening, but he would be there nevertheless—in every critical glance his mother-in-law leveled at Miles's favorite old leather chair, the scarred hardwood floors that needed refinishing, and the walls that were long overdue for new wallpaper. Miles had seen Lance's photograph a couple of times—he was part of the international jet set that constantly got their pictures in the newspaper—and even in the smudgy gray newsprint, he was extraordinarily handsome.

Did Christy ever compare the two of them—hell, of course she did! She'd only had two lovers in her life. Naturally she compared them. And although she was always telling him what a wonderful lover he was, did she really mean it, or was she just being kind?

God, he didn't want *kindness* from Christy! He wanted her heart to sing every time he kissed her—and what the hell was going on with him today, anyway? He was acting like some love-sick kid instead of a mature man who had been married for seven years, long enough to be past this kind of self-doubt. It must have been that *Romeo and Juliet* business—yeah, that was it. Next year, so help him, he was going to cut *Romeo and Juliet* out of the spring curriculum and substitute *King Lear*. . . .

Christy looked up. Her lips curved into a welcoming smile as she dropped the knife on the cutting board and raised her face for a kiss. When Miles held her a little longer than usual, she gave him an appraising look.

"She's just staying overnight this time," she murmured, and he grinned at her and shook his head.

"You could've been burned at the stake for that sort of thing a couple of hundred years ago," he said.

"Oh, it wasn't magic. It was that look on your face—you know, an 'I'm-going-to-be-a-good-sport-if-it-kills-me' look."

"Uh-huh. Like you wear to the faculty wives' luncheons, right?"

"Right. If one more of those blue-haired biddies asks me where I matriculated, I'm going to give her five—right in the eyes."

"Well, I feel the same when some of your associates start talking computerese."

"The ultimate odd couple—the professor and the computer whiz, who lived happily ever after."

"Ever after," he echoed. He put his arms around her and kissed her thoroughly this time. "How about it? Should we make an excuse to go up to bed early tonight, or maybe we could sneak out to the back lawn and have a little private orgy—"

"You two lovebirds never stop, do you?" Jessica said from the doorway. "Or is this exhibition of marital love for my benefit?"

Christy's body stiffened in Miles's arms. He took his time releasing her before he turned to greet his mother-in-law. "Hello Jessica," he said mildly.

Jessica came into the kitchen and perched on a stool. She took out a cigarette and lit it with nervous fingers. "So how's the college game these days?"

"In financial trouble—like a lot of other things."

"Why don't you get into something else—like banking? If you brought home a bigger paycheck, Christy could stay home and take care of Tad."

"Over my dead body he'll get into banking—or anything else besides teaching," Christy said crisply. "Miles is a wonderful teacher—it's what he does best."

"Well, if you say so," Jessica said, shrugging.

Miles felt irritation, but not at his mother-in-law. When something was self-evident, such as the rightness of the career he'd chosen, did it need defending? Since he knew he was being unreasonable, he put it out of his mind and started talking about the weather, always a subject of absorbing interest in Washington State.

During dinner, he was relieved that Jessica devoted her attention to Tad. As he listened while the boy answered her questions about school, he began to relax. Perhaps it wouldn't be so bad, after all—and bless Tad's special gift for bringing out the best in Jessica.

"—and then Miz Baker had us take turns telling what our plans are for summer vacation," Tad said. "Most of the kids are going to summer camp, but of course I can't go this year, so I had to say that I was just staying home."

Jessica frowned at Christy. "I thought you sent Tad to Camp Blue Ox every year."

"We decided to just wing it this year," Christy said, avoiding Miles's eyes. "You know, do the family thing—lots of hiking and camping and maybe spend a few days at the beach."

"Well, surely you could do that and still send the boy to summer camp for a couple of weeks," Jessica said.

"It's money," Tad said, looking glum. He helped himself to more noodles before he added, "We've got all these bills to pay for Grandma Havens's funeral."

Jessica turned another frown upon Christy, but before she could voice her opinion, Christy jumped to her feet and said hurriedly, "I'll get the coffee and the dessert. How about helping me, Tad?"

To Miles's surprise, Jessica let the subject drop, but the rest of the meal seemed to drag as he listened to Jessica's husky voice relating news from the garden club she'd belonged to for the past twenty years. Since her own garden these days consisted of a few pots of fuchsias and azaleas sitting on the tiny patio of her condo, he suspected the club's main crop was gossip, a suspicion he'd never articulated, even to Christy.

After dinner, Jessica and Tad became involved with the complicated rules of the new game she'd brought him. The sight of the two of them, their heads close together at the golden oak table that served as a living room desk, was reassuringly peaceful. Miles was grateful when, at Tad's bedtime, Jessica decided that she would read to her grandson before he went to sleep. It was a mark of Tad's affection for his grandmother that he didn't point out that he was perfectly capable of reading his own books.

Later, Miles was even more grateful when, after a cup of hot cocoa and her tenth cigarette of the evening, Jessica went off to the guest room, saying that she'd had "a tiresome day"—which was either another put-down or an example of her insensitivity.

It occurred to him that Christy had been unusually quiet during the evening. He watched her as she began turning off lamps, wondering if something had happened between her and her mother. More unwanted advice, perhaps. Well, he'd do his best to dispel the goblins—whatever they were.

By the time he had checked all the doors and windows, Christy had gone upstairs. He heard the shower running in their bathroom as he went into Tad's room to make sure he was well-covered. The boy, his face flushed with sleep, was lying on his back, clutching the pillow. Miles removed it gently and laid it on the floor beside the bed. He bent and kissed Tad's warm cheek, thinking how strange it was that the only thing his stepson had inherited from his mother was his incredibly long eyelashes—or did Lance, the Golden Boy of the jet set, have those same dark eyelashes, too?

Angry with himself for the way his thinking had been going lately, he took his own shower. By the time he was finished, Christy was already in bed, the lamp turned off. As he slid under the sheets, his leg brushed her sweet-smelling body, and he felt a surge of excitement. Gently, he ran his hand along the curve of her hip and buried his face in her hair, which smelled like ripe wheat from the herbal shampoo she used.

But instead of turning toward him and slipping her arms around his neck, she murmured, "I'm really tired tonight."

"Hmmm . . . I know just the thing to relax you," he whispered against her ear.

He did the thing she loved, nuzzling his face against her ear, but she rolled away, and this time her voice held sharpness. "I'm not kidding. I'm really not in the mood, Miles."

Miles was silent, too stunned to speak. In the seven years of their marriage, she had never refused him before—had he been wrong to think that she enjoyed sex as much as he did? It had always been such a free and open thing between them—usually he was the one who initiated sex, but often Christy reached out for him first. So the rebuff hit him like a blow in the pit of his stomach. "I'm sorry," he said, and despite himself his voice sounded stiff and hurt.

"Oh, Lord—look, sometimes a person just doesn't feel like being touched. And this has been a really rough day. You do understand, don't you?"

"Of course." He gave her a chaste kiss on the cheek and rolled over on his side, away from her. But it was a long time before he finally fell asleep.

*   *   *

In the morning, Christy's first kiss was longer than usual, and he knew this was her way of saying she was sorry. He told himself that he was getting spoiled and had become too complacent, that he should be more sensitive to Christy's feelings and read her signals better in the future. But it put a restraint on their conversation as they dressed, and he was almost glad when Jessica, already made-up and wearing another of her white suits, this one linen, came downstairs to join them for the cup of black coffee and the one piece of unbuttered toast she allowed herself for breakfast.

Miles studied his mother-in-law as she darted a quick glance at Christy, then at him. There was something stewing behind those eyes, a suppressed excitement that made him wish it were a school day so he'd have an excuse to go off right after breakfast.

Tad appeared, ravenously hungry as always. Remembering his speculative thoughts the night before, Miles tried to look at his stepson with objective eyes. He was an unusually handsome child, with an athletic ability that was as natural to him as breathing. He was also a born leader— and, according to his teachers, the prime instigator of the mischief in his class.

And he was the spitting image of Lance Winthrop. Why, then, was it so easy to forget he was another man's child most of the time? When exactly had he stopped thinking of Tad as his stepson and started thinking of him as his son? Maybe it had been after Christy's miscarriage, the one that had ended for all times the hope that he and Christy would have a child of their own.

His chest tightened, and he braced himself for the old pain. It came—but it was muted now, not as sharp and cutting as it had been at first. Christy, too, was recovering from that old disappointment—or at least, it had been a long time since she'd mentioned the baby they'd lost. . . .

With a guilty start, he realized Jessica was talking, and he made himself listen, knowing that any inattention would be noted and ultimately commented upon.

"—wonder what's behind it? It does seem strange that the man would take a picture of Tad," Jessica was saying.

It was the expression on Christy's face that alerted Miles. For one moment, until she turned away and began filling the napkin-holder, he saw something dark and painful in her eyes. Jessica had seen it, too; her too-taut face held the expression of a bridge player who has just trumped his opponent's only ace.

"He was a real neat-looking guy," Tad volunteered around a mouthful of English muffin. "He had this great tan—like he was out in the sun a lot. I'll bet he's a pilot, or maybe a policeman, the kind that don't wear a uniform."

"*Doesn't* wear a uniform," Christy corrected automatically. Her eyes brushed her mother's face, then moved away. "And I doubt he was a detective."

"So why did he take Tad's picture?" Jessica persisted. "What did he look like, Tad—what was the color of his hair, for instance?"

"Same as mine, only it was more—you know, sun-streaked." Tad stuffed the rest of his muffin in his mouth, chewed, and swallowed it before he went on. "He had these really blue eyes, too."

Miles pushed away his coffee cup; he didn't need to look at Jessica this time to know what her expression would be. So that was the reason for Christy's silence—and maybe the reason why she hadn't wanted to make love last night. Which brought up an interesting question. Why would a visit from her first husband turn her off sex with her second? And why hadn't she told him that Lance had come to see her and—yeah, what the hell did the man want with her, anyway?

                    *   *   *

They had it out after Tad had gone upstairs to clean his room and Jessica had left to return to her condo on the other side of Puget City.

"I would have told you about it yesterday, but I decided to wait until Jessica was out of the house. She has a way of sniffing out things you prefer she didn't know—sometimes I think she has built-in radar."

"You could've told me last night after we went to bed." He was silent for a moment, studying her stiff face. "That's the reason you didn't want to make love, isn't it?"

"Of course not. I was tired—and besides I always feel guilty, having sex when my mother's in the house. I know it's stupid, but there it is. I guess it goes back to all those endless lectures I used to hear about keeping myself pure."

Usually, he would have smiled at her wry tone. Now he felt a sudden irritation at what he knew was an attempt to divert his attention. "For God's sake, Christy! I'm your husband! If we did it on the living room couch in front of Jessica it wouldn't be wrong, only rotten manners. You're a grown woman now, not a kid."

"I told you it was stupid—"

"We've made love before while Jessica was visiting us. In fact, you always seem to need a little closeness after an evening with your mother."

He saw her face close up and knew he had taken the wrong tack—and that he was being unreasonable. Okay, so who said he was perfect? He had a right to blow off steam once in a while. Maybe he should do it more often—

He felt a hand on his arm and realized Christy was smiling at him—a painful smile that didn't negate the troubled look in her eyes. "Okay, Lance was here and it shook me up, but not for the reason you think. He wants visitation privileges with Tad and when I told him no, he said a few things that—well, blew my mind.''

Miles felt a rush of anger. "You mean he threatened you?"

Christy shook her head. "No, that isn't Lance's way. He was very reasonable—he does that, you know. He can sound so reasonable about the most outrageous things that you find yourself feeling guilty and dumb and—and gauche because you don't agree with him. It's a nice trick—it was very effective when I was married to him.''

He looked at her searchingly, noting the shadows under her eyes. "And now?"

"I'm not an impressionable girl anymore, Miles. I saw through his tactics and they didn't work. I told him to leave me—leave us—alone and reminded him about the release he signed. He took it rather well, as if he didn't really care all that much about pushing it any further. Somehow, I don't think he'll be back.''

There was a finality in her voice that told Miles she wanted to drop the subject. He helped her clear away the breakfast dishes and then went outside to so some yard work, but he didn't get to it immediately. Instead he stood by the back porch, staring up at the sky, aware of a feeling of depression, of apprehension.

Christy had sounded so sure when she'd said that Lance Winthrop wouldn't be back—but was that just wishful thinking on her part?

The picnic that afternoon was totally unplanned, and it turned out to be one of their best family outings.

As she often did, Christy put aside her private problems and devoted all her attention to Miles and Tad. Miles knew that this was her way of making it up to the two of them for not being a full-time mother and wife, and he felt a moment's resentment toward Jessica, knowing that she was the main source of Christy's occasional bouts of guilt.

They were sitting under the greening branches of an oak, watching Tad's absorption with an anthill, when he told her, "You're one helluva good mother, Christy—no matter what your mother says. It's quality, not quantity, that matters."

Christy gave him a long, measuring look. "Now who's reading minds, Miles?"

"Not mind-reading—just putting two and two together. First, your mother's visit, followed by this impromptu picnic—and then there is that pucker between your eyebrows. It's a dead giveaway."

Christy laughed, the spontaneous half-giggle, half-chortle that always made him want to hug her. "Okay, Sherlock Holmes, you're right. I *am* on one of my guilt trips—but I also needed this time with just the three of us, too. This is the mortar that holds everything else together—this being with you and Tad, being a mother and a wife, putting the rest aside."

"It's gravy time," he said, grinning back. "Icing time—I feel sorry for everybody who doesn't have what we have, old girl. We're very lucky people."

Unexpectedly, Christy shivered and rubbed her upper arms with her hands. "Good thing we're not superstitious," she said lightly. "Some people believe that kind of remark can draw the attention of evil spirits."

"Uh-huh. And some people believe love and marriage is for the birds. So what do they know?"

He put his arm around her and gave her a lingering kiss. Tad came running up and skidded to a stop in front of them. "Yuk! That kissy-kissy stuff is yukky," he declared.

"You think so, do you? Well, now it's your turn," Christy jumped to her feet, grabbed him around the shoulders and planted a wet kiss on his cheek. He made a gagging sound and collapsed—on top of Miles. In a second, the two of them were rolling on the ground, each trying to stuff grass down the other's shirt.

Later, as they ate their sandwiches and fruit and drank their lemonade, Miles reflected that the picnic had served its purpose very well. Christy had lost that taut look that he associated with any reference to her first marriage—and Tad was having a rousing good time, talking with his mouth full—and not being told to mind his manners, because it was, after all, a picnic—and relating the details, verbal blow by verbal blow, of his latest spat with Cappy, his best friend.

So maybe Lance Winthrop's visit was a whim, and the whole business is just a tempest in a teapot, Miles thought. *And maybe I'm the one who's getting nervy and seeing ghosts where none exist. . . .*

Chapter 5

*Lance Winthrop seldom had second thoughts about any-*thing he did. Whether it was buying a new sports car or speedboat, winning a race, climbing a mountain, or bedding a beautiful woman, he set his sights, then went for the gold, never looking back.

But today, as he sat in the Porsche he'd borrowed from a friend and stared at the old frame house where his former wife now lived, he was aware of a rare uncertainty. It was nothing much of a house—and the inside, what he'd seen of it, was just as tacky. But Christy had been a total surprise. He hadn't been conning her when he'd said she had changed—and for the better.

She'd been a looker, or he wouldn't have married her, not even to get Neville off his back. But she had been immature and, eventually, boring in her eagerness to please.

Now, with maturity, she had acquired—well, *class* was the word that came to mind. Even in washed-out jeans and a cruddy old sweatshirt, she was something to behold. Put the right clothes on her, get her to a good beauty salon, and she would fit in anywhere.

Which was pretty strange when you thought of Christy's background. Oh, she came from old Washington pioneer stock, but her father had bankrupted himself and then been crass enough to die before he could recoup, and Jessica, Christy's mother, was a horror, a real harpie.

So the change in her had been Surprise One—no, Surprise Two. The first one had been when he'd seen the kid and realized he was a carbon copy of his old man.

For a moment, Lance felt a strange tightness in his chest. Hell, the kid was his—he'd known that from the beginning, of course. And now even Neville, who believed nothing that wasn't verified, certified, and down on paper—and even then had his doubts—would flip when he saw those pictures. . . .

Lance took the three Polaroid snapshots of Tad from his jacket pocket and laid them on the seat beside him. This one—with the kid smiling into the camera—could be a duplicate of a photograph in the family album, one of himself at that same age.

So why was he sitting here, beset with a sudden attack of conscience? He had the ammunition to get a few concessions, as well as a whole lot of money, out of the old man. It was long overdue. If he'd had any sense, he would have used Neville's one weakness—his hunger for the perpetuation of the Winthrop line—against him long before this.

Of course, until his blowup with Alissa, he hadn't needed the old man's money. When Neville had cut him off, he'd said a few things that made it pretty hard now to eat crow. So pride and reluctance to let Neville know how hard up he was for money were undoubtedly part of the weird feeling he had of wanting to forget the whole scene.

And of course there was some truth in what he'd said to Christy—that one of the reasons he'd gone to so much trouble to convince Neville he wasn't the kid's father was to keep the old man from breathing down Christy's neck and interfering in her life. Of course, the rest of it wasn't so noble. He hadn't wanted another heir, not even his own son, coming between him and Neville's money.

Lance shook his head, not liking the trend of his thoughts. He had no illusions about himself. He lived by the premise that the Lord helps those who look out for themselves— and screw the rest of the world. And at the present moment, he was in a real jam, down to his last few dollars and living on the charity of his friend, Corky.

Looking back, he realized what a fool he'd been. During the first year of his marriage to Alissa, when she was still so totally crazy about him, he should have insisted that she transfer some of her assets to him. But no, he'd been so cocky, so sure of his hold on her. And besides, it had seemed like too much trouble and he was essentially a very lazy fellow—except when the chase was fresh and his blood was up.

Well, he was paying for his indolence now. When Alissa had locked him out of their Paris apartment—which was in her name, dammit—all he'd had was the money in his personal checking account. He realized now that he should have been more discreet and stopped short of seducing her best friend. There are some things no woman can forgive.

So it was time now to mend fences with his father. That's why he had called Neville a month ago from Paris with the hot item that he'd just discovered that he was a father—and Neville a grandfather—after all. He claimed that gossip had come to him that the kid was his spitting image—which had turned out to be true. Neville, suspicious as ever, had told him he'd be in touch—to stay put until he called.

Well, something must have checked out right, because the old man had finally called and told him to trot back to Washington and to approach Christy with the idea of getting visitation rights with his son. It seems he had pushed the right button, after all. The old man wanted a grandchild, preferably a grandson, in the worst way, right? And he could provide that—had already done it, in fact. It wasn't clear sailing yet, but it would be once Neville saw these pictures. Lance would have the upper hand for the first time in his life. As Tad's father, he was the only one who had a prayer of getting the kid away from Christy. He intended to turn the screws on Neville and milk the situation for all it was worth. What's more, he wasn't going to let it bother his conscience, not one particle. He'd see that Christy didn't get hurt—he could string out Neville's hopes for years—and the old man owed him something, owed him one hell of a debt. Because ever since he could remember, Neville had let him know what a disappointment he was. . . .

For a moment, the old frustration rose inside Lance, tightening his jaw. Neville had never let him forget any mistake he made, no matter how small and unimportant. Even when he was a kid, all his little failures had been paraded before him endlessly, with never a word of praise. No wonder he'd learned the value of a good lie—and how advantageous it was to charm the hell out of the various housekeepers and governesses and cooks they'd had during the years.

And his mother—she'd been soft and weak and an alcoholic, more like a ghost creeping around the house than a real woman. The strange thing was that while she had adored him and given him everything he wanted, it had been Neville's respect and love that he'd yearned for—something he'd never had a prayer of winning, no matter what he did.

Well, those days were behind him now. All he wanted from Neville these days was his money. And he had the wedge, the means, in his own son. He could make the old man jump through the hoop this time—provided he played his cards right.

He started the car and an hour later, having borrowed his friend Corky's motor launch, was nearing the island that gave Neville the privacy he wanted.

Winthrop Island was only one of several such private islands in that area of the Straits, but it was a fortress to end all fortresses. Inaccessible from all but one small docking area and one well-patrolled beach, it was invulnerable to casual visitors. Only those people Neville wanted to see could get past the guard at the high steel fence that blocked off the land end of the docking wharf. Such annoyances as reporters, curiosity-seekers, random picnickers, and, until lately, errant sons were barred. No exceptions.

But Lance's revelation had changed all that. Now the guard, a burly man with hard eyes, tipped his hat with prudence if not respect and said a polite "Good evening, Mr. Winthrop" as he unlocked the gate.

Lance studied the house as he strolled up the path. Built some hundred and fifty years earlier by the founder of the Winthrop family's fortune, it had been spitefully described as "a turreted flight of fancy, transported from Normandy by way of American tackiness."

It was tacky, of course, but there was also a stolidity about its limestone walls and sturdy three-inch-thick redwood doors, its stained-glass windows, its dovecotes and ironwork, that reflected Neville's granite-hard personality. Was that why the old man preferred this place over the ranch near Palm Springs, the Fifth Avenue apartment in New York, the villa near Rome, and sundry other places, including another island, this one just off Greece, that he also owned?

Or maybe it was the climate of Northwestern Washington that Neville felt at home with, Lance thought. Yeah, constant rain and cloudy days were bound to appeal to someone who had the disposition of a dyspeptic bloodhound.

Lance felt his stomach muscles tighten when he discovered he would have to ring the doorbell to get in. Why was the house locked up, here on a virtually inaccessible island? The answer to that question was buried in the complicated brain of Neville Winthrop.

One of his father's bodyguards answered the door. He looked Lance over with flat eyes before he said, "Mr. Winthrop is in the library, sir. I'll announce you."

He turned on his heel and stalked off, leaving Lance fuming. When the old man finally bought it—the bastard would probably live to be a hundred just for spite—he, the heir, intended to clean house. Out with the old garbage, including old employees, and in with the new. Heigh-ho. . . .

A couple of minutes later, the man—wasn't he the one called Brewer? They all looked alike, for God's sake! —returned to tell him his father was waiting for him in the library. Deliberately taking his time, Lance strolled across the tiled floor of the hall. Before he tapped lightly on the library door, and then opened it, he assumed a properly grave expression.

Neville was sitting behind the huge Empire desk that dominated one corner of the room. He was a tall, gaunt man with the agate eyes of a banker—which wasn't so strange, Lance reflected sourly, because that was just what the old man was—among other things.

As usual, Neville didn't bother with the amenities. "Well? Did you get a picture of the boy?" he growled. "And did you have that talk with your former wife? I hope you handled it right. These matters are very delicate."

"I got the pictures and I talked to Christy." Lance said with equanimity. He took the Polaroid snapshots from the pocket of his sports jacket and laid them on the desk in front of Neville. When his father's eyelids flickered, denoting a rare excitement, Lance felt a surge of triumph.

Gotcha, old man! he thought.

"As you can see, the rumors I heard were true. The kid's the image of me." He stopped then, realizing that he sounded too eager. Why was it that he could handle himself with everybody else but invariably fell apart when he was dealing with his father?

Neville grunted; his eyes were expressionless again. "So what did Christy say when you asked her for visitation privileges?" he asked.

Lance shook his head. "No soap. She's still bitter as hell about the annulment. I outsmarted myself there. I thought I was getting out from under a bad situation. Now I'm afraid it will take time before I break her down."

Neville made a chopping gesture with his hand. "How much did you offer her?"

"Nothing. That isn't the right tack to use with Christy. Besides, I didn't know how much—how far you'd go along those lines," Lance said carefully. "In fact, I felt rather . . . intrusive. It's obvious the kid is well taken care of. I talked to him a bit and he's really—well, he's a great kid. Bright and well-mannered and articulate. I'm not sure I should intrude in his life and maybe get him confused— which is what Christy pointed out."

Neville was silent. Something calculating and razor-sharp in his stare made Lance want to wriggle like a schoolboy. Although he didn't make that mistake, he was suddenly remembering the times when as a kid he'd been so terrified by that same look. When the silence continued, he took a surreptitious breath, letting air into his starved lungs. Well, he wasn't a kid any longer. He had learned manipulation from the hand of the Old Master himself. This time, he meant to stick it to Neville and stick it to him good.

"Well, I guess that's that. Sorry, Dad—I did my best."

"Your best is pretty sad—as always." Neville's thin lips barely moved as he issued the insult. "You gave up too quickly. She'll come around. Figure out something she wants badly enough—and then make her an offer."

"How can I do that? I'm busted—flat broke."

"How much do you need?"

It had come too quickly. Lance had been prepared for sparring, for a struggle. He gaped at Neville, who stared back, not trying to hide his contempt as he added, "I said: 'How much?' Don't get too greedy, or I might decide that it isn't worth it."

But it is, you old bastard. A grandson who has your own blood lines is the one thing your money can't buy.

"Well, to make it worth *my* while, I'd need enough to keep me solvent for a long time," Lance said, hiding his triumph.

"Stop wasting my time, boy. Put a figure on it," Neville snapped.

"How about two hundred thousand?" Lance said around a dry mouth. "Then I can make Christy a decent offer and prove solvency if it comes to a court struggle."

Neville brushed his words aside impatiently. "A custody suit would take years. Use some of that charm the gossip rags are always claiming you have. For a beginning, get Christy to agree to visitation rights. Later on, we'll see about something more permanent. For the present, you'll need an edge so you can get your foot in the door. I already have the girl's mother on our side. She's a social climber—she's dying to move in what passes for high society around Puget City. She's been on the fringes for years and she wants in. All I had to do was dangle a carrot in front of her nose. I invited her to use the yacht for the summer and she was gushing like a geyser, promising to talk some sense into Christine. Like mother, like daughter. There has to be *something* your ex-wife wants. What's she holding out for, anyway? She must have given you a hint.''

Lance thought back to his abortive conversation with Christy. ''I think she just wants to be left alone,'' he said truthfully.

Neville's grunt held disbelief. As he leaned forward to pluck a pipe from a walnut rack on his desk, Lance stared at his father's hands. Still strong and powerful, but there was a tell-tale tremor in his fingers. Was there some special reason for Neville's impatience to get control of his grandson? And if so—how could he use the knowledge to his advantage?

Neville finished tamping tobacco into the pipe, then lit it carefully and drew on it several times before he spoke. ''Tell me exactly what you said—and what Christy's reaction was.''

A few minutes later, when Lance had repeated his brief encounter with Christy, both men were silent.

''She wants what's best for the kid,'' Neville said finally. ''That's her weak spot. So you play on that, tell her how much it would mean to——to the boy to be in good with me. That'll bring her around.''

''I don't think so. She's afraid that—well, I think she's afraid the boy will turn out to be like his old man. Or like you, Neville.''

A muscle tightened in Neville's prominent jawline. ''If you want that money, you'd best by God find out what string to pull. And there's a time limit. I don't want this business strung out over the next ten years. I want the boy while he's still malleable. I made a mistake, letting your mother spoil you rotten and not taking you in hand myself. But I've got a second chance now—so don't screw this thing up, or you'll never get another penny out of me. And that time limit is to your advantage, too. If you want to return to Europe to live, you're going to have to settle up those gambling debts—or you might find yourself in a concrete jacket at the botttom of the Seine.''

Lance felt as if a shock wave had struck him. It took all his control to keep his face a perfect blank. Neville smiled—a sour, knowing smile.

''I make it my business to keep an eye on you. You fool! Why did you get in so deep? Those hoodlums play for keeps, and they're going to get their money, one way or another.''

''So how about clearing my debts up for me?'' Lance said easily.

''I'll be glad to—when you get visitation rights for your son. You were a fool to sign away your rights to the boy. My lawyers tell me that there's little chance we could go to court and get custody legally. And don't give me that crap about thinking the boy was fathered by another man. You knew he was yours. I'm not sure what your motives were for lying about it, and at this late date, I don't give a damn. But you'll set things right or you'll lose any chance you had to get me to pay your gambling debts—or of getting back in my will.''

Lance stared at him. ''Getting *back* in your will?'' he said finally.

''I thought that would grab your attention. I wrote you out when you married that floozy, Alissa—but you can get back in easily enough. How does a trust, enough to keep you reasonably solvent for the rest of your life, sound to you—plus being put back in my will for a fourth of my assets?''

"And for this—what exactly do you want?"

"I want your cooperation in getting my grandson for me. Use every trick in the book, every persuasion, every bribe. I don't care what you do, or what steps you take, but I want that boy."

Lance took a long breath. "It's a deal," he said, trying to hide his elation. "But I'll need some money if—"

"I'll deposit twenty-five thousand in your checking account—and don't muck it up this time," Neville warned. "When you let that little tart, Alissa, talk you into a vasectomy, you ended your usefulness to me. That was your big mistake."

Not a mistake, old man, and not Alissa's idea either. Why should I bring more heirs into the world to share in the big jackpot someday?

"Alissa couldn't use the pill," Lance said aloud. "It's against her religion—and in her own crazy way, she's very devout. So to keep the peace, I got the vasectomy. In retrospect, I can see it was stupid, but at the time, I was really crazy about her, so—" He ended the sentence with a shrug.

"More fool you." Neville's mouth looked like a snapping turtle's as he bit off the words.

"Okay, I made a mistake. I'm afraid it's too late to do anything about it now. I checked with the doctors, you know—and there's no chance that the operation can be reversed."

"So you say. But it's not too late to set other things right. You get me custody of my grandson and you'll never have to come around again whining for money. How about that, boy? You'd like that, wouldn't you?"

Lance managed a smile. *Don't let him get under your skin. Keep it cool.* "And I'd be out of your hair, too," he said. "That should be worth a few shekels to you."

"I only pay for service—and I expect full value for my

money. If you don't come across—and soon—I'm cutting
the line for good.''

Neville reached under the edge of his desk and pressed
the button that would summon his bodyguard.

''And now you'd better get on with it. In a couple of
days, I expect a detailed report on your progress. Don't
foul things up again, Lance, or you'll live to regret it—
provided those hoodlums you owe money to allow you to
live at all.''

Chapter 6

During the months following the annulment of her first marriage, when Christy was trying so hard to pull her life together again, she had made the discovery that it was possible to live in compartments, to concentrate on hour-to-hour, minute-by-minute activities to the exclusion of all but the most nagging personal problems.

This single-mindedness had served her well when she'd been trying to juggle motherhood with her return to school and, later, with a job. After she had thrashed out the question of ethics until she was able to justify selling the sapphire bracelet Neville had given her, as well as other jewelry gifts from Lance, she had used the money they brought to support Tad and herself while she learned a trade.

Turning her back on the humanities, she chose the most practical field she could think of and enrolled in a computer programmers' course at Puget City University. Although she had always believed that anything mechanical or technical was totally beyond her ability to master, she found to her surprise that she picked up both the theory and the application of computer science more quickly than any of the other women—and most of the men—in her class. While it wasn't a career she would have considered a year earlier, she had the satisfaction of knowing that she was in an expanding field. As a plus, she found a certain comfort in doing something that followed rigid rules, seldom deviating from the expected, a world of cause and effect, of balance and reason.

Then she met Miles, and suddenly the possibility that she could find the same kind of stability and order in a relationship with a man opened up to her. Despite his quiet steadiness, Miles was surprisingly romantic, and when he read Shelley to her, when he brought her old-fashioned French lilacs instead of hothouse flowers because, he told her, she was a lilac kind of girl, she began to change her mind about never remarrying.

She also discovered that Miles was a sensitive and innovative lover, that his lovemaking left her feeling good about herself as a woman as well as proving that she was getting over Lance. Even so, she considered this as a bonus, something gratifying but having little to do with her decision to risk a second marriage.

More important was the realization that Tad needed a male role model in his life. When she saw how the two of them took to each other, how Tad looked up to Miles, and how patient—and firm—Miles was with her sometimes rowdy son, she knew her decision was clear-cut. A cautious two years after she met Miles, she finally said *yes*.

Her marriage had given her the stability she craved so

much, a peace she tried hard to guard. She continued to follow the same method of partitioning her days—work was work, something separate from her home life. When she left the Computers Now, Inc., offices at four o'clock every weekday afternoon, she left her job behind, and she was just as careful not to take her personal concerns with her when she went to work in the morning.

So she was disturbed, the Monday after Lance's visit, to find that her normal discipline had failed her. What Lance had said, how he had looked and sounded, the hatred that had blossomed inside her, and the sickness in the pit of her stomach when she'd been forced to look at him, to talk to him, and listen to his voice—all these things went around and around in her brain, getting between her and the demonstration and sales pitch she was making to one of the company's best clients for a new data-processing program.

By the time she locked her desk at four and gathered up her purse and sweater, her nerves felt like tiny wires, stretched to the breaking point. With the memory of how she'd always hated to return to an empty house when she was a child, she always tried to arrive home before Tad. It didn't help today that when she stopped to pick up a few groceries for dinner, she had to wait in line so long that she got home half an hour later than usual.

As she dug her house key out of her purse, she paused to look up at the porch roof. The paint was really coming off now. There were crumbs of it all over the porch floorboards, looking like dandruff against the weathered wood. Maybe it was termites—just what their budget didn't need.

With a shrug, she put the problem out of her mind with a mental note to talk to Miles about it later and went into the house. The punk rock music blasting from

Tad's room upstairs told her that he had beaten her home after all.

Her voice determinedly cheerful, she called out, "I'm home, Tad. Sorry to be late."

She wasn't surprised when he didn't answer. It would take a foghorn to penetrate that racket. She went upstairs to her son's room. After a token knock, she opened the door, to find Tad sitting cross-legged on his bed, a large cardboard box open beside him, so absorbed in reading a small booklet that he hadn't heard her knock or the opening of his door.

She came up to the bed, intending to give him a hug, but when he sensed her presence, he gave a guilty start, then instinctively thrust the cardboard box behind his back. There was something so furtive about the gesture that a shock of anger went through her.

"Okay, Tad—let's have it," she said, holding out her hand.

The corners of his mouth drooped as he pushed the box toward her. As she opened the lid, she recognized it as the expensive thing it was—a video recorder that must have cost almost as much as her monthly income.

"Where did you get this?" she demanded.

"It came in the mail—the mailman left it sitting on the porch. It was addressed to me, Mom, so I figured I had a right to open it! And it's just what I've been wanting, too, a video—"

"Who sent it?"

Tad stared at her, the look in his eyes strangely mature. "Someone named Neville Winthrop." He said the name glibly, as if he had studied it long time. "He lives in a place called Winthrop Island—it's one of those little islands in the Puget Straits. I looked it up in the atlas."

Christy discovered she was breathing very hard, that her

heart was pounding as if she had been running. Part of her anger was directed at Tad for deliberately disobeying her orders, but most of it was directed at her former father-in-law. How dare Neville go against her wishes! She had written him, telling him that any gifts to Tad would be returned, and yet he had defied her—but then, when had Neville Winthrop ever paid any attention to other people's rights?

She picked up the brochure and dropped it back inside the box. "You know you're not supposed to open *any* package that comes to the house, even if it is addressed to you," she said tightly. "I'll return this to the post office. There's been a mistake."

"Like the horse—and all those other things you returned, Mom?" Tad said. "You don't want my real father to give me anything, do you?"

She stared at him, too startled to answer.

"He *is* my father, isn't he? That's why those things keep coming to the house. Well, it isn't fair—you don't want me to have anything nice. I think you're a nasty old bitch—" He stopped, but not in time. The word echoed through the room, ugly and lacerating.

Christy felt a rush of anger, the culmination of a dozen irritants and alarms during the past three days. Before she could stop herself, her hand flew out and slapped Tad soundly on the cheek.

For one frozen moment, he stared at her with astonishment in his eyes. Then a wave of red swept over his face. "I hate you!" he shouted. "I wish I could live with my real father!"

Contrite and ashamed, she tried to take him in her arms, but he slid off the bed, ducked around her, and went flying out of the room. It was a moment before she got herself collected enough to follow him. By the time she reached the top of the stairs, the front door had already slammed shut and she heard Tad's footsteps running down the front path.

She hurried down the stairs and flung open the door, frantically calling out his name, but by then he had already disappeared behind the stand of trees that separated their yard from their next-door neighbors'.

The next two hours was a time of accelerated anxiety for Christy. After she had searched the immediate neighborhood on foot, she got into her car and cruised the surrounding streets and roads, then the housing areas farther afield, but Tad seemed to have vanished into thin air.

Finally, forced to admit defeat, she went home. As she drove along Old Orchard Road, she made bargains with herself, with God, that if she found Tad at home when she got back, she would make a lot of changes in herself, be a better mother to Tad, spend more time with him, find the money somehow to send him to Camp Blue Ox, if only for a week.

But when she hurried into the house and called Tad's name from the front hall, hoping against hope that he would answer, it was Miles who came through the kitchen door to give her a quizzical look.

He started to say something, but her expression must have alerted him, because he came to her side swiftly and put his arm around her shoulders. "What is it, Christy? What's wrong?"

Strangely, the question and the concern on his face steadied her and she was able to answer him calmly. "I don't know that anything is wrong, but Tad and I had a—a quarrel, and he ran out of the house. I've been looking all over, trying to find him, only I don't know where he could have gone."

She looked at him expectantly, as if he would immediately come up with the answer.

"Come into the kitchen. I just made a pot of coffee. You look like you could use a cup," he told her.

She let him lead her into the kitchen. She even swallowed a few sips of coffee while Miles, his voice calm and reasoning, questioned her about the efforts she'd already made to find Tad.

At his suggestion, she dredged her memory for the names of Tad's friends—dear God, he did have so many friends—and even a couple of favorite teachers that he might have contacted. She was grateful that Miles made the calls, all of them unsuccessful, because she knew that her own voice would have trembled, giving a lie to the excuse they had concocted for calling—that they were trying to locate Tad because of a minor family emergency.

Finally there was no one else to call. The two of them sat in silence, the coffee in their cups turned cold, staring at each other. Miles's face, always so mobile, had a stiff, unnatural look, and she realized that he was deliberately hiding his own worry.

Fear, like a monstrous black cloud, blossomed in her mind; it seemed to strip the color from the room around her, to put a bitter taste in the back of her mouth. Her pulse felt sluggish, as if the blood in her veins had suddenly turned to ice water.

She fought the fear, fought to hold it at bay as Miles spoke to her quietly, saying the things that she wanted to hear—that this was a safe neighborhood, that they still hadn't exhausted all the possibilities, that if Tad were deliberately hiding, it would be difficult to find him, that when he got hungry, he would turn up. She must have fooled Miles, because when he was finished he patted her hand and his own face relaxed a little.

She realized that he was talking again, and she forced herself to listen, then wished that she hadn't, because the words he was saying seemed to add the stamp of reality to her own spiraling fear.

"Just as a precaution, I think it's time we called the sheriff's department in on this, Christy," Miles said.

Chapter 7

Tad heard his mother's voice calling his name, but it only made him hurry faster.

As he plunged into the strip of trees that surrounded their yard on three sides, he was full of outrage—and bewilderment. In his whole life, he'd never before been struck in the face—or anywhere else. Even when the kids at school roughhoused with each other, they seldom used their fists. Sure, sometimes they shoved each other down and rolled on the ground, trying to push the other guy's face in the dirt, but there was no punching.

And his Dad—when he did something wrong, Miles just talked to him, which made him feel bad enough. His mother, too, hardly ever yelled at him, much less spanked him. So why had she slapped him this time—as if she hated him and didn't want him anymore?

The grievance welled up inside him, almost choking him. It wasn't even as if he'd done something so awful—like stealing from her purse or fooling around with his Dad's stereo. All he'd done was open a package that the mailman had left propped up against the front door. After all, his name had been written on it, as plain as could be: *Master Steven Havens, 3013 Orchard Road, Star Route 1, Orchardville, Washington.*

Didn't *that* give him the right to at least open the box and see what was inside?

And it was such a neat present. He'd been wanting a video recorder for ages. He'd even hinted to Mom and Dad that he hoped to get one for his birthday. Of course, Mom had explained that they cost a whole lot of money, almost a thousand dollars—which he already knew. Even when he told her you could tape TV programs and play them back later, that just about every kid he knew had one, she just shook her head and told him she was sorry.

Then she told him again about the hospital bills for Dad's mom, Grandma Havens, who had been sick a long time back in Maine before she died, that they all had to pitch in and make some sacrifices now—and that if he asked for too many things, it might make Dad feel bad.

Although he hadn't said it out loud, he'd sure wanted to say that he was tired of not having things like the other kids did. Mom had explained all that, too. This neighborhood was the kind where the houses all cost a lot of money, all except theirs, which was so old and tacky—only Mom hadn't said that, of course. So naturally most of the people who could afford to live around here could also afford to buy their kids a lot of expensive things.

"Sometimes more than's good for them," Mom had added.

Then Tad had smarted off and said he didn't think it was fair. According to Grandma Jessica, his real father had lots

of money. Maybe if Mom told *him* how much he wanted
that video recorder, his real dad would buy it for him.

Mom's face got all stiff and funny, and Tad felt rotten
and apologized, but Mom said that that was okay, she
wasn't mad, that maybe they could at least swing one of
those Atari game-players by next Christmas. Tad had
nodded, and he hadn't said that it wasn't the same thing at
all.

Moodily, he kicked the clump of grass at his feet. Well,
he was really in a jam now, all right. Even if he stayed
away the rest of the day, he'd have to go back home when
it started getting dark. Then he'd have to face Dad—and
Mom, too, which was even worse.

Maybe she'd cry. Not that she cried very often, at least
not around him. But he always knew when she wanted to,
because she got that funny smile on her face that didn't
match her eyes. It made him feel so awful that, right
away, he always promised to do better, to start keeping his
room clean or help with the yard work without Dad's
having to ask, or to get good grades instead of horsing
around so much in school.

He never really meant to do bad things. It was just that
Mom expected so much from him, always looking at him
as if she was afraid he'd do something wrong. And Dad,
too, expected a lot—only it was easier with him, because
he didn't put so much pressure on a guy. But Mom—every
time he did something like staying out too late with the
kids, she got that tight look around her nose. It did something to him, knowing that she didn't really trust him.

Maybe that was because of his father—his real one. He
had gone off somewhere before he was born, which was
why Mom was married to Miles now. His grandmother
had told him a lot of times that he looked just like the guy.

Of course, he didn't know if that part was true or not.
Grandma Jessica said a lot of things that—well, didn't

hang together. Like how, a long time ago, her family had owned a big hunk of Puget County. So how come she lived in that dinky little condo instead of a big house somewhere? And how come she drove the same car three years in a row before she bought a new one?

Maybe Grandma was wrong and he wasn't at all like his real father. He'd sure like to know for sure. She never said anything else about the guy, like it was some kind of big secret, and when he asked questions, she just looked funny and told him he should direct his questions at his mother. Which was a big laugh. Mom wouldn't even tell him what his father's name was! She said he was a Havens now, that it didn't matter what name he'd been born with.

But he was pretty sure he knew now. Neville Winthrop—it was a funny name, but that's what had been written on the left hand corner of that package. And who else would send him all those presents? Boy, if his real father ever found out he never got to keep even one of them, he'd sure be mad! And the mare—the resentment swelled up inside Tad, making his temples throb—he'd wanted that mare so bad, and yet his mother had sent her back.

The man who'd driven the truck that brought the mare to the house had called her a chestnut—because of her color, he'd said. Tad had loved her right away. Her eyes were large, sort of soft and friendly, and her nose felt like Mom's good coat, the velvet one she wore on evenings out. When she'd nuzzled his hand, he'd felt—well, real good inside.

And then Mom had come home and she got all excited and told him to go into the house while she straightened things out, that there'd been some kind of mistake. But he'd stood just inside the front door, listening, while she told the man to take the mare back, saying it had come to the wrong house even though the man argued with her and said the kid's name, Steven Havens, was right there on the

papers, plain as could be, and so was the address. And
then, for days aferward, she'd acted funny, hardly talking
or anything, like *he'd* done something wrong.

Boy, if his real father knew how she treated him, slap-
ping him and all, he'd—well, he'd come and take him to
that island to live. He'd like to live on an island. Just laze
around and not go to school and have the kids come over
in a boat to visit him—man, they'd really be green!
But no, he had to live in a crummy old house that didn't
even have a swimming pool. . . .

Tad wandered on, past a row of large yellow brick
houses. At the end of the street, he climbed a grassy hill,
one of a ridge of low hills that surrounded the neighborhood,
then went down the other side.

A new house was being built at the bottom of the hill,
and watching the workmen was usually an absorbing pas-
time for Tad and his friends. But today, as he surveyed the
activity from a perch on top of a pile of dirt, his face was
gloomy. He felt restless and bored, as if he were coming
down with something. When one of the men noticed him
and shouted, "Hey, kid! You'd better get your ass out of
here before you get hurt!" he rose silently and wandered
halfway back up the hill to continue his vigil from the
lower branch of a tree.

Now, that was the kind of house he'd like to live in.
The yard wasn't as big as his, but it would probably have a
sauna, maybe a hot tub, or even a small swimming pool.
Sure, the houses they were building in the neighborhood
were pretty close together, but they had a lot of extras,
too, like air conditioning and big rec rooms. Well, you had
to be rich to live in that kind of place—and Mom and Dad
sure weren't rich.

The construction crew began putting their tools away in
a small portable hut, and Tad realized that it was getting
along toward dinner time. Well, he might as well face

it—he had to go home sometime, especially since he was getting hungry. Not that he felt like he'd done anything wrong. No, Mom had hit *him*, not the other way around.

He flushed suddenly, remembering the name he'd called her. It was a bad word—the kids at school used it all the time for some of the teachers they didn't like—behind their backs, of course. He'd looked it up once in the big dictionary in Dad's den, along with some other words he wasn't supposed to say, and it had something to do with having puppies.

Which meant he'd called his own Mom a dog. But then he'd been really sore—and you said things you didn't mean when you were sore, didn't you? Even his mother did. Once in a while, she said something real sharp in that voice she only used when she was mad, and then later, she always apologized and told him that she'd had a headache or that she was so tired her nerves were all frazzled. So if she, a grownup, could say she was sorry, then he could do it too—and apologize for calling her a bitch.

His feet dragging, he retraced his steps. Taking his time, he climbed the rest of the way up the hill, then went back down the other side, heading for his own neighborhood.

It was an area of large houses, each set back from the road, each surrounded by trees and ornamental plantings and lush lawns. Only a couple of cars passed Tad as he ambled along the side of the road, and he saw no one in the yards or on the sidewalks, which wasn't strange, he reflected, since most of the yard work was done by gardeners and it was probably long past their quitting time.

When he had almost reached the turnoff to Old Orchard Road, he saw a large black car coming toward him, moving very slow. A dark-haired man wearing a suit and tie was driving. When the car pulled up to the curb beside Tad and the man rolled down his window, he automatically slowed his step; then, remembering his mother's warnings about talking to strangers, he started on again.

"Hey, kid—your name is Steven Havens, isn't it?"

Tad hesitated. Did *this* come under the heading of talking to strangers? After all, the man must know him, if he called him by his name. Maybe he was someone who had come to the house to see Mom and Dad, or someone who lived in the neighborhood—or maybe he was the father of one of his friends. . . .

"Yes, sir," he said cautiously.

The man got out of the car. He was smiling, a wide, loose-lipped smile that made Tad feel uncomfortable. His face was moon-shaped, and his mouth was puffy, very red. He took out a wallet and flipped it open in front of Tad's face. Tad's eyes widened when he saw a metal badge.

"My name is Wilkie—I'm a deputy sheriff," the man said easily. "I'm afraid I've got some bad news for you, kid."

Tad's heart leaped, then started pounding very hard. "Mom? Is something wrong with my Mom?"

"There was an accident—she's in the hospital. She sent me out to find you. She wants to see you right away."

"My Dad—does he know?"

"Oh, sure—the nurse called him at the university. He's on his way to the hospital right now. He said to tell you it was okay to come with me."

Despite his worry about his mother, Tad hesitated. Something about the man spooked him—was it the way he kept staring up and down the street? He tried to look into the car to see if it had a police radio, but the late afternoon sun reflected against the glass now and all he could see was his own image.

"Well, I guess it's okay," he said finally.

"Sure it is, Steven. Now, you come along with me and

we'll have you at the hospital in a jiffy. Your mother will be okay.''

He took Tad's arm and hurried him toward the car. Tad looked around, wondering if anyone was watching. Would they think he'd done something wrong, having a cop take him away in a police car? Of course, there wasn't really any way they would know the man was a deputy sheriff. He was wearing an ordinary suit and hat, and there was nothing about the car, like flashing red lights on top or a siren making a racket, to show what it was.

Tad felt a stab of disappointment. He wouldn't mind riding in a police car with the sirens going and lights flashing like crazy—but then, they probably didn't do that sort of thing unless they were chasing criminals. But it *was* odd that there was no insignia on the car. Was Mr. Wilkie an undercover man, or was it different with deputy sheriffs?

Well, it had to be okay, he thought. After all, Mr. Wilkie had showed him that badge, so he really was a deputy sheriff. He knew his name, too, even though it was funny that he'd used his school name, Steven, instead of calling him Tad, like everybody else did. And he knew about Dad working at the university—how would he know that if Mom hadn't told him?

Tad climbed into the front seat; he hoped the hospital wasn't too far away.

Chapter 8

It was Miles who made the call to the police.

With Christy's hands so numb that she didn't even dare raise the coffee cup to her lips, she was sure she couldn't have talked coherently enough to give the information they'd need. As she listened to Miles's calm voice tell some nameless stranger that he wanted to report a missing child, she fought against a rising tide of panic.

"They're sending someone over," Miles said turning away from the phone. "Even though it's only been a few hours, they're getting involved because of Tad's youth."

Tad's youth—yes, he is so young! So very young. . . .

"Is it going to be all right?" she said pleadingly, needing his reassurance. "Will we find him, Miles?"

"We'll find him. He's—I'd guess that he's hiding out somewhere, maybe at a friend's house. There's a lot of places he could go. I'm sure this is some child's trick to gain attention.''

"But Tad isn't like that! He's never done anything like this before.'' Almost with relief, she felt a stir of anger. "But if it's true, then so help me, I'll—'' But the brief flare of anger died as quickly as it had come and her eyes filled with tears. "Oh, Miles—I can't stand not knowing. I just can't stand it.''

He put his arms around her. "Hold on, honey. It will be all right.''

He was still holding her a few minutes later when the front doorbell rang. Christy was out of her chair and flying toward the hall before Miles could move. She flung the front door open, Tad's name on her lips, but when she saw the woman standing there, she could only cling to the doorknob, too disappointed to speak.

"I'm Sheriff's Detective Lombard.'' The woman's voice, like her appearance, was pleasant but very businesslike. "I understand you've called in a complaint about a missing child?''

Since Christy's voice seemed to have failed her, she motioned the woman inside, and a few moments later they were sitting across from each other on the living room love seats. Miles's hand was clasping hers; she was thankful that he had taken on the job of answering the detective's questions.

"And his age?''

"He turned ten two weeks ago—''

We had a party for him—all his class came. He's very popular, you know—his teacher says he has leader potential. . . .

"His height and weight?

"We measured him on his birthday and he was just a shade under—''

He's still a little small for his age, but so was I until I was past twelve. And they do say a boy is always taller than his mother, don't they? But even if he isn't, it doesn't really matter, because he carries himself so well that everybody thinks he's much taller.

"Any distinguishing marks—you know, birthmarks or scars?"

"None—oh, I take that back. He does have a small crescent-shape scar on his right thumb—"

It happened that time he fell off the swing—remember how upset I was and how calm you were, Miles? But that's why I married you, isn't it? Because I knew that you would always be there, steady and solid and supportive, the exact opposite of Lance.

"Do you have a recent photograph of your son? Full-face if possible, and preferably in color?"

"The snapshots taken at his birthday party are the most recent—I'll get them for you."

Miles gave Christy's hand a squeeze before he stood up. She felt a fresh wave of panic, as if something had wrenched apart inside her, when he left the room. She wanted to say something to Detective Lombard, to offer her a cup of coffee or a little wine or a mixed drink in a civilized way, but she was sure that if she opened her mouth, she would start screaming.

I'm not strong at all—I always thought I was so strong, but now I know the truth. I'm a coward, a quivering coward, where Tad is concerned. . . .

Numbly, she stared at Detective Lombard. The woman was youngish—perhaps in her early thirties, and her dark-brown hair was arranged in a simple, underplayed style; her make-up was subdued. In her gray blazer and matching skirt, she could have been a secretary or a teacher. She was wearing a wedding ring—did she have children? If so, did she worry about them, dream up scenarios in which *she* was the parent and someone else, another police officer, was writing down a description of her missing child in a notebook?

Detective Lombard broke the silence first. She asked how long it had been since they'd last seen their son, and to Christy's surprise, her voice sounded almost normal when she answered. "It's been over five hours now. At first I was concerned but not too worried. Then, after I'd looked all over the neighborhood, I returned to the house, hoping that he'd come home on his own, but of course he hasn't. Miles called everybody we could think of, but no one had seen Tad. That's when we knew we had to have help."

"You were the one who first thought of calling the sheriff's office?"

"No, Miles suggested it first. I knew he was right, but taking that step seemed to—" Her voice faltered.

"To make it more real? Yes, I can understand that. But you did the right thing. Even if—I'm sure it's a false alarm, but even so, the sooner we put out a bulletin on a missing child, the better. Usually, in these cases, the child turns up within twenty-four hours. He's probably hiding somewhere—especially if there was some sort of trouble at home."

"We had a quarrel. He ran out of the house—that's why I started looking for him immediately, you see. But it was as if he'd vanished into thin air."

Miles came back into the room and handed Detective Lombard several snapshots. She studied them carefully, then laid aside two of the clearest ones.

"He's a very good-looking youngster," she observed; there was an odd note in her voice that sent a fresh wave of fear through Christy. "He doesn't really look like either of you, does he?"

Since Christy didn't want to explain that Tad looked like

his real father, she nodded, then she asked, "What comes next, Detective Lombard?"

"The first thing we do is send out a bulletin to all law agencies in the area. A child that young out alone at night is bound to be noticed. Meanwhile, you call everybody you can think of that he might have gone to—neighbors, friends, and relatives."

"There's only my mother—and she lives on the other side of Puget City. He wouldn't go there."

"Probably not, but I suggest you call her anyway. And check with his friends, anyone he has the slightest acquaintance with."

"But we've already done that. No one has seen him since he left school this afternoon."

"Kids have been known to cover up for each other, so get the parents of his friends involved. Tell them the truth, that Tad is missing and you think he may be hiding out with someone. If there's anything going on, they'll smoke it out. And if he hasn't turned up by morning, we'll call for volunteers and put together a search team. It shouldn't take long to scour the woods and Granite State Park. Since the park's only three miles or so from here, it seems an obvious place for him to head if he wants to hide out."

"And if we don't find him there," Miles asked, "what will the police do next?"

Detective Lombard gave him a long sober look. "Look, I'm going to level with you and tell you how my superiors will view this business. We're in the business of solving— and sometimes preventing—crime. And being missing is not a crime. It has a very low priority with the—the Powers That Be. Until there's some evidence that—well, that something has happened to the child, we can only help organize search parties, put out bulletins—and notify the FBI so Tad's description will be included in their national crime computer. And be prepared for some questions that will seem insensitive and even cruel to you."

"What does that mean?" Christy said.

Miles's hand tightened around hers. "Detective Lombard is warning you that she has to follow standard police procedures. There are cases involving child abuse where—where the parents are responsible for the disappearance of a child."

Detective Lombard nodded. "Exactly. I know it's an unpleasant subject to talk about, but some parents lose control of their tempers and seriously hurt or even—well, things get out of control. Afterward, they panic and try to cover up by reporting a child missing."

Christy put her hand over her mouth, feeling sick. "Oh, my God! Are you saying that you suspect me of—" But she couldn't say the words out loud.

"No, I don't think any such thing. But I have to follow certain procedures that are spelled out in the police manuals. It has to be a matter of record that I asked you point blank if you—or your husband—did anything, accidentally or otherwise, to cause the disappearance of your son."

"No! You're a woman and married—do you have children?"

"Two—a boy nine and a girl seven."

"Then how can you ask such a thing?"

"It's her job, Christy," Miles said.

She turned on him, her eyes blazing. "At a time like this, how can you be so—so damned reasonable? Don't you feel anything at all?"

As soon as the words were out, she would have done anything to be able to recall them. She reached out to touch her husband's hand. "I'm so sorry—I know how much you love Tad. I don't know why I said that—"

"It's okay. And this isn't the time for—we can't afford to waste any time, Christy," he said quietly.

She took her hand away, feeling rebuffed—and yet knowing he was right. Tad was the important thing now. Nothing else mattered except finding him as quickly as possible.

"Then you do understand that I have to ask certain questions?" Detective Lombard said. "And there's more. I'd like permission to look around your house and grounds. That should be a matter of record, too."

"Do anything you have to do—but please hurry!"

After Detective Lombard had left the room with Miles, Christy huddled on the sofa, her eyes fixed on the phone, begging it to ring.

Her mind seemed shattered, filled with sharp shards of memory that had a cutting edge—Tad on his first tricycle barreling up and down the driveway, his eyes filled with dreams that she couldn't share. Tad going off to school that first day—and coming home with the news that he had *this* many best friends now, Mommy—and then he'd held up all ten of his fingers. And Tad at six, sleepy and a little cross, telling her that from now on, he was too old to need help with his bath. . . .

Oh, God, take anything else, but don't take Tad away from me! It would be too cruel.

She put her hands over her face, fighting panic, fighting the ugly suspicions. So many things could happen to a child—drowning and falling out of a tree and getting hit by a car and other things too terrible to think about.

And Tad was so trusting, so sure that everybody he met was his friend. He was used to people responding to him immediately because of his infectious grin, so he naturally gave back warmth in return.

Surely, surely no one would hurt a child like that—or would that charm, that beauty, be the thing that—no, no, she wouldn't think of *that*! She had to believe that he was all right, that he was staying with a friend, someone from school that she hadn't thought of, a new boy in his class perhaps. . . .

Miles's face looked gray and stiff when he returned to the living room. Detective Lombard asked more questions, and now Christy was the one who answered them, glad to have something to occupy her mind besides her own lacerating thoughts. It seemed to her that Detective Lombard's attitude had subtly changed, that she had lost some of her professionalism—or was that wishful thinking?

"Did your son say anything at all before he ran out of the house?" the policewoman asked finally.

"No, he just looked at me with a—a hurt expression as if he couldn't believe that I'd actually slapped him. I ran after him and called his name, but by then, he'd already disappeared behind the trees."

"You struck him?"

"Why, yes—didn't I tell you that? He called me a—a name, and my temper got the best of me. It's the first time I've ever hit him, but I lost control and—oh, what difference does it make? The important thing is to find him before something worse happens."

"Yes, that's the important thing." But there was a subtle coolness in the woman's voice now.

"It wasn't a hard slap. And it's the first time, too. We—Miles and I don't believe in physical punishment, so Tad has never even been spanked. But my nerves were so on edge today that when he called me that name, I lost my temper."

"What exactly was the argument about? What started it?"

Christy's mind moved sluggishly; it all seemed ages ago—the gift that Neville had sent to Tad, his disobedience, her outburst of anger, the slap. . . .

"He opened a package that came in the mail," she said. "Tad is strong-minded, but he doesn't often deliberately disobey our orders. I—I overreacted, I'm afraid, and he stormed out of the house—'' She stopped, her throat suddenly thick as she remembered the shock on Tad's face after she'd slapped him.

''Why would he disobey you this time, I wonder?''

''The package was addressed to him. He couldn't resist, I suspect.''

''What was it? A late birthday present?''

''A gift from his grandfather. When I told him I would have to send it back, he was very angry.''

''I don't understand. Why would you send back a gift from the boy's grandfather?''

''Because—oh, it's very complicated, and it hasn't anything to do with Tad's disappearance.''

''Why don't you let me be the judge of that, Mrs. Havens?''

''Oh, very well . . . until a month ago, Tad's grandfather—my former husband's father—has been completely out of touch with his grandson. Then, out of the blue, he started calling me, wanting visitation rights with Tad. There are reasons—very good ones—why I don't want Tad to have any contact with my former father-in-law, so I refused. When the presents started arriving, I sent them all back, including a horse that came a week ago.''

She paused to take a deep breath before she added, ''I gave Tad instructions that he wasn't to open anything that came in the mail, not even if it was addressed to him. Usually, I'm home first, so I make sure he doesn't see the packages, but a couple of times he was here when they arrived. He's been very curious—I guess he couldn't resist this time. Which is why I was so angry—''

''Could he have gone to see his grandfather?''

''Oh, no. Tad has no idea he even has a grandfather.''

''I don't understand.''

"My first husband and I—oh, do you have to know all of this?"

"I think you'd better tell me everything that could possibly help, Mrs. Havens. This isn't the time to keep secrets, no matter how embarrassing."

Christy knew she had no choice, but her voice was tight as she said, "My first husband wanted an annulment of our marriage so he could remarry in the Catholic Church. In return, he signed away all legal claim, including visitation rights, to his son. Lance, my first husband, told his father that I was pregnant by another man when he married me and his father believed him. I'm sure he regarded the annulment as additional evidence that Lance was telling the truth. I don't know why Neville is suddenly so interested in Tad. I suspect Lance had a change of heart and told his father the truth—possibly with the idea of getting money out of him. At any rate, that chapter of my life is closed. I don't want it reopened now."

"Then your first husband has no interest in Tad? He refuses to acknowledge that he's the father?"

"Oh, he admits it now, but he's a little late. He came here a few days ago, wanting to see Tad—" She stopped, her eyes widening. "Oh, my God—is *that* it? Did Lance take Tad because I wouldn't let him see him? Is that the answer?"

"You don't know that, Christy," Miles said quickly. "Why would he do anything so stupid? After all, he's shown no interest in the boy until recently. It was probably a whim of some kind, his coming here."

"No, you're wrong! I'm sure Lance took him—"

Detective Lombard snapped her notebook shut. There was an air of finality about the sound. "I suggest you get in touch with Tad's father and find out if he has the boy. If so, let us know immediately so—"

"Hold on, Detective Lombard!" Miles's voice, usually

soft-spoken, held an edge of authority now. "I don't think you should jump to any conclusions. We have no reason to believe that the boy's father took Tad. That kind of assumption could waste valuable time."

When Christy started to speak, he gave her hand a warning squeeze. "So what do we do next?" he went on. "Should I call the local radio and TV stations and ask their cooperation—or does the sheriff's department do that?"

"It's a little premature for—" The officer stopped, gave Miles's stiff face a long look, then shrugged. "Very well. We'll take care of that. And you're right. Radio and TV bulletins often do the trick, especially if a child is staying with a friend. But I have to warn you that it can also bring the kooks out in droves and—"

She paused, then switched subjects. "But meanwhile we'll check up on the boy's father. Most child disappearances are instigated by disgruntled spouses. And maybe we'd better talk to his grandfather, too. It couldn't hurt. How about starting with your former husband's name and present address, Mrs. Havens?"

"His name is Lance Winthrop. I don't know where he's staying—possibly with his father on Winthrop Island—"

She broke off when she saw Detective Lombard's eyes narrow. The woman looked around the sparsely furnished living room, then at Christy's tense face. "Are you saying that Neville Winthrop—*the* Neville Winthrop—is the boy's grandfather?"

It was Miles who answered her. "Yes—and I doubt that the Winthrops have anything to do with this. There's no question of a custody suit. Until a couple of days ago, Lance Winthrop showed no interest whatsoever in his son. I suspect he came here on a whim—you did say he took your refusal good-naturedly, Christy, didn't you?"

"Yes, but you don't know Lance. He doesn't care who he hurts as long as he gets his own way—"

She realized her words had a hard, brittle sound, and she stopped, blinking hard.

Detective Lombard got to her feet. "Well, I'll get things rolling. And try not to worry too much. Kids have a way of getting misplaced, but they usually turn up okay." When she smiled, her austere face took on warmth. "My oldest kid's a born explorer. A couple of years ago, he wandered off during a picnic, and it was three hours before we found him, sleeping under a tree. So I know something of what you're going through now. I didn't know whether to kiss him or blister his behind."

"I know what I'd do if Tad walked in right now," Christy said with a shaky laugh. "I'd hug him until he was dizzy."

"Well, try to get some rest." Detective Lombard hesitated. She looked at both of them in turn before she added, "Look, this is the private citizen in me talking now, not the police officer. Because of the prominence of your former father-in-law, this business is bound to—to stir up a lot of attention. So I'm going to give you some advice. Be very careful what you say to the press if you don't want this turned into a three-ring circus. On the other hand, be completely honest with us, the police. Even if there's something that could be humiliating or embarrassing, don't hold back."

"We've told you everything," Miles said grimly.

"Then my next advice, speaking as a private citizen, is to stay on top of things. We tell the parents in such cases to let us handle the investigation completely, but—well, I could get canned for saying this, but if it were my kid, I'd get involved. Doing something constructive can keep you from—from brooding too much. Waiting is hell—and the busier you stay, the better."

She paused again, as if weighing her words before she added, "After twenty-four hours, the sheriff's department will report Tad's disappearance to the FBI, but things have a way of getting fouled up where bureaucracy is concerned. So check with the bureau in a couple of days—if Tad hasn't shown up by then—and make sure the particulars have reached their national crime computers. And be prepared. With a grandparent as wealthy as Neville Winthrop, there's always the possibility that your son has been kidnapped for ransom.''

At Christy's gasp, the detective gave her sober look. ''And if Tad has been taken for—let's say he was kidnapped by a barren woman who wants a child, which happens sometimes, then it could be a long while before you get him back. Remember that kids change very fast. So now's the time to put down on paper every detail about Tad you can think of. You're sure you'll never forget anything about him, but there have been cases that have stretched out into years. So make a list now of Tad's mannerisms, the way he walks or holds his head, anything unique about his appearance. Is he sociable or shy? Does he have any special gifts or learning disabilities, a stutter, or a special way of laughing or smiling? What is his level of interest in sports, his natural abilities—and also his shortcomings? Someday, you might need these things— and, by the way, do check with the hospital where he was born and see if you can get his footprint. It's the best identification there is.''

''You talk as if you think it'll be a long time before we see Tad again,'' Christy protested. ''I can't believe that! I won't believe it—''

''It's just a precaution, Christy,'' Miles said. He exchanged glances with the officer. ''And Detective Lombard is being very honest with you and giving you the best advice she can. Listen to her.''

Detective Lombard nodded. ''I'm sticking my neck out,

saying some of this, but—well, I was a woman before I became a cop, and I'm also a mother. If you decide to put out flyers, offering a reward or such, let us know what you're up to. We can't advise you to hire private detectives, and in fact, it's the official policy to tell you not to do it. For one thing, it's very expensive. But if you go that route, let us know, so we can cooperate. And if you give any interviews on TV or radio, or print up any flyers or take out ads in newspapers, for God's sake, don't give your address and phone number. The nuts come out of the woodwork at times like this. Refer any information to us. We'll check it out. This way you can avoid extortion attempts—"

"You mean people are so low that they would actually try to extort money from the parents of a missing child?"

"Most people are decent and well-meaning, Mrs. Havens, but some of them, a very small minority, will do anything to make a fast buck. And there's another group that could be pretty hard on your emotions—the parents of other missing children. They can be very supportive, but sometimes they'll call and beg you to take along their kid's picture when you're doing your own searching. And who can blame them? If anything happened to my kids, I'd do the same thing, go to any lengths to find them. But protect yourself from all the mental strain you can. You'll need your strength for when your boy comes home."

Miles studied her, frowning. "Do you think this is a kidnapping for ransom?" he asked abruptly.

Detective Lombard shook her head. "I think your boy will turn up when he gets good and hungry, possibly within the next twenty-four hours. But in case he doesn't— the Winthrop name is synonymous with wealth. It's possible that he's been kidnapped for that reason."

"I just can't believe it," Christy said. "Very few peo-

ple know who Tad's father is—and besides, wouldn't there
be a ransom note?''

"It may come later. I think we'd better keep your phone
monitored, just in case. Meanwhile, I'll start the ball
rolling so we can organize a search party as soon as it gets
light.''

"I'll go with you and give you a hand getting volunteers.
My students will help, I'm sure," Miles said. "And then
I'll do some searching on my own." He looked at Christy.
"You'll have to stay here—in case Tad comes home."

An involuntary protest rose to Christy's lips, but she
suppressed it. Tad's safety came before her own reluctance
to be left alone.

"I think it's time you called Jessica and asked her to
come over," Miles said, as if reading her mind. "She'll
be company for you, and she can also help you with the
phone once the bulletin comes over the radio."

"We'll set up a monitor on your phone as soon as
possible," Detective Lombard said, glancing at her watch.
"Just in case a ransom demand is made. And my best
advice to you, Mrs. Havens, is to take it easy. You'll need
all your energy in the morning. I know you can't sleep,
but do try to get some rest."

She put her pad away in her blazer pocket; later on,
Christy was to think that her final words had a prophetic
ring as she added, "And now the only thing you can do is
try to relax. It could be a long wait."

Jessica arrived an hour later. Without her usual careful
make-up, with her hair tied up in a scarf, she looked like a
stranger. Smoking one cigarette after another, she paced
up and down the living room floor, her lips pressed tightly
together, as if she were afraid that if she opened them
she'd say something unpleasant.

It was almost a relief when Jessica finally spoke. "What I don't understand is why you made such a fuss over a present. What harm could it possibly do if Tad got a few gifts from Neville—or Lance? After all, Miles and you can't provide much in the way of luxuries for the boy— and you won't let me give him anything more than a game or something small, even for Christmas or his birthday. I guess I'll never understand you, Christy, never in a million years."

Or I you, Mother.

Christy felt a telltale prickling under her eyelids. Murmuring some excuse, she retreated to the downstairs bathroom and had her first cry since Tad's disappearance. When the tears finally stopped, she dashed cold water on her face, not bothering to comb her hair, and returned to the living room, to find Jessica curled up in Miles's old Morris chair, her eyes closed, her face so slack that Christy knew she must be dozing.

Christy dropped onto one of the love seats. She leaned her head against the back and closed her eyes to rest them, although she was sure she couldn't sleep. As if her nerves were jangling to some of Tad's punk rock, she felt jumpy, and her head throbbed, keeping time with her pulse. When she found it hard to breathe, she realized that she was having an anxiety attack. Quietly, she rose and went to take one of the tranquilizers the doctor had prescribed after she'd lost the baby, then returned to the love seat.

Whether it was the pill or her own exhaustion, she fell asleep, and it was almost dawn when she finally awoke with a start that jarred her whole body. She looked around wildly, half expecting to find Tad standing there, but nothing had changed. Jessica was still asleep, and the lamps were still on—it was only when the phone rang again in the kitchen that she realized what had awakened her.

Her first reaction was guilt. How could she sleep when Tad was still missing? She hurried into the kitchen to snatch up the phone, and said a quick "Yes?" into the mouthpiece.

"Is this Mrs. Havens—Mrs. Miles Havens?" a man's voice asked.

"Yes, it is. Who is calling, please?"

"This is John Taylor—at KPUG. Would you please fill me in on the disappearance of your son, Mrs. Havens? I understand that he's the grandson of Neville Winthrop—"

Somehow she answered the newsman's questions as politely—and briefly—as possible, following Detective Lombard's advice. After she got rid of him, she sat there, feeling numb, the quiet pressing in around her. The silence frightened her, and finally she went back to the living room to awaken Jessica, just to have company.

It was the sight her mother's sleeping face, looking strangely defenseless, that stopped her. For all the relentless facials and creams and massages, the expensive facelifts and hair touch-ups, Jessica was beginning to show her age. Another woman might give in and grow old gracefully, but not Jessica. She'd go down fighting the wrinkles, the age spots, the middle-age spread. Was this why, despite Jessica's constant criticism and unwanted advice, she had never shut her mother out of her life? God knows, Jessica's goals and interests were not the same as hers, but no one could deny that her mother was a fighter.

And so am I, Christy thought suddenly. *I won't give in to this thing. I'm going to fight back, do everything I can to find my baby, and I'm not going to lose hope—not ever.*

Knowing she must keep busy or go out of her mind, she returned to the kitchen to make fresh coffee. She was sitting at the table, her head resting on her folded arms, when Miles came home.

His face had a gaunt, exhausted look. For the first time since she'd met him, she was aware of the ten years difference in their ages. Briefly, her heart contracted with fear—until he gave her a tired smile.

He kissed her, then sank down into a chair. "No news so far, Christy. I came home to change into something more suitable for hiking and to bring you up to date. Then I'll be heading out again. The sheriff's deputies will be canvassing the neighborhood as soon as it gets light. They'll interview everyone within the radius of several miles. Someone may have seen something that will give them a lead."

"You said search *parties*—how many are there?"

"Two of the local boy scout chapters are organizing a sweep of Granite State Park, and there were enough volunteers at the university to make up three more parties. They're going to cover every inch of this area—they should be getting underway any minute now. It's possible Tad found a boat and went out on Granite Park Lake, then lost his oars and is drifting around out there somewhere. The state police are sending a helicopter out to make a sweep of the lake."

He paused to rub his hand over his face. "The bulletin will be on the six o'clock news—and then all hell will break loose, I'm afraid. But we haven't any choice. The more people who know about Tad's disappearance, the better the chances of finding him quickly."

A few minutes later, the announcement that a child was missing came over the kitchen radio. To Christy, listening, the newcaster's words seemed to hold an element of déjà vu. How many times had she heard something similar on the air about another child? She'd always felt pity for the parents, but inevitably the incident had soon faded from her memory. There were so many appeals, so many tragedies—sometimes the child was found, but so often she never knew how it all turned out. How would this one end? In happiness—or as some terrible tragedy?

She felt a coldness on her face and only then realized that tears were running down her cheeks. To stem them, she hid her face against her knees, bending forward as if she were in pain. Miles's warm hand lifted her to her feet and then her face was pressed against his chest. His sweater reeked of cigarette smoke, and she realized that he, who disliked cigarettes so much, must have spent hours at the sheriff's office in an overheated room filled with smokers.

"It'll be all right, Christy. We'll find Tad—just hold on to that thought."

She scrubbed her face with the palms of her hands. "How can you say that for sure?" she said dully. "How can anyone say that?"

"I say it because I believe it—and you have to believe it, too. And now—how about fixing me a couple of pieces of toast while I change my clothes?"

The calls started almost at once. From neighbors and friends. From Miles's colleagues and students at the university, and from her co-workers at Computers Now—all offering to help in the search for Tad. There were also calls from strangers—from curiosity-seekers and well-wishers and cranks—and from the news media. As Detective Lombard had predicted, the connection with the Winthrops was too big a story to go unnoticed.

But no ransom demands came, and when Detective Lombard called at midmorning, it was to tell Christy that nothing had been discovered so far to indicate foul play. A construction worker on a nearby project had seen a boy of Tad's description, but other than that, there were no leads.

A little to Christy's surprise, Jessica volunteered to field the calls. Crisply, she dispensed with well-wishers, using the valid excuse that the line should be kept open. Other calls she referred to the police, and twice she simply hung up the phone without speaking.

The doorbell rang constantly. People came and went— familiar faces, some not familiar. People asked Christy questions, and she must have answered them in a reasonably sensible way, because they nodded and went away. Once, someone put a mug of coffee in her hand, and she took a drink, only to realize it was loaded with sugar and cream, which she detested, but she finished it off anyway, because what did it really matter? She got used to bright voices murmuring the same reassurances, giving her the same advice, that she should try to get some rest, as she wandered restlessly from room to room, trying to outrun the dread, the fear.

Once, when she came into the kitchen, someone told her she must eat and keep up her strength, and she tried to force down a sandwich, only to find it was impossible to swallow. Miles came and went, his face increasingly tired, but when she insisted that he lie down for a while, he shook his head and told her that he would rest later.

Detective Lombard returned that afternoon during one of the times when Miles was there. "I've been assigned to the case permanently," she told them. "We're pretty shorthanded, but I've asked for a twenty-four–hour watch on your house, at least temporarily, to keep some of the nuisance visitors away. Meanwhile, I have a bit of news. Sheriff Ardmore called Neville Winthrop and asked for your former husband's address. He says that as far as he knows, his son is in Europe—possibly in France."

"But Lance is here—in Puget City," Christy protested.

"Mr. Winthrop claims he's been out of touch with his son for several years. However, he gave us a couple of local addresses—friends Lance might be staying with. We're checking on it now."

"If Lance did take Tad—is that the same as kidnapping, even though he is Tad's father?"

"You'd better believe it—although in that case, it would be called child-stealing." Detective Lombard smiled at Christy suddenly. "There's a lot of people out there trying to help—"

The phone rang, interrupting her. Jessica answered it, listened a moment, then silently handed it to Detective Lombard. Christy watched the woman's face as she said a few words into the mouthpiece. When the policewoman frowned, the fear rose inside her like a malignant cloud.

When Detective Lombard hung up the phone, she looked up and met Christy's agonized stare. "It's okay, Mrs. Havens!" she said quickly. "That was the sheriff. He's located your former husband, but I'm afraid it's a dead end. He's been on a cruise on a friend's yacht for the past several days—there are a dozen witnesses who will swear he never left the yacht during that time."

"Lance's friends would lie for him," Christy said sharply. "They'd think it was some kind of lark. So their word means nothing—"

"I'm afraid it does. The owner of the yacht is Corky Lafferty, the State Attorney General—and one of the guests was Art Rinehart, the mayor of Puget City."

Christy shook her head stubbornly. "Corky would say anything Lance tells him to—and Mayor Rinehart could be mistaken."

"I think it's very unlikely. The yacht has been out at sea for several days and just docked this morning."

"I don't care about that. I have this gut feeling that Lance took Tad. Maybe he hired someone to do it. I don't know how he managed it, but I'm sure he has my baby!"

"Really, Christine, you're being a little absurd," Jessica said. "Just because you have this grudge against Lance—well, do use some judgment about the accusations you make."

The phone rang again, and Jessica, who was nearest to it, snatched it up and snapped, "Yes, who is it?" into the receiver. Christy saw her face stiffen. "For you, Christine," she said, holding out the phone.

"Yes?" Christy said into the mouthpiece.

"This is Lance—are you okay? I just heard what happened and if there's anything I can do—"

"You've done enough!" she said shrilly. "I want my baby—bring him back to me, you hear!"

"Hey, that's crazy. Why would I take the kid? Sure, I'd like to see him, but—"

"Don't lie to me, you bastard! You can't get away with this—you and your friends can fool the police but not me. If you don't bring him back, I'll—I'll come looking for you with a gun!"

"Christy, you're hysterical. Now, calm down and think about what you're saying. The way I move around, what on earth would I do with a kid?"

"Who knows how your mind works? I only know that you have Tad and I want him back—"

Miles took the receiver from her hand. Above the roaring in her head, she heard him say, "This is Miles Havens, Christy's husband. She's been going through hell, Winthrop. If you know anything about this—"

Lance must have interrupted him, because he broke off and listened silently for a while, his face expressionless. Christy wanted to snatch the phone from his hand, but a sudden awareness that the room was full of neighbors and friends stopped her. She turned away from their embarrassed looks, knowing that none of them believed that Lance had taken her son—and that she hadn't helped things by losing her temper, by her wild accusations and threats.

A few minutes later, when Miles finally hung up the phone and turned to look at her, she knew something else—that Miles didn't believe her either.

Chapter 9

They had been driving along a narrow country road for about fifteen minutes when Mr. Wilkie reached under the seat and took out a thermos bottle.

"Here, kid, you look thirsty. Pour yourself a drink of cola. You can find some paper cups in the glove compartment."

Tad knew he should refuse. He wasn't supposed to drink soft drinks because they were bad for his teeth. But he was too polite—and too thirsty—to say anything. He got a paper cup from the glove compartment and carefully poured it half-full of the cola, but as soon as he'd taken a sip he was sorry. For one thing, it was too sweet. For another, it tasted funny—sort of flat, like the bubbles had all gone out of it.

But he finished it off anyway, because he didn't know

where to dump what was left in the paper cup, then settled
back in his seat, wishing they would go faster. Instead,
Mr. Wilkie seemed to slow down even more, not even
trying to pass an old farm truck up ahead that was just
crawling along. And it wasn't as if there were a lot of
other cars on the road. No, they hadn't passed one for
quite a while now, or seen anything much except trees and
fields and a few farmhouses. In fact, as Tad looked around,
he realized that it was a road he'd never been on before.

Well, it must be a shortcut to the hospital—and despite
his anxiety about his mother, he was glad that he had time
to do some thinking and decide what was he going to say
to Mom when they got to the hospital. And what would
she say to him? That she was sorry she'd slapped him?
Yes, she'd say *that* for sure. She always said she was
sorry. And then it would be his turn to tell her that he
shouldn't have called her a bitch or argued about sending
the video recorder back either, and that he was sorry, too.
He really was sorry—and scared, too. What if something
bad had happened to Mom? What if he never got a chance
to apologize and tell her that he loved her?

He realized the man was watching him out of the corner
of his eye, and he swallowed hard, not wanting to cry in
front of a stranger.

"How long before we get to the hospital, Mr. Wilkie?"
he said.

"They took your mother to one of the big ones in the
city—why don't you just relax and before you know it,
we'll be there. Close your eyes—it'll make the time go
faster."

Although it didn't make sense to Tad—why would closing his eyes make the time go faster?—he discovered that
his eyelids felt tired, as if they were weighted down with
something heavy. He turned sideways, facing away from

the man, and drew his knees up to his chest, closing his eyes.

It sure was crazy—he'd been wide awake just a few minutes ago, but now he really did feel sleepy. Well, he wouldn't take a nap, but he'd rest his eyes. . . .

A lot of things were happening around Tad, but his eyelids were still so heavy that he couldn't get his eyes open to take a look around. For one, a cold draft blew against his face, making him wonder if Mr. Wilkie had opened the window on the driver's side of the car. And under him, the car was rocking gently back and forth, just as if he were in a giant cradle. The rocking movement went on for a long, long time before it finally stopped, and then someone was lifting him, carrying him like a baby. And he could hear people talking, but they sounded as if they were a long way off.

He heard his name. Not Tad, but his school name— Steven. And then a voice, a sort of rusty voice, was asking questions, and Tad was glad that the man was talking to Mr. Wilkie instead of to him, because man, he sure did sound mad. . . .

Later—a minute or an hour or maybe even several hours later—he felt something soft and cushiony under him, and he was sure he smelled flowers, not real ones, but as if someone wearing perfume or maybe aftershave lotion was bending over him.

Light flashed against his closed eyelids, then went away. Maybe he had fallen asleep downstairs on the couch, watching TV, and Dad had carried him up to bed—no, that couldn't be! He was too big for Dad to carry him up the stairs, and besides Dad was at the hospital with Mom, and Mr. Wilkie had come to get him and drive him into the city to see her. . . .

Something brushed his arm; with a startled cry, he opened his eyes and stared around wildly.

No—no, he wasn't in his room. In fact, he'd never seen this place before—or anything like it except maybe on TV or in a movie. For one thing, it was bigger than the rooms at home, and the furniture looked heavy and sort of fancy. The walls were covered with wood paneling, and there were lots of pictures. Some of them were really neat—clowns and circus things and old-fashioned balloons, the kind people used to ride in.

Hanging from the corners were models of airplanes and rocket ships and even a space capsule. They weren't the kind he had at home, the ones he and Dad made up from kits. These looked real, as if they were made of metal. One whole wall was covered with bookcases, but instead of books, the shelves were stuffed full of model kits and games and sports equipment and other neat things, more than he'd ever seen together in one place except maybe in the toy department of a store.

Maybe this is a dream, he thought. *Maybe I'm still asleep—*

"How are you feeling, young man?"

Tad blinked, only then realizing he was lying on his back on a white spread that looked—and felt—like fur. Instinctively, he looked down—and saw that someone had taken off his shoes.

He turned his head and found himself staring into a pair of steel-gray eyes. The man standing by the bed was a stranger—and he was also very old. Fine lines radiated out from the corners of his eyes and mouth, while deeper ones cut through the middle of his leathery-looking cheeks. His lips were thin and straight and unsmiling, and although he held his body very straight, Tad was sure he was even older than Grandma Havens had been before she died.

"I guess I fell asleep in the car," Tad said, finding his tongue finally. "Can I see my Mom now?"

"Not yet—why do they call you *Tad*? Isn't your name Steven?"

"Steven's my name at school, but the rest of the time, everybody calls me Tad. It's short for Tadpole," Tad said politely. "My dad started calling me that when I was real little—and it stuck."

"Your dad—you mean your stepfather, don't you?"

"I guess he's that, but only because I was already born when he married my mother. Otherwise, he'd be my real dad."

The man grunted. He regarded Tad so closely that he felt uncomfortable, as if he'd done something wrong.

"Are you the doctor? Can I see my Mom now?" Tad asked.

"She isn't here. I'm afraid my man Wilkie lied to you. Your mother is fine. There was no accident."

Tad stared at him, dumbfounded. "But—but why did Mr. Wilkie say she was hurt?"

"Because he wanted you to get into his car without you making a fuss. He had orders to find you and bring you here to see me."

A suspicion flowered inside Tad. "Are you my—?" But the idea was too impossible. His father couldn't possibly be this old—or could he?

"My name is Neville Winthrop and I'm your grandfather. My son is your father."

"You're my *grandfather*?"

"I am—and it's about time we became acquainted. Stand up, boy, so I can get a good look at you. I want to see what kind of material I've got to work with."

Feeling shy, Tad slid off the bed and stood up. The man took his face between his hands, staring at him. His hands felt cold, very dry, and an odd odor, not really unpleasant, but sort of musty, made Tad's nose twitch. He wanted to pull away, but he didn't want to hurt the man's feelings. He was glad when his grandfather released him, nodding his head.

"You're the mirror image of your father. I just hope the resemblance ends there," he said. "What kind of lad are you, I wonder? Spunky, I'd guess—and smart. Know how to mind your manners, too. That's good—I can do a lot with a sharp boy who has some grit—and also some respect for his elders."

Standing beside the old man, who was so tall, Tad felt very small—and suddenly afraid.

"I think I'd better go home now," he said in his politest voice. "My mother doesn't like me to stay out after dark, especially when she doesn't know where I am."

"Oh, your mother knows you're here. She was in on the whole thing."

"But—but she didn't say anything about it to me. She didn't even tell me who you were when she took your present away from me. That's why we had that—why we yelled at each other and I ran away."

"We set this thing up earlier, before you came home from school."

"You mean she told that man to lie to me? But Mom never lies—never!"

"I'm afraid she did this time. It was her idea, having my man bring you here. She thought a good scare would teach you a lesson—but all that's behind you now. From now on, you'll be living here on Winthrop Island with me—at least, for a few days. And you're going to have a great time. I bought those things for you so you wouldn't get bored." He gestured toward the bookshelves. "Anything else you want, just ask for it. Within reason, of course."

"I don't understand, sir. You mean I'm going to visit you for a while?"

"Not for just a visit. From now on, you'll be living with me." The man smiled at him, but Tad didn't feel any better. "In a week or so, we'll be leaving the country—as soon as I can arrange things. How'd you like to live on a real Greek island, boy, one where everybody works for your grandfather—and no outsiders are allowed to butt into your business?"

"If you don't mind, I'd really rather go home now, sir," he said.

"Well, I'm afraid that won't do. Your mother and I have an agreement. I'm a very wealthy man, you know—or maybe she never told you that?"

Tad shook his head numbly.

"Well, I am. In exchange for a quite a lot of money, your mother and stepfather agreed to let you come and live with me."

"Don't you say that! She'd never do that—" Tad choked on his words and couldn't go on.

"Here now, Steven. No tears. I can't abide a sniveler. Buck up and accept the truth. Your mother wants what's best for everybody, including herself. Since you obviously haven't been happy at home lately, she decided you'd be better off living with me. And don't blame those two for taking my money. Money is important. Don't ever run it down."

Tad swallowed hard, still fighting tears. Despite himself, he remembered the conversations with his mother about mortgage payments and obligations and Grandma Havens's funeral expenses. Had Mom and Dad sold him to this man for enough money to pay all their bills? And when Mom had slapped him today—had she done it on purpose so he'd run away and Mr. Wilkie could pick him up? Maybe she was ashamed to come right out and tell him the truth, that she wanted him to go live with his grandfather.

Hurt seethed through him—and then rage, the strongest

of his life. If she didn't want him—if *they* didn't want him—then maybe he didn't want them, either.

A wave of nausea seized him. "Where's the bathroom?" he asked thickly, feeling as if he wanted to throw up.

The man pointed to a door. "Through there—that damned fool Wilkie! I didn't authorize drugs—what's so difficult about handling one ten-year-old boy?"

But Tad wasn't listening. He flew across the room, through the door, and into a tiled bathroom where he bent over a washbasin and was sick for a long time. When he finally stopped vomiting, he felt as if he were completely hollow inside. After he'd washed his face and cleaned everything up, he went back into the bedroom, feeling weak and shaky.

The man—no, he'd better start thinking of him as his grandfather—was still there, standing by the window, looking out. He turned and gave Tad a long stare. "Are you feeling better now, boy?"

"Yes, sir—I'm okay."

"Well, you'll be back to normal by morning. It's long past your bedtime—why don't you get ready for bed? There's a supply of pajamas in that chest over there—your mother told me what size to buy."

Tad went to get the pajamas from the drawer. He felt rotten—like someone had kicked him in the stomach. If Mom had told his grandfather what size pajamas to buy, then the other things he'd said must be true. Mom and Dad really didn't want him anymore.

Was it because he forgot to pick up his room sometimes or because he was always sneaking cookies just before dinner and playing the punk rock station on his radio so loud that it gave Mom a headache—and made Dad shake his head and say that thing about sic transit gloria something?

Or maybe it wasn't any of these things. Maybe they wanted to be alone, just the two of them, without having to bother about him. Sometimes, when they were laughing together at some joke he didn't understand, or when they looked at each other in that funny way, like they had some secret together, he felt lonely, as if he was on the outside of the house, looking in at them through the window . . .

"Just in case you start wondering if I'm telling you the truth, boy, I think you'd better take a look at this paper," his grandfather said. He laid a piece of paper on a desk near where Tad was standing. "You can see your mother's signature there at the bottom, and if you'll read it you'll note that it gives me custody of you until you're eighteen. I know you're confused right now, but after you've had a good night's rest, take a look at it."

He didn't seem to notice Tad's silence as he moved toward the door. "One of my men will bring you up a snack from the kitchen—a hamburger and french fries and a hot dog, too. Your mom tells me these are some of your favorite foods, but I've forgotten what you want on the hamburger."

"Special sauce—and chili on the hot dog," Tad said automatically. His stomach growled, and he realized he was very hungry.

The man snapped his fingers; there was a funny look in his eyes as if he'd just heard a joke but he didn't want to laugh out loud. "Of course—that's exactly what Christine told me. Well, I've got a bad memory sometimes, but that's because I'm getting a bit long in the tooth."

He hesitated, then added, "How much did your mother tell you about me—and your father?"

"Nothing. I don't even know his name. I never heard of you either until I saw your name on that package—and all Mom said then was that there'd been a mistake."

The man's lips tightened to a thin line; Tad felt cold, looking at him. "Well, at least she hasn't filled you full of a lot of lies about us," his grandfather said. "I guess she told you she deserted your father after she met Miles Havens?''

Tad started to say ''No,'' but he was afraid his voice would choke up on him, so he compromised and shook his head instead.

''I'm afraid it's the truth. Your father was heartbroken when she ran off with that fellow, especially since she took you along, too. I don't like saying these things about your mother, but it was too bad she refused to allow your father to visit you all these years.''

Tad tried to sort out his grandfather's words. He wanted to defend his mother and say that his mom wasn't like that at all, but he wasn't sure of his grounds. Maybe she'd been lying when she'd told him that his father had left her, that it wasn't at all as if his father had rejected *him*, too, since he hadn't even been born then. Of course, if it was true that she had run off with Dad, he could understand that. Dad was a really cool guy. But why hadn't she let his real father see him? It just didn't make sense—none of it did.

''Well, put it out of your mind, Tad. I'm sure that she intended to keep you with her until you were a grown man. But Christine does have a fickle nature—do you know what that word means?''

''No, sir.''

''It means she gets tired of people easily. Like she got tired of having you around. Which is why she turned you over to me to raise. And we're going to get along fine, aren't we? I'm a very rich man. You can have just about anything you want, including that chestnut mare your mother sent back. By the time you're a man, you'll be able to handle the money you'll inherit from me someday—provided you mind your p's and q's. Money is what makes the world go around, boy—but it's also a big responsibility, too. You're a sharp boy—you'll learn fast. And this time,

I'm not making the same mistakes I made with your father.''

A knock at the door interrupted him. The man that came into the room was a stranger to Tad. He was a large man, more muscular than fat, with a bald head that seemed at odds with his youngish face. Silently, he set a covered tray on the desk, then stood there, looking at Tad's grandfather.

''This is Cotton. From now on, he's your special helper. Anything you need, just tell Cotton and he'll get it for you. For your own safety, until I've made arrangements to fly us out of here, I want you to do everything he says. There are people who—well, let's say that being rich has its problems and I've made a few enemies. So mind what Cotton tells you. One of his duties is making sure you're safe.''

At his nod, the man called Cotton turned silently and left the room. Tad puzzled over his grandfather's words for a moment, then turned his attention to the tray. At his grandfather's nod, he lifted the dome-shaped lid, sniffing hungrily. A hamburger and french fries, and the hot dog— and a bowl of chili, too, which was another of his favorite foods. His mother must have told his grandfather this, too.

Well, that didn't make him feel better. It made him feel awful. If she didn't want him around anymore, then he didn't want to live with her, either. He'd just put her, put both of them, out of his mind.

After all, it was pretty cool, having a rich grandfather. He bet he was even richer than Cappy's father, even if Mr. Howard did own that big department store in Puget City. Boy, when Cappy found out that he was going to inherit a whole lot of money someday, wouldn't he turn green?

He started to ask his grandfather if he could invite Cappy and some of the other guys over soon, but on second thought, he changed his mind. Maybe he'd better be careful about asking any favors for a while. Because what if his grandfather decided he didn't like him either? Where would he go? Who would take care of him then?

Silently, he went over to the desk, sat down in the chair, picked up the hamburger and began to eat hungrily.

Chapter 10

Lance didn't hear the news until the morning after Tad's disappearance. Corky Lafferty, an old friend from his Harvard days who was also the present Washington State Attorney General, had invited him along for the shake-down cruise of his new yacht. They had docked early that morning in Puget Basin, and Lance was still sleeping off a rather arduous night.

Since Corky, who had ambitions for higher office, was using the cruise to pay off several political favors, the guests included a federal judge, two prominent local attorneys, and the mayor of Puget City, a widower who had an eye for the ladies. It also included several single girls from Corky's office.

One secretary, a leggy honey-blonde, had been particularly accommodating to Lance. Although he was not much

given to abstract thought, it had occurred to him more than
once lately that the tabloids had it all wrong about his
being a chaser. These days, he seldom bothered pursuing
women, since they did the job for him. In fact, he was a
prime target for ambitious girls who wanted to add Lance
Winthrop's scalp to their list. It was as if his reputation
had a life of its own, a momentum that kept scoring one
girl after another without any effort on his part.

Not that he objected. A warm body in bed was a warm
body in bed—and he had an inexhaustible libido. But there
was a side effect that sometimes became embarrassing. He
had bedded so many willing girls that they tended to blur
into one collective image—nubile bodies, lustrous eyes,
and since he was a leg man, long, elegant stems, as he
privately called them. He was hard put, when meeting one
of his former lovers even a few weeks later, to remember
her name, so he often used generic terms—darling, love,
sweetcakes.

Lance enjoyed life to the fullest—or rather, he amended,
he would if he could figure out a way to keep the gravy
train rolling. In the meantime, he had a few problems to
solve.

After Alissa had dumped him, he'd known it was fence-
mending time with the old man. And he knew that the best
way to do it was to provide Neville with a ready-made
grandson, the thing the old man wanted most.

At first, the thought of using his own son to get money
from his father had given him a bit of trouble. His conscience, although rusty with disuse, had stirred sluggishly,
and he'd rejected the idea out of hand. But then his
favorite casino had banned him because he couldn't pay
his gambling debts. A few not-so-subtle threats from other
creditors had forced him to leave his old stomping grounds
in Europe, and his scruples flew out the window.

It hadn't taken much effort to convince Neville that Tad

was his grandson, even before he'd produced the snapshot. His offer to set things right with Christy, to talk her into giving him visitation rights, had found a willing ear. The fact that she'd turned him down the first time he'd approached her was only a minor setback. He was confident that he could eventually bring her around. After all, she'd been crazy about him once—some of the old feeling might still be there. And if it wasn't, then he would try something else—like appealing to her conscience.

He had gone off on Corky's shakedown cruise without a cloud on the horizon and had enjoyed to the fullest his three days of fun and games and bunk-hopping with the agile girls from Corky's office. After the others disembarked before dawn that morning, he stayed behind with Corky, hashing over the events of the cruise and having one last drink, which led to another and then a few more. Toward morning, they finally crashed in their respective berths for a few hours of sleep.

It was almost noon when Corky, looking bleary-eyed and bloated, shook him awake. Lance groaned and pulled the covers up over his head.

Corky yanked the covers down again. "Come on, old buddy—wake up!"

Lance opened one eye and stared balefully at his host. "What's going down, Corky? The boat sinking?"

Corky was short, on the stocky side; with his pug nose, his pale eyebrows, and freckled hands, he could have been an adult version of Tom Sawyer, a deceptive look that he hoped would win a few elections for him in the future. Right now, he fairly brimmed with curiosity.

"What've you been up to? There's a county cop on deck, waiting to talk to you."

"To me?" Lance searched his conscience. No unpaid speeding tickets—at least not in Washington, certainly not recently. . . . "Hell, I don't know what he wants. Couldn't you get rid of him?"

"No way. He wants to see you right now."

Lance groaned again, but he rolled off the bunk, slid into jeans and a sweatshirt, and went into the head to splash cold water on his face. In the mirror above the sink, he saw that his eyes were red-rimmed and his face had a grayish cast. *Too much booze, too much sex, too little sleep—and let's face it, old buddy, you don't bounce back quite as fast as you used to. . . .*

He went up on deck, to find a middle-aged man looking grim and purposeful and not at all intimidated by the luxury of his surroundings.

"Lance Winthrop?"

"Yeah—who are you?"

The man showed him an ID card that identified him as Sheriff's Detective Markoff of Puget County.

Lance returned the laminated card. "What's this all about, officer?"

"You haven't heard the news?"

"News? What news?"

"Do you have any knowledge as to the whereabouts of Steven Havens?"

For a moment, Lance's mind went blank. "Steven Havens—who the hell's that?"

The man's eyes narrowed. "According to the boy's mother, Christine Havens, he's your son."

"Oh . . . sorry, officer. My mind slipped a cog there for a moment—" 'He broke off as realization came to him. "Hell—you mean the kid's been kidnapped?"

"We don't know what happened. So far, no one's contacted his mother and stepfather with a ransom demand. We're assuming it's—we're following normal police procedures. That's why I have to ask you again if you have any idea where the boy is."

"Hold off a minute, officer. Did Christy put you up to this? Hell, she knows I wouldn't do anything stupid like kidnapping my own kid. Sure, I asked for visitation rights, and I do think it's about time I got acquainted with Tad, but I wouldn't—with my life-style, what the devil would I do with a kid underfoot?"

The man stared at him coldly. "Then you deny any knowledge of his disappearance?"

"Of course I deny it. When did all this happen?"

"Yesterday. He was last seen at five o'clock yesterday afternoon. There's been no trace of him since."

"Well, until early this morning, my friend's yacht, with me aboard, was heading for the docks here at Puget Basin at about ten knots—and there's a dozen or more honest citizens who will confirm that, including my host, who's State Attorney General, and Art Rinehart, the mayor of Puget City." He gave several more names, then added, "How is Christy taking this? She must be frantic."

The man shrugged. "These things are always rough on the parents. I'm not in charge of the case, so I haven't met her."

"God—what a rotten thing to happen," Lance said. He hesitated, then added, "I wonder if—what can I do to help?"

"You'll have to talk to the parents about that," the man said.

After he was gone, Lance used Corky's ship-to-shore phone to call Christy. Since his own conscience was clear, he was totally unprepared for her anger—and her accusations. He tried to convince her that he knew nothing about the boy's disappearance and was aggrieved when she obviously didn't believe him. After he'd exchanged a few words with her husband, who seemed like a decent chap, he hung up and then sat there for a while, frowning at the phone while suspicion, like a crawling worm, moved through his mind.

Corky trotted in from the galley. Lance told him the facts absently, his mind playing with his suspicions.

Was it possible that Neville had become tired of waiting for him to produce the boy legitimately and had done something about it—like arranging for a kidnapping? God knew Neville could swing it if he wanted to. His men were completely loyal to him—as long as the money rolled in.

One reporter who'd been roughed up by them when he'd tried to crash the island had referred to them as "Winthrop's bullyboys"—a very apt name. But—hell, the whole idea was stupid, much too risky. And Neville never did stupid or risky things.

Or *was* it so risky? If Neville spirited the boy out of the country and took him to Aristos, his island in the Mediterranean, who would be the wiser? In eight years, Tad would be of age—and by then, no doubt, totally in Neville's pocket.

And Neville was ruthless—God knew, he was that. He was also not a well man. He'd made it plain that time was an important factor in his desire to get control of his grandson. Maybe he didn't have time to waste trying to wiggle his way into Tad's life through legal means.

And that brought up a rather painful personal question: Did some of the blame for this fiasco strike close to home? By going to Neville and telling him that he'd been mistaken and the boy was his, after all, had he opened up a can of worms?

Lance felt a discomfort that was new to him. Despite his treatment of Christy, he had always retained a deep respect for her. In fact, if things had gone differently, if he hadn't met Alissa at just the time when Christy had stopped being fun and become a drag with her morning sickness and her troublesome pregnancy—well, he might even have stayed with her.

And if you had, old buddy, you really would have messed up her life. . . .

But maybe he did owe her something. He didn't want to see her go through hell because of something he'd started. He'd never intended to try to take the boy away from her—just to use Tad to extract money from Neville. Well, maybe this was the time to pay an old debt—provided it didn't ruin his own prospects. It was even possible that he could use this business to his own advantage. Yeah, the situation did have certain possibilities. . . .

He waited until Corky had wandered off to see a friend whose sloop was berthed nearby before he used the ship-to-shore phone again. He asked the marine operator to get his father's number on Winthrop Island, only to be informed by a male voice he didn't recognize that Neville was "indisposed" and was not accepting phone calls.

"Tell Mr. Winthrop that his son would like to come out to the island to see him this afternoon," Lance said.

There was a long wait; and then: "Mr. Winthrop won't be available for a few days. Because of flu among the personnel here, the island is off limits to visitors at present, sir."

"I see—well, give him my best," Lance said easily.

His suspicions confirmed, at least to his own satisfaction, he hung up, then sat there, trying to decide what to do next. If he called the police in on this, he could kiss Neville's money good-bye forever. On the other hand, if he confronted Neville in person, maybe he could turn him around without risking too much. And if that didn't work—well, he'd think of something. He always did, didn't he?

He located Corky and borrowed his motor launch for the five-mile ride across the straits, but an hour later, when he presented himself at the dock gate of Winthrop Island, the guard on duty was adamant.

"I'm sorry, Mr. Winthrop, but your father's orders were that nobody, including you, is to be admitted."

"Not even the police?" Lance said.

"The police, sir?"

"Yes, I understand my son is missing—eventually, the police are going to come here to talk to Mr. Winthrop. What are your orders then?"

"I don't know nothing about that," the man said. "If the cops come here, I'll call the house for more orders."

"Well, just a thought. And have a good day," Lance said blandly.

He returned to the motor launch, which he'd moored at the end of the dock. As he roared across the straits toward Puget Basin, his mind moving over various plans to penetrate the security of Winthrop Island, it occurred to him that there were a few advantages to being a dilettante. You knew a little bit about a lot of useful things. Maybe he should have taken up cat burglary as a profession. God knew he had the right skills for it.

After a longish nap, he again approached Corky, who was more than willing to lend him the motor launch and scuba gear for what he believed was one of Lance's amorous adventures. Once his preparations were made, he joined Corky in a drink—and another rehashing of the cruise. It was getting dark by the time he finished off his whiskey, gave his friend a conspiratorial wink, and went roaring off in the launch.

An hour later, he anchored the boat near a channel marker buoy that was located a few hundred yards off the rocky coast of Winthrop Island. After he'd donned the wet suit and the other equipment he'd borrowed, he slipped into the cold waters of the bay. He felt no qualms about this part of the venture. He'd scuba-dived off this particular beach dozens of times in the past, and these waters were as familiar to him as the back of his hand.

When he reached shallow water, he switched off his underwater torch. Normally, this beach was patrolled every hour, day and night. If his suspicions were correct, then the intervals would have been shortened, since this stretch of beach and the dock were the only places on the rockbound island where a boat could safely land.

The water lapped against Lance's mask as he eased his head above the surface. At the far end of the crescent-shaped beach, the light of an electric torch cast a yellowish beam across the sand. He ducked lower, waiting until the guard had paced the full length of the beach and the beam of light had disappeared into a growth of scrub pine. Then he rose out of the water and made a dash for the shelter of the rocks. He stripped to his jeans and sweatshirt, shivering in the cold evening wind, then hid the diving suit and gear in a crevice in the rocks.

Pausing often to look around, he moved cautiously up the rock path toward the house, which had been built on a small rise that gave its windows a panoramic view of the bay.

Again he paused, this time to listen. Since he was wearing dark clothes, he wasn't too worried that anyone would spot him—and even if they did, he wasn't in any mortal danger. No matter what Neville's opinion of him might be, he still had only one son. No, that didn't worry him. But if he were caught lurking in the ornamental shrubs, he just might get roughed up a little before he could identify himself—and he'd prefer not to risk having his face wracked up by one of Neville's bullyboys, thank you.

He stayed in the shadows as he circled the house. Somewhere along the way, he made the discovery that he was enjoying himself. Fast cars and boats, sexy women, and high places—a challenge of any kind always gave him a rush. That's why he'd never gone in for drugs. He wasn't suicidal—he always calculated the risks first and if he decided to go for it, he made his preparations carefully—but it was the danger element that was his drug, that got the old blood pumping through his arteries. . . .

He had almost reached the original starting point of his slow circuit of the house when he spotted Tad's shadow against the light in a second-floor window. Hell, that was *his* old room! In fact, he still slept there during his rare visits to the island—or he had until he'd married Alissa and had become persona non grata to the old man.

Had Neville put the kid in that room on purpose? He did have a rather macabre sense of humor sometimes—he probably thought it fitting or ironic or something, since he intended to replace the son who had been such a disappointment to him with the grandson for whom he had big plans.

Lance shrugged off his sudden spurt of anger. After all, it gave him an advantage—provided he decided he wanted to talk to the boy on the sly. He'd cut his climber's teeth escaping from that very room after he'd been locked in for some infraction of Neville's rules. How many times had he edged along that ledge, then up the ornamental trim of the overhang to get to the attic window above, then down the back service stairs to the kitchen for a late-night raid on the refrigerator or, sometimes, the old man's private liquor supply? There'd been an excitement in those boyhood escapades, a satisfaction in bettering the old man, that his later adventures had never equaled.

The thing was—did he really have anything to say to Tad? Maybe it was better to beard the lion in his den, now that his suspicions had been confirmed. Since he knew to what lengths the old man was willing to go to get possession of his grandson, a whole world of new possibilities had opened up to him.

This kidnapping business wasn't intended simply as a means of looking the boy over. No, Neville had burned his bridges when he'd abducted Tad. And that meant—hell, he must be planning something permanent, such as taking Tad out of the country.

The old bastard—what a hypocrite he was! Well, he'd always known that about Neville, hadn't he? Even while the old man had mouthed a lot of platitudes to a growing boy about obeying the rules, he'd shown an absolute contempt for the law where his own interests were concerned.

Lance felt a rush of triumph as sweet and visceral as the stirrings of sex. Neville had put a weapon into his hands, one that just might accomplish everything he wanted. By now, Neville had surely been contacted by the police— how else had the sheriff's deputy known where to find him?—and he would have lied, denying any knowledge of Tad's disappearance—which made him as vulnerable as hell. . . .

Since he couldn't have done the job himself, his men had been involved, and the kind of loyalty that's paid for with a paycheck stretches only so far. If the whistle were blown on Neville, he would be in big trouble. Oh, he wasn't in any kind of danger of going to jail. Men with Neville's clout never went to jail. But his credibility, his image, was vulnerable. And Neville did like to keep a good public image—and a low profile. That was the problem about being so closely identified with your own super-respectable banking firm. It made you vulnerable to scandal.

Lance smiled to himself. *Gotcha, old man!*

The next question was—how to play out his hand? Why, the simplest way possible. By marching in there, bold as brass, and confronting Neville in person. . . .

Dropping all attempts at stealth, Lance whistled cheerily as he strolled toward the front portico. As always, the door was locked—only Neville would lock the doors on an island that was guarded like a fortress—but this time Lance had taken the precaution of bringing along one of the ornate brass keys that would open that door.

The key was a relic of those months during his first marriage when he'd been trapped on this godforsaken island, being bored out of his gourd while poor Christy was suffering pregnancy pangs. He'd swiped it from the key rack in the butler's pantry and had used it to make his nightly escapes. Those gambling bouts with old buddy Corky and, later, his rendezvous with Alissa had kept him sane. When he'd burned his bridges and left for good, he'd taken the key with him—as a souvenir, a way of thumbing his nose at the old man.

Lance winced. His triumph had been a hollow one. In her own way, Alissa had been as much of a tyrant as Neville. Well, all that was going to end shortly. When he walked away this time, he intended to be on top of the heap. . . .

As soon as he unlocked the door, he heard music coming from the library. Since it was Rachmaninoff, he knew the old man was in there, poring over his stamps. Beethoven when he worked with his coins. Chopin for his Japanese netsuke, those tiny carved ivory and wood trinkets that were Neville's fetish. And Rachmaninoff for stamps, the fabulous collection that was rumored to be one of the most valuable in the world.

And that, since Neville *was* a creature of unbending habit, meant that he would be alone.

Lance crossed the cavernous entrance hall with its black-and-white harlequin tiles. He didn't bother to knock before he opened the library door and slipped through.

Neville, wearing one of his velvet smoking jackets, was seated behind the huge Empire desk that had belonged to the first of the Winthrop tycoons. He was bending over a stamp album, and he didn't look up as he snapped, "What is it, Logan? I told you I didn't want to be disturbed—"

"Sorry to intrude, Neville. I see you've already recovered from the flu."

Neville froze. For a moment, something—surprise? consternation?—flickered across his face. But his voice was even, without emotion, as he asked, "How the hell did you get in here?"

Again, Lance discovered he was enjoying himself. Danger did that to him—and he was in a very precarious position indeed at the moment. "Why, I came through the front door. No problem—should there have been?"

"My men wouldn't have let you past the dock, so you got on the island some other way."

"Oh, that. Well, I swam ashore. I was out boating with some friends and I decided to pay you a little visit. They're still waiting for me out in the bay. I told them that if I didn't return in three hours to call the police."

"You're lying, of course. Your clothes are dry—and there are no friends waiting for you, either. But no matter. You can leave now. I'm too under the weather to receive guests."

"You consider me a guest? Your only son?"

Neville's face lengthened. He reached for the button that would summon his man, but he didn't press it, because Lance said quickly, "We have some business to discuss—the matter of *my* son this time. That was very tacky of you, kidnapping Tad. Don't you have any guilt at all for the anguish you're putting Christine through?"

Neville stared at him, his eyes unreadable. To Lance's surprise, he didn't deny the accusation. "She had her chance. I wasted enough valuable time, trying to make contact with the boy through his mother. And you must know by now that I seldom worry about other people's feelings—it's counterproductive."

"So you admit you kidnapped Tad?"

"Why not? You won't tell anyone—and if you did, who would believe you?"

"You might be surprised there. There are such things as polygraph tests. By the way, did you know that they give those tests to the parents of a missing child? A commentary on modern life, wouldn't you say? And pretty traumatic to the people involved, too."

Neville regarded him thoughtfully. "This concern for your former wife is a little late in coming, isn't it? Especially since you treated her so shabbily."

"Touché—or maybe not touché. You might say that I did Christy a favor when I left her for Alissa. The boy's probably been better off with a stepfather. Of course, you'd be a better judge of that than I. What kind of kid did he turn out to be, anyway?"

A little to his surprise, Neville answered his question readily. "He's sharp—a lot like I was at his age. Accepted this business without a whimper—at least, in front of me. Good material—yes, I can do a lot with the boy."

Characteristically, Neville dismissed the subject with a chopping gesture of his hand. "So what's your price for cooperation? I'm warning you—I don't intend to be gouged, so don't get greedy."

It had come too quickly. Again, Neville had thrown him for a loop. Lance chewed on his lower lip, his thoughts whirling. Had *this*, a payoff for his silence, been in the back of his mind all along, the real reason he'd come here—to cash in on the situation? When he'd told himself that he wanted to set things right for Christy, to thwart the old man's plans at the same time he did a bit of private blackmailing—had he been lying to himself? Now he felt the stirrings of greed—and all sorts of possibilities went through his mind.

"I'm still waiting for the fee you promised for our last deal," he hedged.

"You didn't earn it," Neville pointed out. "You were supposed to talk Christine into visitation rights—and then you were to bring the boy here so I could look him over."

"You didn't give me enough time. I had everything under control—"

"You went off with your friends on a cruise when you should have been attending to business. That's when I decided to take matters into my own hands."

"Well, I played my hand the way I saw it. And rushing in and spooking Christy was the worst thing I could have done. You should have given me more time to—"

Again, Neville chopped off his words with a gesture. "It's a moot question now. Eventually, I intend to take the boy to Aristos."

"You can't keep this a secret forever. Too many people know about it. How many men do you employ here on the island—ten? Fifteen? And everybody on Aristos knows what's going on at the villa. It's just a matter of time until someone blows the whistle on you. Eventually, you'll have to give Tad back to his mother."

"I pay enough protection to keep the Greek authorities off my back for a long while. And time is on my side. It'll take years to get a custody suit through the international courts, and by the time that's resolved, if it ever is, the boy will be old enough to make up his own mind where he wants to live. I intend to turn the corporation over to him someday. You can bet he'll decide to stay with me."

At Lance's silence, a thin smile altered the straight line of Neville's mouth. "Oh, yes. I intend to train Tad—by the way, I detest that name—to train Steven for the responsibility of managing a multibillion-dollar banking empire. I want a Winthrop at the reins after I'm gone. I failed with you, but I won't fail with my grandson. He's not like

you—you were weak, like your mother. But this boy—
well, he's like me. Bullheaded and strong and sharp as a
fox.''

Lance felt a wave of heat to his head—which surprised
him more than anything else this day. Ever since he was a
boy, he'd known that, in his father's eyes, he didn't
measure up—so why, at this late date, did Neville's contempt sting so much? Why did it make him want to pick
up that bronze bust on the old man's desk and heave it into
his face—

"Well, boy? Got your tongue caught in your zipper?
What's your price? And I'm warning you again—don't get
greedy. For what I pay out in wages, my men will do
anything I tell them to—and you're in a very shaky
position.''

Lance took a deep breath, forcing back the rage. Losing
his cool would gain him nothing. Outwitting the old man,
making him pay in the only coin that held value to him—
yeah, that was the way to go. . . .

"My price is the same as before. And for a fat bonus,
I'll go even further. You'll need help in keeping the boy
happy and in getting him to cooperate—and I do have a
way with kids.''

"Very well. I'll—what do gamblers call it? Sweeten the
pot? How about making that bonus enough to provide you
not only with security, but with a very high-bracket income for the rest of your life? Say—a million-dollar
annuity?''

Lance stared at him, stunned. This kind of payoff was
out of line with the cards the old man held. "Why the
generosity?'' he said finally. "What else do you want
from me?''

"I want you to step out of the picture, once I take the
boy to Aristos. In return for the annuity, you promise—in
writing—to buck any legal attempt on Christine's part to

get the boy back. By the time it goes through the courts, with all the delaying tactics my lawyers can provide, he'll be in his teens—and under my control. In addition, I want a signed statement from you that you won't contest my will. I think another statement, this one undated, agreeing to stay away from the boy, is also in order.''

He paused, his eyes flicking over Lance. ''I don't want him infected with your playboy philosophy of life. I intend to make him into the kind of man who can take over for me someday. First I'll show him the rewards of being enormously rich—and then I'll make sure he knows how to deal with the responsibility of controlling that kind of power. I only make a mistake once—and this time, the second time around, I intend to make sure nothing interferes with my plans to train an heir so that what I leave behind won't be squandered on gambling and women. Which is why I'm making you this offer—and a very generous one it is, too, boy.''

Lance was finding it hard to maintain his outward cool. Everything he wanted was within his grasp. Hell, he didn't care about the old man's banking empire! He had no desire to control his various enterprises. It was money, lifelong security against the kind of humiliation he'd suffered in the past, that he wanted, craved, hungered for. . . .

The question was—how could he be sure that Neville would keep his end of the bargain? The old man's word was like Washington State weather—subject to constant change.

On the other hand, this situation was an ongoing thing, wasn't it? At any time during the next few years, he had the power to drop the custody suit and bow out of the picture. Then Neville wouldn't have a legal leg to stand on—and even the Greek politicians he had in his pocket might have second thoughts about protecting him if both Tad's parents were on the other side of a lawsuit—and if both of them were willing to swear that Neville had no legal rights to the boy, since Lance hadn't fathered him.

No, Neville didn't hold all the cards. In fact, in one area, he was very vulnerable. For all his money, his influence, he had one Achilles' heel—he wanted the boy in the worst way.

Lance took a long breath, let it out slowly. "It's a deal, Neville," he said.

Chapter 11

A week after Tad's disappearance, Miles resumed his classes at the university. Christy, not yet able to face the open sympathy—and the covert curiosity—of her co-workers, postponed her own return to work, although she knew that it was only a matter of time before she must go back. Even in the midst of their troubles, their day-to-day expenses never stopped. Bills arrived as usual in the mail, along with the flood of letters and notes and cards, and they had to be paid, come what might. Life had to go on—how many times had someone said those words to Christy in the past few days?

Already the barrage of phone calls, the letters, and messages had begun to taper off. At first, the house had been flooded with friends and neighbors. Someone did the laundry and others brought in food—food that Christy could only nibble at. She got tired of saying "thank you," of putting on a brave face, of making meaningless conversation, but paradoxically, when people stopped coming, when the phone seldom rang, she longed for warm bodies to fill the empty rooms, for voices to dispel the silence.

Although she understood that people must move on to their own concerns, their own lives, there were hurts—some small and some that cut much deeper.

Two days after Tad's disappearance, she returned home from a session at the sheriff's office and went into the kitchen in time to hear one neighbor say to the friend that had been the most supportive, "I can't help wondering why the sheriff asked both of them to take those lie-detector tests. It seems—you know, funny."

And her friend had replied, "Well, maybe the police know something we don't—you ever think of that?"

A second later, the friend looked around, to see Christy standing in the doorway. Her face had turned dark red, and she'd stammered something incoherent that probably was an apology. Since then she hadn't been back to the house, nor had she phoned—but her words were permanently etched on Christy's mind. They came back to her late at night, when her defenses were at their lowest, ruining the little sleep she was able to get.

But now, with Miles back at work and her mother off at the shopping center, having her hair done—as well as a facial and a manicure—Christy would have welcomed even the nosiest and least diplomatic of her neighbors, just to have someone to talk to, a voice to chase away the quiet.

In the living room, she switched on the stereo, turning it up very loud. So loud, in fact, that when the phone rang, at first she thought it was part of the symphony she'd been listening to. When she realized what the buzzing sound was, she made a dash for the kitchen and was out of breath when she said, "Yes?" into the mouthpiece.

"May I speak to Mrs. Havens, please?" It was a woman's voice, hesitant and apologetic.

"This is Mrs. Havens."

"My name is Lucille Dubois. You don't know me, but—well, I heard what happened and I just want you to know that you aren't alone."

"Thank you," Christy said automatically. There had been many of these calls—strangers reaching out to say they were sorry, that they were praying for her and her child.

"I—well, I went through the same thing when my baby was taken from our backyard. So I know something of what you're going through. If there's anything I can do to help—"

"Your baby—did you get him back?"

"Her—her name is Laurie, and no, not yet. But I haven't given up hope." There was a feverish quality in the woman's voice now. "We—my husband and me—heard about an abandoned child they found in Illinois. We're flying out there this afternoon. Maybe this time—the description is pretty close, although the hair is a different color. But hair can be dyed, of course—"

"I wish you luck, Mrs. Dubois. How old is Laurie now?"

"She'll be eight in two weeks—but I'm sure I'll know her when I see her. There was this little triangular birthmark just above her left heel. And she has such beautiful brown eyes. Surely, they wouldn't have changed. . . ." Her voice trailed off.

"I wish you luck," Christy said, her voice catching.

"Yes—well, it's a chance. That's what keeps Jack—that's my husband—and me going. When you wait for a missing child, you wait until you die, they say. And it's true. I hope—well, I hope this doesn't happen to you, that your son will be home soon and then you can forget all this.''

"We pray that happens," Christy said.

"If—well, if you should ever feel like you want to talk to someone about it, do call me. There's a group of us in the Puget City area that meet regularly and just compare notes. It helps. It really does. Sometimes, when we exchange stories of the dumb things people say to us, you can even laugh a little. Sharing things like that does take some of the—the hurt out of them.''

"I'm sure you're right—"

"It isn't that people mean to be cruel, but they—well, I think they're afraid that your troubles will rub off on them, that somehow you'll bring them bad luck. A few months after Laurie disappeared, we had a birthday party for Tommy—that's our oldest child who was five at the time. We invited some of the neighborhood kids, but none of them turned up. Their mothers wouldn't let them come to our house.''

"I'm sorry—"

"You have to keep up your courage, but it's so hard. Sometimes we talk about giving up, moving away, changing our name even, but of course we can't. So we just live from day to day—''

Christy realized suddenly that she couldn't bear to hear any more, even though she sensed how well-intended Mrs. Dubois's call was. So she broke in to ask for the woman's phone number, promising to keep in touch.

But after she'd hung up, she sat for a long while, staring into a future that loomed like an endless nightmare. Eight years from now would she still be waiting for the phone to ring, waiting for a knock at the door, for a grown son to return to her, a son who would be a stranger?

Or what if Tad never returned? Would she and Miles

spend the rest of their lives following leads that led nowhere, trying to find their child? Wouldn't it be better in the long run to know that Tad was—

''No! Never!'' she said loudly, setting up echoes in the empty kitchen. She would never give up hope! Somewhere in the world, Tad was alive—whether close by or thousands of miles away. And right now, he was grieving for them, waiting for them to find him and take him home. And they would find him—they *would*! No matter how long it took, how much energy and hard work, how many sacrifices, she and Miles would get him back. What's more, she wasn't going to sit back passively and wait for the police to find him, either. . . .

By the time Jessica returned from the beauty shop, Christy had made her plans, but she waited until her mother had gone to bed that night and she and Miles were alone before she laid them before him. Although Jessica had been a surprising comfort to her, she wanted no audience while she tried to convince Miles to go along with her decision to spend everything they had in a search for Tad.

In preparation, she had called several detective agencies in the city, and while the daily rate they charged had taken her breath away, she never faltered in her determination to go through with her plans. In fact, she had her arguments marshaled on how they would pay for the search, how they could raise the money for a reward—a second mortgage on the house, the sale of everything of value they owned, her return to work immediately.

But to her surprise, her carefully prepared arguments weren't needed. As soon as she broached her plan, Miles agreed that she was right—and then he told her that he'd already taken one step toward financing it.

''I talked to administration today. They've agreed to let me take on extra classes not only during summer session, but at the Adult Education Center, starting the middle of June,'' he said. "And I can get fifteen dollars an hour doing private tutoring—I already have four students lined up. If we take out a second mortgage on the house, we should be able to swing the detective agency fees, a reward of at least five thousand dollars, and still meet our bills.''

"You've already been considering this? You don't think it's a waste of money?''

"Tad is my son, too,'' he said. "Why are you surprised?''

"I—I'm not,'' she said. "It's just that—well, you're always so practical. I thought you'd figure we should let the police handle it.''

"If I were practical, I wouldn't be teaching English to college kids, Christy. I'd be pushing papers around for some high-powered firm in the city.'' There was something in his eyes, a measuring look that she'd never seen there before as he regarded her thoughtfully. "Sometimes I wonder what you see when you look at me, Christy.''

"I see a wonderful human being. A good man, to use an old-fashioned phrase.''

"But not a very exciting one. You had that with your first husband, didn't you? Is that why you married me, Christy? Because you thought I was the exact opposite of Lance Winthrop?''

She felt a stir of anger, but she suppressed it and gave him a truthful answer. "Yes, you're different from Lance—and you don't know what a relief that is to me—but I married you because I loved you—''

"But not because you were *in* love with me?''

"You're putting words into my mouth, Miles! And why are you bringing this up now, of all times? Don't we have enough to worry about without quarreling?''

He rubbed his face with the heels of his hands as if to clear his thoughts. "You're right. But eventually, we'll have to have this out, Christy. I hoped—well, I was sure that you'd worked Lance Winthrop out of your system, but this idea you have that he took Tad—there's absolutely no evidence of that. I think you're obsessed with the man—and I keep wondering why.''

"Because I know how devious he can be. And convincing. He could have gotten Corky Lafferty to lie for him. Corky was Lance's little shadow at Harvard—and still is, even though he's Attorney General now.''

"And Art Rinehart? The mayor's too shrewd to risk his political career. In fact, he'd only just met Lance at the time of the cruise. So it's unrealistic to—''

"A few minutes on the phone, and you believed everything Lance said. You thought I was being hysterical. No, you didn't say so, but I saw it in your eyes. Okay, he does have an airtight alibi, but isn't it possible he hired someone else to kidnap Tad? Maybe that's why he took those pictures of Tad—it would be easy for him to hide him on Winthrop Island. Because I wouldn't be a bit surprised if Neville wasn't in on it, too.''

"Against all evidence to the contrary? There was no sign of the boy when they searched the island—and the man did volunteer to let them do it, you know. It's just too hard to believe that a man of Neville Winthrop's stature would—''

"You have no idea what he's really like! As for the police searching his estate, Tad could have been taken out of the country by then—or maybe he was hidden somewhere in that old house. It would be so easy to fool the police—they're so damned in awe of the Winthrop name! When he offered to let them search the place, he had them in his pocket—and made me look like a hysterical woman. He's a very clever man—why won't you believe me?''

"Christy, Christy—you must know you're grasping at straws. Why do you persist in this?''

Christy looked at him, and suddenly her eyes filled with tears. "Because I *have* to believe it—don't you see that? If Lance took him, then Tad is safe. But if he didn't—oh, God, then he could be dead or suffering in the hands of some—"

Miles reached her in three steps. He pulled her to her feet and held her contorted face against his chest. "I'm sorry—I should have realized what was going on inside your head. And maybe you're right. If so, the boy will turn up safe and sound when Lance gets tired of playing games."

And because he was trying so hard to make things easier for her, Christy nodded, pretending to believe that Miles believed his own words.

That night, for the first time in a long while, she reached out for Miles after they went to bed. Since the night she had rebuffed him, although he always kissed her before they went to sleep, he hadn't tried to make love to her. While she knew the reason for it, that he thought she needed time, she felt neglected, lonely.

Tonight, when she nuzzled against his back and slid her arm around his waist, his heart gave a big leap and he turned to her eagerly and took her in his arms.

Thankfully, she nestled against him, taking comfort in his warmth. But when he touched her breast, she felt a secret resentment. What she really wanted was comfort, to have Miles tell her again that everything would be all right, that they would find Tad soon, and then to fall asleep in his arms. Although she knew it was irrational, it seemed so callous to have sex when they didn't know where their son was or what he was doing or if he were suffering or—

Her body must have stiffened because Miles pulled away, looking down at her. The tears came, flooding her cheeks, and he pulled her close again, murmuring reassurances against her hair. But she sensed his disappointment, and because she loved him—and because she owed him so much—she fought the tears until they finally stopped.

She kissed him then, letting her body yield against his, sending the message that she was willing to make love. But as he responded, doing the things he knew she liked, she found herself wanting to pull away, to roll over and go to sleep. In the end, she had to fake her response, and when it was over, although Miles kissed her as usual and told her to get some rest, she knew she hadn't fooled him, that he'd sensed her lack of response and was hurt by it.

After Miles's breathing became regular and deep, she lay awake, making plans for the day ahead. In the morning she would call her boss and tell him she was ready to return to work. And tomorrow afternoon, as soon as Miles's two-o'clock class was over, they would drive into Puget City and hire a detective—the best one they could find. Even if it took every penny they could rake up, even if they had to sell the house they had worked so hard for, they had to do this thing, had to do everything in their power to get their son back.

Chapter 12

Tad was playing with the electric train when a knock came at the door.

It was his second day on the island, and he was feeling tired. For the last two nights, he hadn't slept at all well, even though the big four-poster bed, with its thick comforter, downy pillows, and silky sheets, was much roomier and softer than his narrow one at home. He just hadn't been able to get comfortable. He'd squirmed around, turning this way and that, his mind filled with things that had happened in the past two days—the quarrel with his mother, Mr. Wilkie's lies, what his grandfather had said the night he'd come here. And he'd been trying to figure out just what he'd done that was so bad that his parents had turned against him. Was his grandfather right—were they tired of having him around? Did they simply want to be alone?

His eyelids smarting, Tad fiddled with the train's control panel. He didn't care what they thought. He really didn't. If they didn't like him anymore, then he didn't want to live with them. And anyway, it was really great here. Already, he had nicer things than any kid at school, even Cappy and Allie. Nobody he knew had a train set like this one with everything, from the gold-plated smoke funnel on the engine to the bright-red caboose in the back, just like an old-time narrow-gauge steam engine—only a lot smaller, of course. Everything was calibrated so it was authentic—or at least that's what it said in the instruction book.

And the tapes that came with the video player—he'd had to stay in his room yesterday because his grandfather was afraid he was coming down with something, so he'd watched four movies, one right after another. Man, just wait until the kids got a load of some of those movies! A couple were so new that they hadn't even been shown in Puget City yet, much less on cable TV. The video games Mr. Cotton had brought in for him to play with—they were full-sized and exactly like the ones in the arcade near school, only you didn't have to use quarters.

And just *wait* until the guys saw—Tad felt a sudden sinking inside his chest. Because Cappy and Allie and the other kids would probably never get to see the authentic calibrated steam engine or the video games or the movies that weren't even in the downtown movie houses yet. He probably wouldn't see his friends again—not if his grandfather took him away to that other island halfway around the world. . . .

And why had the door been locked last night? He'd gotten up once to go to the bathroom and for some reason—maybe because he was so sleepy?—he'd tried to open the hall door and that's when he'd found out it was locked.

Maybe he'd better tell his grandfather about that. Yeah,

it had to be some kind of mistake. It was one of the things that kept him awake because being locked in a place where he couldn't get out made him feel—yukky. When he saw Mr. Cotton he'd ask him to be careful and not do that again. What if there was a fire and everybody forgot he was there?

He heard the knock then, but before he could get up from the rug, the door opened and Mr. Cotton came into the room. At first, Tad had been a little scared of him because he was so big and also because he looked so—so unfriendly. But this morning, he was smiling—or at least it looked like a smile.

"How are you feeling today? Still got your stomachache?"

"No, sir. I feel okay."

"Any more headaches? That sort of thing?"

This time, Tad just shook his head.

"Well, in that case, your grandfather expects you in the breakfast room in fifteen minutes, Master Tad."

Master Tad! Boy, wait until he told—no, he had to stop thinking like that. He wasn't going to tell the kids *anything*, not ever, not unless his grandfather let him write to them. . . .

"Yes, sir," Tad said aloud, realizing that Mr. Cotton was waiting for an answer. He hesitated, then added, "What should I put on? I couldn't find my jeans and stuff when I got up this morning."

"I gave them to Cooky to put in the laundry." Mr. Cotton pointed toward a tall chest with brass pulls. "Everything in those drawers—and in the closet—belongs to you now. Wear anything you want."

He went to open the blinds. Tad stared at his broad back, at the expanse of shiny skin on the top of his head. He'd never seen a man without any hair at all. Mr. Cotton didn't even have eyebrows. Did he shave all over? He looked kinda young to be so bald. And what did Mr.

Cotton expect him to do about dressing? Surely, he wasn't supposed to do it right in the same room.

Feeling self-conscious, Tad got a pair of jeans from a drawer and chose one of the plaid shirts he found hanging in the closet. There were labels on the back pockets of the jeans and the shirt had a fancy yoke, just like the cowboys wore in movies and on TV. He felt—well, he felt really cool, knowing they belonged to him, especially after he found a whole row of boots in his size. Boots with all those studs and decorations cost a lot of money. He knew that, because some of the kids at school bragged about their custom-made boots and jeans with labels. Mom said that their parents were paying for advertising, not quality— whatever that meant. He hadn't argued with her, but he'd always been a little ashamed of his own jeans and shirts from the Penney's store at the shopping mall.

In the end, he dressed in the bathroom, and when he came out, Mr. Cotton was still waiting for him.

"I'd better show you how to get to the breakfast room, Master Tad. This house is so big, you could get lost if you don't know your way around."

Tad followed the man's broad back along a thickly carpeted hall, past a row of paintings in heavy wood frames. Tad found most of the paintings dull and uninteresting, especially those of people dressed in old-fashioned clothes, but there were a few of ships and animals and what looked to be sea battles. He wished he had time to study those more closely.

His feet dragged a little as they started down a flight of wide, curved stairs. He wasn't really looking forward to another meeting with his grandfather. The fact was, he was a little scared of him. Oh, sure, Grandfather Neville had given him all those presents, and he'd promised that he could have a chestnut mare when they got to that other island, but—well, he'd just have to get used to being around him. After all, he'd be living with him from now on, not his Mom and Dad.

Unexpectedly, a flood of grief welled up inside Tad, so strong that he stopped in his tracks, his eyes watering and his face twisting as if he were in pain.

Mr. Cotton turned to look back at him. "What's the matter, Master Tad? You got another bellyache?"

Ashamed that the man had seen his tears, Tad shook his head quickly, blinking hard. They went on, and a few minutes later he was being ushered into a sunny room filled with potted plants. A latticework partition shaded the round glass table and iron chairs where his grandfather, looking tall and intimidating even when he was sitting down, was reading a newspaper.

When he saw Tad, he folded the paper and laid it beside his plate. "Well, did you get a good night's sleep?" he asked, looking at Tad over the edge of his glasses.

Tad wet his lips. "Yes, sir," he lied.

"You feeling better today? No nausea or headaches?"

"No, sir."

"Well, sit down, boy. What you need is a good breakfast under your belt. I understand you didn't eat much yesterday. That's no good at all, no good at all. A growing boy needs his food."

"I—I wasn't very hungry, sir," Tad said.

Mr. Cotton pulled out a chair for him, and he slid into it awkwardly, not knowing where to look or what to do with his hands. Doubtfully, he took in the display of china and glasses, the cloth napkin. Was he supposed to use it the way he did a paper napkin? After a moment's hesitation, he picked the napkin up and put it across his lap the way his mother had taught him to do in company.

To Tad's relief, his grandfather returned to his newspaper. He discovered he still wasn't very hungry, even when Mr.

Cotton set a plate of pancakes, one of his favorite break-fast foods, in front of him. He added several of the curls of butter that came with the pancakes and poured a generous amount of syrup over them, but the smarting behind his eyelids was back, making his eyes ache.

At home, pancakes were reserved for Sunday morning breakfast—and then his mother made the top pancake on his stack into the shape of a rabbit or a cat or, sometimes, just increasingly small circles so that it ended up looking like a pyramid.

A sob escaped his throat. Mortified, he covered it up with a cough, then choked on the bite of pancake in his mouth and had to drink a glass of water before he could breathe right again. By this time, the desire to cry was gone, chased out by the fear that the racket he was making would make his grandfather mad.

"You okay, boy?" His grandfather was watching him over the edge of his glasses again.

"Yes, sir," Tad said. "I guess a piece of pancake went down the wrong way."

"Why don't you practice calling me Grandfather—or if you prefer, Grandfather Neville. We're going to be good friends, the two of us. Right now, I know you're feeling a little disoriented—a little strange, but that'll change quickly. You'll love Aristos. It's a beautiful place—there's lots of things for a boy to do there."

"Aristos?" Tad asked.

"My island in the Mediterranean. Where I'm—well, let's say where I'm King of the Hill. No one's allowed on the island without my permission—including reporters. Everybody there works for me. You might even say I own them. And someday it will all belong to you, Steven."

He went on talking, saying how important Tad's real name was. A silly name, suitable only for a weakling, could hurt a man's chances for success, while a good strong name like Steven—of which he approved although he'd prefer it spelled with a *ph*—was as good as money in the bank.

It was adult talk, and although Tad listened politely, his mind wandered. He felt an ache in his back from sitting up so straight, and he wished he could go to his room—or maybe outdoors to walk around the yard.

He stared out the window at what seemed to be a park with lots of green lawn and flowers in stone jars and bushes trimmed so they were all square at the corners. His breath caught sharply as a man strolled into view from around the corner of the house. In the morning sunlight, his hair glistened like gold, and he moved gracefully, like one of the big cats at the Puget City Zoo. *I'll bet he's a lion tamer or maybe one of those big game hunters,* Tad thought.

His grandfather followed his stare. "I think it's time you two met," he said. He rapped on the window, catching the man's attention. When he beckoned, the man hesitated, then nodded and strolled toward them. Although he wasn't smiling, somehow Tad got the impression that he'd just heard a funny joke.

"I know that guy," Tad said excitedly. "He took my picture once when he came to our house. Mom said he was a door-to-door salesman."

A look of annoyance crossed Neville's face. "He's not a salesman—your mother didn't want you to know who he really is."

Before Tad could ask any questions, the man came into the room through a sliding-glass door, and Tad thought how strange it was that suddenly the room seemed much smaller. Not because the man was all that big or tall. No, it was something else—the way he walked or maybe it was his smile—his teeth so white and his skin so tan.

He's really cool, he thought.

"Hello, Tad," the man said easily. He sat down at an empty place and picked up a napkin. "Are you getting acclimated to the higher altitude here on Winthrop Island?"

Tad stared at him, not sure what he meant. He finally nodded, feeling shy.

"I was just telling Steven that it was time you two got acquainted," Grandfather Neville said. Although his words were pleasant, he was frowning now—but not at Tad.

The man didn't seem to notice. "And you're wondering who I am, Tad?"

Tad felt as if he were in the middle of an electric storm. "Yes, sir," he said finally, settling on the safest answer.

"I'm a relative of your grandfather's—which makes us relatives, too."

Tad blinked hard. "Are you my uncle?" he said.

"Not really—but that's near enough for now." He shook hands with Tad, just as if they were two men meeting for the first time. His hand was strong, warm from the sun, and Tad smiled back at him, liking him more every minute.

"And since this relative stuff is as new to me as it is to you," the man went on, "why don't you just call me Lance?"

Tad felt bedazzled, as if he had been sitting in the sun too long, as Lance added, "We have a lot to learn about each other. For instance—do you like sports?"

"Yes, sir—especially baseball."

"Well, baseball isn't exactly my game, but I'm a whiz at tennis. Are you into that, too?"

Tad nodded. "I like it, but the only time I get to play is when Dad takes me to the public courts or I go to see one of my friends who has a court in his backyard. There's one at the Country Club, but we don't belong, so I can't use it unless someone invites me to play there.''

"Well, we'll change all that. What say we knock a few balls around after your breakfast has been digested? We have a great court here—and since it isn't raining today, we might as well take advantage of the sunshine.''

Tad nodded eagerly. "That'd be great. Dad isn't into sports very much, but he likes to fish, and he does play tennis, and he showed me how to—'' He broke off, suddenly embarrassed.

"You and your stepfather—how did you two get along?''

Tad looked down at his plate. "Okay, I guess,'' he said listlessly.

"Well, I'll be here for a few days, so there's no reason why you and I can't have some fun. How about skeet shooting? Have you ever done any of that?''

Tad shook his head. "Mom doesn't like guns.''

"She wouldn't mind this. It's purely for sport—and we shoot at clay pigeons. Or we can try archery—that's a lot of fun.''

Tad hardly noticed when his grandfather left the table, taking his newspaper with him, although he remembered his manners enough to rise when the older man did. He discovered he had an appetite, after all, and he finished off his pancakes and even had some toast and scrambled eggs just to keep Lance company while he ate.

Later, they played tennis for a while; then, at Lance's suggestion, they went swimming to cool off.

Lance called the place where they swam "the lagoon,'' but it looked like a big green pond to Tad. Surrounding it on three sides was a grove of trees, not pines but the kind that lose their leaves in winter. Now there was so much shade that the only place to get a tan, Lance told Tad, was on the log raft in the middle of the lagoon.

At first, Tad wondered if he was supposed to swim nude, like the boys did at school in the indoor pool, but Lance took him to a building made out of logs and told him this was the bathhouse. To his surprise, there was a bunch of swimsuits there, including several in his size.

"I see the old man thought of everything," Lance said with that funny smile he got when he said anything about Grandfather Neville. "Which makes him quite an adversary—remember that when you deal with him, kid."

After they had changed into swim trunks, they went into the water. It was very cold, even though the sun was shining. As Tad watched Lance diving off the raft, he thought he looked just like one of those old-time Olympic heroes they'd read about in school, the ones people used to knock the city walls down for after they'd won a race. Later, Lance helped him with his backstroke, showing him how to stretch out his arm, how to cup the water with his hands, and, when Tad caught on right away, Lance told him he was a natural, a chip off the old block.

They were lying on the raft, drying off in the sun, when a stunning idea came to Tad. "Are you—you're my father, aren't you?" he blurted out before he could reconsider.

Lance smiled, the tiny lines beside his eyes deepening. "I am, indeed. Do you mind?"

Mind? Was Lance kidding?

"No, sir!" he said so explosively that it shook the raft. "Do I call you—what do I call you?"

"You call your stepfather *Dad*, don't you?"

Tad felt his face stiffen. "Not anymore, I don't."

"Well, just so you won't get confused, why don't you continue calling me Lance? Later on, if it feels right, you can change that to *Pops* or *Poppa* or whatever suits your fancy." Again, he had a funny look on his face as if he was laughing at some joke he'd just remembered.

"Okay, sir—I mean Lance. I never knew anyone called that before. It's a funny kind of name."

"For me, it's very funny. The original Lancelot was the perfect knight. I'm a little less than perfect."

Privately, Tad disagreed. He thought his father was the greatest, and again he felt regret that he couldn't show him off. How he'd like to see Cappy's face if he ever came to the Father and Son Dinner with his real dad! And how could Mom have left Lance for someone else, even Miles? It didn't make sense. Sure, Dad was okay, but he didn't have any—well, he wasn't really anything special to look at.

"What is it, kid? Is something bugging you?"

"I—I was just wondering how come you never came to see me."

Lance didn't answer for a moment. "What did your grandfather tell you?"

"That Mom wouldn't let you."

"I'm afraid that's the truth. Christy thought you'd be better off if I stayed away."

"But you're a grown-up. You don't have to do what she says. You could've come anyway."

"I didn't want to make trouble between you two—or with your stepfather, either. It's pretty easy for a youngster to get mixed up."

"But lots of kids I know have divorced parents and they see both of them, no matter who they live with. It doesn't bother them at all—well, not much."

"It was your mother's decision. I wanted to get to know you but—" Lance shrugged, looking sad.

"Then you really did want to see me?"

"Of course. You're my kid, right? And fathers and sons—well, they should get to know each other and be friends."

Friends? He'd never thought of it like that before, but he and Miles had been really good friends—until two days ago.

"What else is bugging you, Tad? Maybe I can help."

"It's just that—well, I think it's really gross, the way Mom and Dad dumped me on Grandfather Neville just because they need money to pay some bills."

Lance was silent for a while; he was staring out at the horizon, his eyes shielded by his hand.

"Everybody has to do . . . what they have to do, Tad," he said finally. "You can't decide what's right for someone else. Your mother had her reasons—maybe she decided you would be better off with your grandfather. He can do a lot of things for you that she can't afford to do."

"But I—I miss her," Tad confessed, unconsciously lowering his voice. He blinked his eyes hard, feeling miserable and ashamed at the same time. "I felt real bad when I found out that she—that they just gave me to Grandfather Neville without asking me what I wanted. And it was mean, having Mr. Wilkie lie to me and all. I was scared, thinking Mom had been hurt in an accident. It really makes me feel bad, them tricking me like that."

"It happens to everybody eventually. People have a way of letting you down. Why don't you try to put them out of your mind? It won't be easy, but you can do it."

"Is that what you did when Mom left you for—for Miles," Tad said, the bitterness welling up inside him.

Lance's eyebrows rose. It was a while before he said, "Yeah—that did hit me pretty hard. It took a while to get over your mother. But life goes on and you find other things to do and you become interested in other people. And one good thing came out of our marriage—you."

His smile was so warm, his voice so sincere, that suddenly Tad didn't feel so lonely and mixed-up anymore.

And when Lance added, "We're going to get along fine together, Tad, and become great buddies," he felt good all over.

He gave his father a shy smile. "My real name is Steven. I don't much like being called Tad anymore. That's a kid's name," he said.

Chapter 13

During the days following Tad's disappearance, Miles watched helplessly as his comfortable world fell apart.

Although Christy never mentioned the erosion of their social life, the cessation of the solicitous cards and letters and the phone calls with offers of support and help, he knew it must cut deeply. For her sake more than his, he resented the faithlessness of their friends—or maybe, he thought (as always seeking the most appropriate word), it was their frailty.

He couldn't even blame them all that much. Hadn't he been guilty of the same frailty in the past?

That time one of his colleagues had been accused of molesting a pupil—he had stayed aloof. Reserving judgment, he'd called it. And when the girl had confessed that she'd lied because of a failing grade, somehow he'd always felt uncomfortable around the man after that, even though he'd phoned his fellow-teacher immediately with congratulations that he'd been cleared of the charge. In fact, he'd felt a little resentful because he'd just discovered that he needed a lesson in not making too quick judgments.

Would it be the same if—*when* Tad returned? Would people still stay away because they felt embarrassed for their own all-too-human failings?

Although he was able to protect Christy from most of the intrusions of the press and curiosity-seekers, from the crank calls that came to the house, it was impossible to shield her once she had started back to work. They had argued about that—if the polite words they'd exchanged could be called an argument—and Christy had pointed out that they needed her wages more than ever now, and then she'd added that she couldn't stand being alone in the house now that her mother had gone home and he was at work.

Whatever trials she encountered at work, she never spoke of at home, but during the days following her return, he watched her face grow paler, her finely boned body become thinner, saw her eyes grow more haunted, and he realized that some of it was caused by the thoughtlessness of other people.

He, too, had been the target of curious looks, of sudden silences when he came into the faculty lunchroom, of the politeness that was more damning than overt suspicion would have been. He could ignore all that, but Christy—it had to be harder for her. If only she would talk about it instead of going around surrounded by that ghastly calm. . . .

A week after she'd returned to work, he came home a little late to find her sitting in the kitchen, staring at the door, her expression so frozen that he knew immediately that she, so sensitized to disaster, had already dreamed up a grim reason for his tardiness.

"Sorry I'm late, Christy," he said quickly. "Old Hopkins had the floor at the staff meeting and you know what that means. There's no way of shutting him up, once he gets started on one of his tirades against government intervention in the universities."

He bent to kiss her, but she turned her face away and his kiss landed on her cheek. "I'll put dinner on the table," she said tonelessly.

Unexpectedly, he was swept by anger. Did she think she was the only one hurting? God knows, he didn't deserve to be shut out by Christy. Without thinking, he seized her face between his hands, forcing her to look at him.

She tried to pull away, her eyes cold. "You're hurting me, Miles," she said in a controlled voice.

He let her go then, but he stopped her when she started to get up. "I think we'd better have this out, Christy. You act as if I've done something terrible by being half an hour late. Hell, I'm always a little late on staff meeting afternoons—and this one was the last of the school year, the one where we discuss budgets for the fall term. And you know it's almost impossible to phone once I'm trapped in the conference room. So come off it, will you? Don't add to our problems by acting like a—a possessive wife."

It was the wrong thing to say. He knew it the minute the words left his mouth. The muscles in Christy's throat tightened and her eyes darkened, and for a moment she looked almost like the shrew he'd implied she was.

No—no, be honest. She looks vulnerable, like someone who's just been badly hurt. . . .

As quickly as it had come, his irritation vanished, replaced by another emotion just as disturbing—physical desire. He hadn't tried to make love to Christy since the night she'd lain in his arms as unresponsive as a rag doll.

The humiliation of not being able to satisfy her still lingered—and she hadn't made any overtures toward him, either.

Part of him understood—or at least, he was pretty sure he did. When something was bugging him, his instinct was to seek comfort in Christy's arms, while she—well, she withdrew into herself. Realizing that their natures, their needs, were different, he had been patient, never showing his own desire for physical intimacy, even though he had missed their former uncomplicated sex life. But God, he was only human! He was a man of strong sexual drives— and it was all directed toward Christy, had been since their first meeting.

That day he'd first met Christy on the campus, he'd been sure she must be the most beautiful woman in the world. Later, he had realized that she wasn't really that— her face was a little too thin, her mouth too generous, her hair too thick and heavy for her small head. But she had something—call it quality—that was devastating when combined with the earthiness, the natural sexuality he hadn't expected, and that had taken him totally by surprise.

When they'd made love that first time, two months after they'd started dating, he'd been prepared to hold back, to keep his strong drives in check—only to discover that Christy's passion matched his own. Together, they had made sex something beautiful, out of the ordinary. Was that all gone now? Leached out by the traumas of the past few days?

Or had the erosion of their marriage started even before Tad's disappearance? No, he would have known if that were true. Oh, he'd always been aware that there was something within Christy that she never truly shared with him, that she withheld some part of herself even during their most intimate moments together. He'd read some-where that even in the best of marriages, one partner loves more than the other, and he'd been resigned to be that one.

But this—this coolness between them lately—he didn't know how to handle. And he wasn't sure how much more he could take. He wanted Christy as much as always, maybe even more now, but she'd obviously lost all sexual desire for him.

Miles realized that he was still staring at Christy. Her eyes were wary, as if she had seen something in his face that she didn't like. Abruptly, he turned away and went to get the evening paper from the front steps. When he returned to the living room, he hid himself behind it, not offering to help with dinner as he usually did. On a back page, he found a small blurb about Tad's disappearance. It was the first mention in three days, but it said only that the search was continuing, that there was nothing new to report.

Christy came to the door to tell him dinner was ready. Her eyes moved to the newspaper in his hands. "Is there anything about . . ." Her voice trailed off as if she couldn't say Tad's name out loud.

"A couple of paragraphs. Just a rehash." Christy's face sagged and his compassion stirred. "We'd know first if there was anything new," he reminded her gently.

"I know, but I just keep hoping." She hesitated, then added, "Lucille Dubois called again—she's the woman whose baby was stolen from her backyard. She wants us to join the group she and her husband belong to, the one with parents of missing children. I told her I'd talk it over with you."

Miles took his time answering, not sure how to best express his doubts. "Look, we've posted that reward, and the police are doing all they can," he said finally. "And Jake Judson is a competent private investigator, the best we could find. What good could it do to—to expose yourself to more stress? You're going to hear a lot of grim stories from those people, Christy. Are you up to that?''

"It might be—comforting to share what I feel," she said.

Unaccountably, his anger stirred again. "Hell, Christy, you can't even open up to me, so why would you be different with strangers?" he said.

Her eyes looked stricken. "I'm just hanging on, Miles," she said. "I can't—don't you see that I'm doing the best I can? I'm hurting so inside that—that I haven't dared talk about it."

"Not even to me, Christy? What kind of relationship do we have if we can't share our feelings? Every time I try to talk to you, you retreat. And when I kiss you, it's like touching a statue."

"I'm sorry. I'm doing my best to—to cope with this thing. Can't you be a little more understanding of what I'm going through?"

"What *you're* going through? Singular? Tad was my son, too. Why do you keep forgetting that? Is it because you've never really thought of me as Tad's father?"

She gave him a stony look. "Why don't you say what you're really thinking? That it was all my fault, that if I hadn't slapped him, he wouldn't have run away—"

Her face crumpled and she turned and ran from the room; a moment later, he heard her footsteps on the stairs. He started to follow her, but then he stopped. What would he say? What apology could he make that wouldn't sound like a lie? He didn't blame her for Tad's disappearance—but would she believe him when her own conscience must be playing hell with her?

And he wasn't sorry he'd made that remark about Tad's being his son, too. It was something that needed to be brought out in the open, this feeling he had that she sometimes forgot how much he cared for the boy. So what could he, in all honesty, say to her? That the thing he was *really* sorry about was that their quarrel hadn't cleared the air, that it had driven them further apart?

After the quarrel with Miles, although they were polite to each other, Christy sometimes felt as if she were completely alone in her grief, her fear. She wanted desperately to restore the warmth of their former relationship, but it seemed to have slipped away, as lost to her as her son was.

Although she knew that if she approached Miles for sex he would respond, the price was too high. She felt empty—both unloving and unlovable. To let him make love to her was beyond her acting ability just now. For one thing, she felt an almost paranoid distaste for being touched, she who had always been so eager to make love before.

And there were other changes. Sometimes, she found herself vacillating about the simplest things. At the shopping center supermarket, she would pause for the longest time in front of a merchandise display, unable to remember whether they needed soap or breakfast cereal or coffee.

Or she would start to fix dinner and then, a few minutes later, find herself standing in their old-fashioned pantry, trying to decide whether to have rice or potatoes or pasta for dinner—and unable to make even this small decision.

Her work suffered, too. She forgot things, lost her train of thought at the most inappropriate moments, found herself saying words that had nothing to do with the conversations she'd been having with a colleague or client.

She told herself she was emotionally wrung out, living on her nerves, that it was no wonder she didn't want to make love, so why was Miles so—so insensitive? Had she hit upon the truth with her accusation, stated in anger? Did he blame her for Tad's disappearance—the way her own mother did?

Oh, Jessica never said it out loud, but it was there in the things she didn't say, the assurances she didn't make. Well, she did come around often, offering her support, even doing small chores, although she loathed housework. And she called every day, too, never staying on the line long, but—still, doing her duty, being supportive, which was more than a large majority of their friends had done.

What had Lucille Dubois told her the first time she'd called? That people seemed almost superstitious about associating with the parents of a lost child? Did they think that kind of tragedy and rotten luck rubbed off? Or did they suspect, in their secret hearts, that somehow she or Miles or both were child-abusers, that they had gone too far and killed their son? Or was it something much more simple, much more understandable? Were their friends and neighbors and colleagues simply ill at ease around them because, as they went on with their own normal lives, they knew that nothing would ever be the same for the Havens family again?

Christy rubbed her head wearily, thinking of chores she should be doing. Since it was Saturday, she had slept a little later than usual, and when she'd finally dragged herself out of bed she'd found a note from Miles, saying he had to see about some car repairs that couldn't be postponed any longer, not to expect him back for several hours.

So she'd found herself alone, faced with a dozen household chores. How strange that she had once looked forward to Saturdays, had even enjoyed getting the house in order and cooking up a storm for another week. Now every piece of furniture in the house seemed to reproach her, calling up memories that grew more hurtful with every passing day.

Well, no help for it. Housework, like taxes and—no, she would *not* think of that word. In fact, she intended to work so hard scrubbing out the bathrooms, vacuuming floors and scatter rugs, washing windows, and polishing furniture that when the day was over, she'd be so tired she'd fall asleep immediately without having to take one of those pills the doctor had given her. . . .

When the rest of the house was immaculate, she paused to fix herself a cup of tea, steeling herself for a chore she had put off too long. Since Tad's disappearance, she hadn't touched his room. But when he came back, wouldn't it bother him if his chest and bed were covered with dust? Wouldn't he expect to find his clothes hanging up, ready for him to put on, and clean sheets on his bed?

When she finished drinking her tea, she went upstairs and pushed open the door of Tad's room. A familiar odor—rubber shoes and model airplane glue and something indefinable that she thought of as little-boy smell— washed over her, and she had to lean against the door, fighting weakness, before she could go inside.

But once she had embarked upon her task, there was almost a relief in having finally faced up to it. She put away a scattering of clothes and games, the radio set Tad and Miles had been building, then changed the sheets on his bed, vacuumed the plaid rug, dusted the furniture and the floorboards.

She was folding Tad's favorite sweater to put away in a drawer when the pain came upon her so suddenly that she gasped and clutched her chest, thinking in that first confused moment that she was having a heart attack. Then, realizing what it was, she sat down on the edge of Tad's bed, rocking back and forth, her face convulsed with grief.

She so seldom cried—and then only when she was alone. With others, she was stoic, reasonable, unemotional. But now, the pressure, the fear, built up and up until finally it burst from her lips; a scream tore at her throat.

And then she was crying, the tears running down her cheeks and dripping on the front of her sweatshirt.

When the storm was over, she wiped her face with the hem of her shirt, and discovered she felt better—and ashamed that she did. Were her emotions so shallow that a few tears could banish her yearning for Tad? No, that wasn't it. The fear, the grief, was still there. It was just that she had held it all in too long. Was that what hurt Miles so, that she wouldn't let go in front of him, wouldn't talk about her feelings to him?

As if the thought were a catalyst, her mind opened, and suddenly she was remembering another time of grief. The baby she'd lost—no, that *they* had lost. Why did she keep shutting Miles out, putting him in a separate category? They had both lost that baby—and Miles had been as devastated as she, maybe even more so. Because of course she already had a child, flesh of her own flesh, while Miles didn't—and never would have now.

He had never reproached her for the miscarriage, even though she had been warned that she must be very careful, that the chances for carrying the baby to term would be decreased if she became too fatigued. But she had felt so good that day, so full of energy, that she had cleaned the house from top to bottom—and then had climbed up on that wobbly stool to hang those freshly laundered kitchen curtains—

But Miles had never shown in any way that he blamed her. Even when they'd found out that the operation that had saved her life had also made her barren, that there would be no babies, it was Miles who had comforted her. He had held her in his arms, telling her over and over again that it didn't matter, that they had Tad—and each other. And she had felt so cherished, so loved—why couldn't she accept his comfort now?

A truth so deep—and so simple—came to her. She had

always known that the reason she'd married Miles had been to add stability to her life and Tad's. Oh, she'd felt very lucky that someone as fine as Miles loved her, wanted her—and was willing to raise Tad as his own son. But she hadn't been *in* love with Miles, even though the sex between them had been so good.

Now she knew something else: Somewhere along the way, at some point during the past seven years, she had fallen deeply in love with her husband.

Why hadn't she realized this until now? In her own secret thoughts, she had called what she felt for Miles affection and companionship or, that catchall phrase, a good relationship, when all along it had been plain old-fashioned love.

She had even deluded herself about their sex life. She'd been surprised when she found herself so responsive to Miles's lovemaking, but she'd chalked it up to his sensitivity, to her own naturally passionate nature.

But for sex between a man and woman to continue to be good for so long it has to be fed by love, to be constantly renewed by love. If the love isn't there, then the whole relationship eventually falls apart. So why hadn't she realized that what she felt for Miles was real love, the kind that has nothing to do with gratitude or companionship? Why had she fought this knowledge so hard, even to the point of denying herself to Miles? Was she afraid of opening herself up to hurt and disillusionment again?

She leaned against Tad's desk, her eyes closed, breathing deeply. So much pain—she had suffered so much these past few days. She couldn't face losing Miles, too.

So it was time to move on, to mend the breach in her marriage. To lose Miles now was unthinkable. Whatever the reason for her—her frigidity—she must fight it, confront it, and overcome it. The best way to prove to Miles how much she loved and needed him was to restore the intimacy of their marriage bed. . . .

That afternoon when Miles got home, Christy had thought it all out and was waiting for him. She hadn't changed into something sexy—that would have been too artificial, too contrived. But she greeted him with a long kiss, a lover's kiss, something she hadn't done for a long time. At first, she sensed his reservation, but then his lips relaxed under hers and he was kissing her back, holding her tightly.

They talked—about the car repairs, about a comical remark one of his private students had made, and then she related a bit of office scandal—and all the time, she was trying to tell him with her eyes, her voice, her smile, that she wanted him, wanted things to be right between them again.

They went upstairs early, walking side by side, his arm around her waist, and she felt curiously nervous, almost as if it were that first time again. In their room, he undressed her, removing her clothes slowly, as if it were a ritual, something that had special meaning to him, and she remembered that the first time they'd made love, it had been the same.

She didn't help him. She stood motionlessly, a half-smile on her lips, holding everything destructive—fear and grief and worry—at bay. And when he bent his head to kiss her bare breasts, then the soft mound of her stomach, she buried her hands in his hair and arched her back, opening her thighs to him, letting him feel the slow quivering of her body as the fever began to build inside her.

He groaned and cupped his hands over her hips, and when she felt the tremor in his hands, she was proud that it was her body, her skin, her flesh, that made this strong man tremble. . . .

He had made love to her a thousand times, but tonight it was different. As if every inch of his lean body, every stretch of muscle, and every fiber and bone were an extension of her own body, she felt his desire as well as her own. And when he touched her, it was in a new way. Always before he had been careful with her, as if she were fragile, something easily bruised and broken. But tonight she knew what it meant to be the object of Miles's full passion, and something primitive and hungry in herself responded—wildly, mindlessly.

His caresses became more inventive, and she knew the relief of being fully aroused, of losing herself in sexuality. Nothing else mattered; the outside world had ceased to exist. Nothing intruded upon their complete submersion in each other. There was only the two of them, a man and a woman exploring the boundaries of their own sexuality, their own fascination with each other's bodies, stretching the sweet agony to the very limits.

When he entered her, possessing her fully, she felt as if she were flying—and with the duality that was so new, she knew Miles felt the same, as if the roaring in their ears were a high wind buffeting them about, building and building until it finally reached the out-of-world sensation that comes only a few times in a person's lifetime—if ever.

It was only later, when she was lying in Miles's arms, her heart still racing, her breath still tremulous, that she felt a stirring of guilt. How could she feel so happy when Tad—but no, she wouldn't think of that now. Later, she would grieve again, be beset with all kinds of fears and imaginings, but for now, she would just be a woman in the arms of the man she loved. . . .

But it was Miles who forced her to face her guilt. He raised up on his elbow and stared down at her. They had left the lights on and she could see the dampness on his forehead—and the tenderness in his eyes.

"You aren't feeling guilty for taking this time out for yourself, are you?" he asked quietly.

She rolled her head from side to side in denial. "This has nothing to do with Tad."

He kissed her then. "But it does, Christy. When Tad comes home, he'll expect to find that nothing's changed. That's why we have to keep our marriage strong."

"He will come home, won't he?" she said, her voice pleading.

"We have to keep thinking he will."

"Oh, Miles, how can I stand it? Sometimes I'm so afraid, so weak," she whispered against his throat.

"You're the strongest person I know. But it isn't weakness to admit that you have fears. And you've been living with this—this thing for the past three weeks. It's always with you—waiting for the phone to ring, part of you hoping it won't, because it might be bad news, and another part of you praying that it will, because maybe it's someone telling you that Tad is coming home."

"You do understand, don't you?" she said wonderingly.

"Of course. Didn't you know that?"

"I know how much you love Tad, yes. It's just that— well, no one expects a man to be as—as sensitive as a woman."

"I'm a human being, Christy. I hurt like anyone else— and I'm not afraid of showing it. Right now, I want to hear you say that you love me—and that you forgive me for letting you down lately."

"There's nothing to forgive. And I do love you. I know I've told you that before and I meant it, but this time— suddenly, I understand what it means to be *in* love. It's not affection or liking or—or sexual need. It's being half of a whole. Knowing that someone is always on your side, even if they don't approve of everything you do, just as you'll always be in their corner, rooting them on."

"And that's how you feel about me?" There was a hunger in Miles's voice that gave her a guilty pang.

"Yes—you believe me, don't you? You aren't still thinking that—that I have any reservations?"

"I believe you, Christy." But there was a shadow in his eyes now, and she was silent, knowing that Miles had sensed that something was still missing from their marriage. Something, some factor she couldn't put a name to, was still creating a barrier between them—and she didn't know what the hell to do about it.

Chapter 14

*T*ad lay on the log raft in the middle of the lagoon, watching Lance as he dived off the edge of the raft.

Something was troubling him and he wished he could figure out what to do about it. So far, he hadn't called his father anything except Lance. It didn't seem right to call a grown-up by his first name and yet—he still couldn't bring himself to call him *Dad*, either. Even though Miles didn't like him anymore, that name belonged to him. Of course, there were other names he could use, like Pop or even plain old Father, but they didn't seem right, either. Much as he liked Lance, somehow he didn't seem like a father.

Tad stared at Lance as he surfaced from his dive, snorting the water from his nose and mouth. In all his life, he'd never known anyone even a little like him. Sometimes it was hard to believe that he and Mom had once been married. Not that she was old or anything, but—well, Lance wasn't like most grown-ups. Sometimes, when they were talking together, it was like being with another kid.

And he could do anything—*anything*! Like winning that big race in—well, somewhere in Europe. Then there was the time Lance had climbed that mountain in Africa, the first white man ever to do it. Not that he bragged about those things. No, it all came out when he was talking about places he'd been, people he'd known, stuff he'd done. There was a reason why he talked about himself so much, too. Lance said he wanted his own kid to know where he was coming from—you know, understand him and his life-style.

His kid. . . .

Yeah, that sounded real good. In fact, it made Tad feel warm inside and not so lonely for—not so lonely. Of course, that was dumb anyway, feeling sad, because he'd been dumped by his mom and dad—no, *not* his dad. He had to remember that from now on. His dad was Lance Winthrop, and he was a lot more exciting than Miles could ever be. Right from the beginning, Miles probably had just pretended to like him to get on Mom's good side so she would marry him. And it must have worked, because when she got a chance, she had chosen Miles—and a lot of money—instead of him, her own son. Well, he wasn't going to think about them anymore. Not ever again. . . .

And anyway, Grandfather Neville wanted him. He thought he was something special. Good material, he said—which sounded funny but was really a compliment. Someday, his grandfather was going to leave him a whole lot of money in his will and let him run this really big banking business he owned. And other things—like a copper mine and some oil wells and a computer company and a couple of newspapers, too. It was great, having a lot of money—and power. You could order people around and make them do what you want. Yeah, Grandfather Neville had set him straight about *that* a couple of days after he'd come to the island.

They had been in the dining room, Grandfather Neville, Lance, and Tad, eating lunch, when Cotton had come in with some more hot rolls to go with the soup and salad. When he'd asked if Tad wanted another roll, he'd said, "Yes, sir," as he always did, and that's when Grandfather Neville had corrected him—and right in front of Cotton, too.

"Cotton works for me—and indirectly for you. You don't call subordinates *sir*, boy. Nor *mister*, either. You can call him Cotton—and when you want something, just tell him what it is and he'll get it for you. That's what money does. It gives you the right to give orders to the people who collect a salary from you. On the other hand, you have to have enough money so you can pay them every week. But make no mistake—when you pay the piper, you call the tune."

"You think that's the sort of thing you should be telling a kid his age, Neville?" Lance was smiling, but somehow Tad didn't think he meant it.

"He's not too young to know how heady power can be," Neville said. "First the carrot, then the stick."

"And the stick? What form does that take?"

"Discipline—hard, strict discipline. Which starts as soon as we get to Aristos. But he'll get his rewards right along, too, as well as the discipline, which is how I should have handled you. You've never understood that wealth has its price. Your mother isn't here to make a wastrel out of this boy, and by the time I get him raised, he'll be—"

"A carbon copy of Neville Winthrop?" Lance said.

"Exactly. And since we've made our deal, it behooves you to keep remembering it. No monkey wrenches in the works, Lance, and be very careful what you say to our little friend here or you'll be back freeloading off your friends.''

Tad watched, feeling a little scared, as Lance's face turned all funny. Not ha-ha funny, but the other kind. He didn't understand the conversation, but he did know they were fighting over him, and it made him feel bad. He felt a little disappointed when Lance just shrugged and went back to eating his soup. He would've liked him to argue a little more or something. Of course, Lance had to get along with Grandfather Neville because of all that money, and also because a guy wasn't supposed to argue with his own father, even if he was an adult. Still—well, after that, he hadn't been quite so much in awe of Lance somehow.

Water splashed over him as Lance flung himself up on the raft, looking like a wet seal. His body was sleek, well muscled and yet slim. Not the same kind of hard leanness that Miles had. Miles wasn't into any exciting sports like auto racing and mountain climbing and skiing, but still he kept in good shape, too.

What was it Miles had told Tad once? That the losers get the same amount of exercise as the winners—and sometimes, like in bowling, a lot more? He never seemed to think it was all that important to win. ''I don't have the killer instinct,'' he'd said, smiling. ''To quote a very old proverb: 'It isn't whether you win or lose but how you play the game.' ''

Well, I like to win, Tad thought, *and I'm going to be good at everything—like Lance. Only I'm going to be smart, too, and not make Grandfather Neville mad at me. And then someday, I'm going to own all this and a lot more, too, and then they'll be sorry that they gave me away. . . .*

Lance wasn't sure when the feeling of discomfiture had first surfaced. He had come to the island originally to talk his father into returning the boy to Christy. But that altruistic impulse had died when Neville dangled one of his carrots in front of his nose.

So of course he was cooperating. He wasn't his father's son for nothing. He knew the power of money—and not having to come crawling to Neville ever again for a handout was worth putting aside a few scruples for.

He'd set out to charm the kid, to keep him happy, and make him accept Neville's version of the truth. And it hadn't been too hard to convince Tad that he, his father, was some kind of hotshot hero.

Jack of all trades—and master of the ones that don't have any market value, he thought cynically.

Of course he could always scratch for a living as a ski instructor in Aspen. And he'd make a damned good tour guide, showing middle-aged ladies around Europe. Yeah, he'd be good at that. Unfortunately, his tastes were too rich for the pay of an ordinary working man—thanks to the old man. Hell, he couldn't live a week on a year's wages as a ski instructor or a tour guide.

And it was a moot question, because he was back in the game with a big balloon payment waiting up ahead for him, which made it all so strange that he felt so—so uncomfortable about lying to Tad about Christy and that guy she'd married. Well, it was a little late in the game to develop a conscience. In fact, things like scruples were pretty expendable when you were down to your last few bucks—which he was, since Neville had reneged on that seed money he'd talked about earlier. And it wasn't as if Neville intended to mistreat Tad. Hell, the kid would have the world on a string in a few years. He was doing his son the biggest favor of his life.

So why did the feeling, as if he were watching a lamb being led to slaughter, still persist?

As he sunned himself on the warm logs of the raft, he

studied Tad with appraising eyes. Good-looking kid. A chip off the old block, all right. Which was the thing that had convinced Neville that the boy really was his grandson. And, he was beginning to realize, the resemblance wasn't only physical. Sometimes it was like looking at himself in a mirror—and he didn't much like what he saw there.

"So, kid, how goes it?" he said. "You having fun?"

"Yes, sir—I mean, yes, Lance."

"Oh, you can call me *sir* if you like," Lance said dryly. "I'm only in Neville's pocket, not on his payroll."

Tad gave him a puzzled look, and Lance let his mouth stretch into the grin that he'd discovered years ago was the most effective way to disarm other people and keep them from asking him what he meant by his throwaway remarks. "Anything you need?"

Tad shook his head. "When I want something—you know, like a glass of milk and cookies or a different movie for the video player—I just tell Cotton and he gets it for me."

Lance winced at the unconscious arrogance in his son's voice. *You learn quick, little man.*

"So it's *Cotton* now, is it?" he said lightly. "It doesn't bother you to order a six-foot man around?"

Tad shrugged. "He's there to—uh, serve me. That's what Grandfather Neville says."

Unexpectedly, Lance's anger flared. "He's a human being with at least a few sensibilities. Don't let my father—"

He broke off, realizing that he was a fine one to lecture Tad. When was the last time he'd worried about the sensibilities of the Cottons of the world?

"Part of those responsibilities your grandfather has been talking about is seeing that the people who work for you are taken care of," he said mildly.

"Well, Cotton makes a lot of money." Tad's tone was defensive. "I heard him telling Cooky that if it wasn't for his fat paycheck every week, he'd chuck this crummy job. And then Cooky said that they both get three times what they'd get anywhere else and lots of time off to spend it, so they'd better keep their—uh, traps shut or they'd blow a good thing.''

"Uh-huh. Do you make a habit of listening in on private conversations?" Lance asked.

Tad flushed. "It wasn't on purpose. I was just fooling around with—it was just an accident that I heard them talking." He fidgeted with his flippers, looking at Lance out of the corner of his eye. "You won't say anything to Grandfather Neville, will you?"

"Not to worry. I don't exactly swap confidences with your grandfather."

Despite his light tone, Lance was puzzled. The kid was hiding something—maybe this called for a little probing.

"I can't help wondering what your mother would say to some of the changes in you lately," he said.

Tad's mouth set in a stubborn line. "She wouldn't care. She's glad to get rid of me. Now she and Dad—Miles— can be alone and they have enough money so they don't have to worry about paying off Grandma Havens's hospital bills or the mortgage and other things."

"You really believe they—" Lance broke off.

"Besides," Tad went on, not noticing the interruption, "I didn't do anything wrong. Grandfather Neville listens in all the time with that gadget in his desk drawer. He even showed me how to work it, but—well, I guess I'm not supposed to fool around with it unless he's there. I—I didn't do it on purpose, listening in to what they were saying in the kitchen. It was just that I was looking for a pair of scissors so I could start a scrapbook of racing car pictures and Grandfather left his desk drawer unlocked and—well, I pushed this one button without thinking and then I heard them talking. I only listened for a little while.''

Lance felt chilled. So Neville was up to his old tricks, keeping tabs on the people who worked for him—and he was already teaching Tad those same tricks. Was that part of the carrot—or part of the discipline?

''You don't think it's wrong to bug other people's private conversations?'' he asked.

Tad shrugged, his face sulky. ''What's wrong with it? It's okay when you're the one paying the bills. You have a right to know what's going on in your own house.''

''That sounds like a quote from my esteemed parent.''

''Grandfather Neville said that when he showed me how to use the—he calls it a gadget.''

For a moment, he looked very mature as he added, ''Cooky is always giving me cake and pie and stuff and talking real nice, but he doesn't like me. He told Cotton that if I belonged to him, he'd turn me over his knee and give me a good walloping.''

''Well, that's the penalty for listening in on private conversations. You hear a lot of things you don't want to know. Of course, like you say, if you're paying the bills, it's okay. But just think—if your grandfather is listening to us right now, he knows you've been fooling around in his den.''

Tad gave a furtive glance around, then shook his head. ''It's only connected to places in the house. I read those little buttons and I didn't see anything about the raft. And anyway, I don't think he'd mind, not really. He said that knowledge is power—and that I'd better get used to using it early on. That means you should—well, if you're boss, you should act like it. As soon as this island belongs to me, I'm going to fire Cooky first thing. You just wait and see if I don't.''

''I see a lot of things, kid.'' Lance felt a little nauseated.

"I see myself—and it's not a pretty picture. I've been closing my eyes to what's really going down here, just what he's making out of you, but I guess there's a limit, even for me. Your grandfather made one of his rare mistakes in judgment. I'm not as degenerate and far gone as he thinks—or as I thought I was."

Tad stared at him, looking a little scared. "What does that mean, Lance? Are you sick or something?"

Lance gave him a crooked smile. "I have a great idea," he said, ignoring Tad's questions. "How would you like to learn how to use scuba gear, Tad?"

At Tad's excited nod, he laughed and added, "And since I'm about to start doing the father thing for the first time, I think you should begin calling me Pop—or any similar term of your own choice."

Chapter 15

Until now, Tad's dealings with Lance had been pure fun.
Although his father had given him a few pointers on the
tennis court and had helped him with his crawl and his
backstroke when they went swimming, he hadn't persisted
when Tad got bored with the lessons and wanted to do
something else. But for the past two days, he had been
acting like—well, like a teacher or something, and Tad
wasn't sure he liked the change.

There were so many things to learn, to remember, about
scuba diving, and after an hour of being drilled on how to
put on and clear a face mask, how to breathe just so, how
to check every inch of the equipment—and all this before
they even went into the water—well, he wished they'd do
something that was more fun, like skeet shooting or just
fooling around in the water or maybe lazing around on the
raft. He finally voiced his objections.

"I didn't know you had to learn so many things when you went scuba diving," he said sulkily after Lance had showed him, for yet another time, how to use spit on his mask to keep it from fogging up in cold water. "I thought it would be more fun."

"Now that's the mistake a lot of people make, Tad." Although Lance didn't raise his voice, Tad sensed that he was very serious. "Becoming expert at a sport is hard work—it just looks easy to outsiders. Mountain climbing, for instance. Sounds very gung-ho, right? All that glory and being the first on top of the mountain, looking down on all those ants below. But as much time is spent getting ready and checking your gear as climbing. The same with any sport, including skiing or skydiving or car racing. One percent thrill and ninety-nine percent preparations. When your life is on the line, you either learn to keep your equipment in perfect order or you don't live to grow old bones."

"Well, I don't think I want to go in for sports if it's that much trouble," Tad said, feeling grumpy and put-upon. "And even if I did, I'd pick something like football or baseball, where you can make a whole lot of money. None of that amateur stuff for me. It's just a waste of time."

"Another quote from your grandpa?"

"No, it's something I figured out for myself. Grandfather Neville doesn't like any kind of sports, even professional. He says it's just an excuse some people use to become a bum." Tad hesitated; then, afraid that he had hurt Lance's feelings, he added quickly, "He didn't mean you—or at least I don't think he did."

"Well, to each his own. And bums don't get very far in sports, amateur or professional. It's hard work, no matter which one you go in for, even for a natural athlete—and you're that, kid. Just like your old man."

He hesitated a moment, then added, "Since you want to

go for the money, I suppose this means you've also ruled out the academic life, such as becoming a college professor like your stepfather?''

''I don't want to be a teacher. You don't make much money teaching.''

''You're right about that, I'm sure. But your stepfather might argue that there are other compensations. Tell me—what's he really like? You haven't talked much about him, you know. He must be a pretty dull duck, since he doesn't go in much for sports.''

Tad felt uncomfortable. Dull? Dad? ''Miles is—well, he's good at what he does. All the kids at PSU want to get into his classes even though he makes them work really hard. But he makes things you read in books interesting—you know? When he reads out loud, it's a lot better than watching TV, even cable stuff.''

''But it's obvious he hasn't been much of a father to you. I'll bet he's really strict, right?''

''We have—*had* a lot of fun together. Sure, I had to do chores and stuff like that, but we did other things, too—you know, like going fishing or, sometimes, we'd just take a walk and talk. Mom works, but we always did something on Sundays, the three of us, and lots of times they let my friends go along, too.''

''You miss them, don't you, Tad?''

Tad looked away. The hard, crusty feeling was back. He wanted to cry, but not in front of Lance.

''They don't miss me,'' he muttered. ''They were glad to get rid of me. Grandfather Neville says that someday, when they find out how rich I'm going to be, both of them will go to court and try to get me back, but then I'll be old enough to tell the judge I want to stay with him. He says I can tell them to go to hell.''

Lance was silent for so long that Tad felt uncomfortable.

When he finally looked around at his father, Lance was staring right at him, a funny expression on his face.

"If I let you in on something, will you promise not to tell?" Lance said abruptly.

Tad felt a stir of excitement. He loved secrets—and he was good at keeping them, too. "I promise," he said earnestly.

"Not even to your grandfather? Are you sure you wouldn't snitch to him?"

Tad mulled over his words. Did a promise to keep Lance's secret mean he would risk making his grandfather mad at him? He wouldn't want to do that—on the other hand, he wanted to please his father, too.

"I won't tell," he said, making up his mind. "Cross my heart." He made the sign he and his friends used. "Honest, I won't. I know lots of things about the kids at school that could get them in a whole lot of trouble if the teachers found out and I've never snitched once."

Lance nodded. "Okay, I believe you. I'm going to tell you something that'll make you feel differently about your mom. Your grandfather told you that she ran off with Miles, didn't he? That she's the one who wanted the divorce?"

Tad's heart gave a painful leap; as he nodded, he suddenly found it hard to breathe.

"Well, it isn't true. I was the one who ran out on both of you the day you were born. I had been having an—I had met this woman, and she was very sexy and very rich, too, so when I got the opportunity, I cut out. And to get your mother to agree to the—the divorce so I could marry the other woman, I signed away the right to visit you. Your stepfather adopted you later, so he's your legal father now. That's why I had no right to come see you. And that's why your grandfather kidnapped you. He knew it wouldn't do any good to try to get custody of you through the courts.''

Tad felt a painful restriction in his throat. "Kidnapped me? But my mother and Dad—'' He broke off, staring at his father's sober face.

"They have no idea where you are. In fact, your mother is undoubtedly going out of her skull right about now, afraid that you've been—that something bad's happened to you. And according to a newspaper article I read, your dad had posted a reward that I'm sure he can't afford and hired a private detective to help the police try to find you. They're spending every cent they have, mailing out flyers to police departments all over the country, taking out ads in the big city newspapers, that sort of thing.''

"They want me back? They didn't give me away?''

"They want you back the worst way. And no way did they give you away.''

"But Grandfather Neville said—was he lying all along?''

"All along. That's why there are no TV sets on the island. Neville doesn't want you to hear any newscasts. And that day Cotton and I took you for a cruise in the bay in one of the motor launches? The sheriff and his men searched the island, at my clever parent's instigation, that day. It's also why the guards watch you all the time—and why we can't go boating out in the bay, where someone might see us. Haven't you wondered why every radio in the house is broken? That's so you won't tune to a newscast and hear something about yourself.''

"And the newspapers—I asked Cotton if I could see the Sunday funnies and he said they got thrown out. I thought it was funny when it happened two Sundays in a row,'' Tad said slowly.

"Your grandfather plans to smuggle you out of the country and take you to Aristos. I thought I had more time to break this to you gradually, but he told me at breakfast today that a helicopter was flying in early tomorrow morning to take you into Canada. From there, he'll fly you to Europe in one of the corporation planes. Once you're out of the country, it could be years before your mother finds out where you are. By that time, Neville intends to have you completely alienated from your parents."

Tad tried to absorb all this, but some of Lance's words were too big for him. "Then everything he said about Mom was a lie?" he asked, returning to the important thing.

"It's time you knew that your grandfather will use any trick, tell any lie, do anything, legal or illegal, to get his own way."

Tad felt a flash of heat to his head. Without any warning, he flew at Lance and pounded his chest with his fists. "You knew this all along. You lied to me, too—I hate you! You're an awful man!"

Lance fended him off easily. "Whoa! I'm not all bad. As soon as I suspected what had happened, I came here to get you and take you back to your mother. Unfortunately, Neville wasn't easy to convince, and now I'm as much a prisoner as you are. He even keeps the phones locked up so I can't call off the island. And when I tried to use one of the motor launches, he told me flat out that I couldn't leave until you were gone. Even when we went off the island that day, he sent Cotton along to make sure I didn't get any ideas. Maybe I could handle the man in a fair fight, but he packs a gun. I'm not the hero type, kid. Being on the wrong end of a gun scares the hell out of me."

"But why didn't you tell me the truth? At least you could've done that. Why did you let me think that Mom and Dad had given me to Grandfather Neville?"

"He made me an offer I couldn't refuse, Tad. Unfortunately for him, he also made a slight mistake in judgment.

Even for a dedicated opportunist like me, there's a few things that stick in the craw. And putting Christy through any more hell than she's already been through is one of them. Seeing you turn into a carbon copy of my father is another. One Neville in the world is enough. You've already picked up some of his tricks—that business about eavesdropping on Cotton and Cooky, for instance.''

Tad flushed and looked away. ''I didn't really mean—it was just that—''

''Sure. That Neville made it seem so reasonable. That's how they work, Tad—people like your grandfather. But you knew better. You couldn't be your mother's son and not know right from wrong. So take my advice—for what it's worth. Choose your mother and stepfather as role models, not Neville.''

''I want to be like them, really I do. And like you, too.''

For some reason, his words seemed to make Lance mad. He frowned and shook his head. ''For God's sake, try to see me objectively, kid. On a scale of one to ten, I'd rate about a 'one' for being trustworthy. I don't know your stepfather, but I suspect he's a pretty decent guy. So count your blessings that your mother didn't turn around and marry someone just like me.''

Tad stared at him, trying to pin down an elusive idea. ''Do you still love Mom, Lance?''

''Love her? I'm not in love with her, but yes, I love her, I guess. Not that I wouldn't go crazy, being married to her. Oil and water, kid—oil and water. Two things that just don't mix.''

The sun broke above the top of the trees surrounding the lagoon and glittered on Lance's hair as he grinned suddenly. ''And if you ever repeat this conversation to your mother, I'll deny it to my last breath.''

"Okay," Tad said. "I'll bet—yeah, I'll bet Mom and Dad will want to be friends with you when we get back."

"So you've decided to return to your mother? You'll be giving up the chance to be super-rich, Tad. You might regret it someday."

Tad thought about the train set, the video games, the sports equipment—and about the motorboats and racing cars and skiing trips to Switzerland his grandfather had told him he could expect when he was a little older. He coveted them, all those things, in the worst way.

On the other hand—what good were they if he couldn't show them off to his friends? Watching a movie alone, even if it hadn't come out yet in Puget City, wasn't nearly as much fun as—say, kicking a football around with the guys in the schoolyard or going fishing with his dad.

With a sigh—and not a little regret—he relinquished all those neat things and said, "I want to go home—are you going to tell Mom and Dad where I am so they can come and get me?"

"It's not that easy. Neville's bullyboys are watching us all the time. Right now, if you'll glance over toward the bathhouse, you'll see Cotton's bald pate shining like the full moon in the shadow of that larch. No, I couldn't make a move until after dark tonight—and by the time I get to a phone, provided I make it that far, it might be too late to stop Neville from taking you off the island. So we'd better make a run for it tonight, the two of us. But it's going to be tricky, kid. I just hope—" He broke off, looking worried.

"How will we get off the island? It's a long way to swim," Tad said doubtfully.

"It seems Neville isn't infallible after all. I left my friend's motorboat anchored at a buoy out in the bay. I've been keeping an eye on it with field glasses and it's still there—or it was a couple of hours ago. Either Corky forgot to report it missing or—well, never mind that. The important thing is that it gives us an option. As part of the carrot Neville's been dangling in front of you, he gave me carte blanche to order any kind of sports equipment you took a fancy to—which was another mistake on his part. we'll get off the island the same way I got on—using scuba gear.''

Tad stared at him. ''Is that why—''

''You've got it. That's the reason why I had Cotton go into Puget City for a wet suit in your size and why I've been pushing you so hard to learn how to use it. All we have to do is reach Corky's boat without being caught. Unfortunately, there's a full moon tonight and clear skies are forecast, or we could swim to the boat. But I'm afraid we'll have to go underwater for at least a few hundred yards, kid.''

Tad's face must have shown his qualms, because Lance laughed and slapped his shoulder. ''Don't sweat it. If you get tired, you can hold onto my belt. It'll be a little hairy, but I'll get you back to your mother. And once you're home, I don't think Neville will try anything illegal again.''

''You don't think he'd—you know, try to kidnap me?''

''He took the chance this time only because he was so sure he was above suspicion—which has proved out, since his tactics, inviting the sheriff and his men to search the island, worked all too well. I don't think even Christy seriously suspects him now. She's too busy blaming me.''

''Wait till she finds out how you helped me,'' Tad said. ''She'll stop being mad at you then.''

''Uh-huh—well, anyway, with the truth about Neville out, and the illusion blown that the great man wouldn't stoop to such a vile thing as child-snatching, he'll have lost his edge. Not that he'll give up. No, he'll use other tactics, such as a little judicious bribery, but I think another kidnapping is out. Who knows, kid? You might end up his heir, after all."

Although he was smiling, Tad had a funny feeling that he didn't mean it.

Tad felt cold suddenly. When he shivered, Lance flung a towel around his shoulders, and said, "So easy does it for now. We'll finish your cram course on scuba diving and then I want you to rest for the remainder of the day. Conserve your strength, because you'll need it tonight. If everything goes okay, you'll be back home by morning— and then you'll have enough yarns to dine out on for the rest of your life."

Tad lay in the darkness of his room, staring at the dim outline of the hall door. Following Lance's instructions, he was wearing jeans and a dark sweater under his pajamas. For some reason he couldn't explain, he had chosen his own clothes instead of the ones his grandfather had provided for him. After he'd turned out the lights and crawled into bed, he'd spent the time trying to keep his courage up.

When Cotton checked up on him at ten o'clock as usual, he'd pretended to be asleep, but his heart had pounded so hard that he was sure it must be shaking the covers. He didn't relax until he heard the door close and the key turning in the lock.

Then he waited, too scared to fall asleep, for what seemed hours. Although he was too warm with so many clothes on under the covers, he was afraid to throw off the sheet, for fear Cotton would make an unexpected check on him the way he sometimes did. Outside his window, the moon rose, filling the room with a gray light that distorted the familiar chests and bookshelves and chairs, giving him a queasy feeling in his stomach as if he might barf any minute.

Ordinarily, he would've been glad to see the moon,

since that meant it wasn't raining and he probably could go swimming in the lagoon the next day. Now he wished it would cloud up and maybe even rain so the guards would stay inside tonight and not make so many rounds.

What would happen to them if he and Lance got caught? Would his grandfather do something bad to Lance? He was pretty sure *he* would be safe from punishment, because he was just a little kid. But if they got caught, Grandfather Neville would really be sore at Lance. *Really* sore.

Why was Lance taking such a chance for him, anyway? Was it because he—well, because Lance was his father? He had sounded like he was laughing at himself when he'd talked about losing all that money Neville had promised him, which was kind of weird, because Lance really liked being rich. He didn't make any bones about that.

Tad made a solemn promise to himself. When he got back home, he would tell Mom and Dad how Lance had helped him and then he'd ask them if maybe his father could come see him sometimes. Surely, when his mother knew what Lance had done, she would get over being mad at him. It wasn't right, Lance's taking off like that and leaving Mom and him and marrying some other woman, but still—adults did dumb things. Half the kids he knew had stepmothers or stepfathers, sometimes both, so that meant parents were going off all the time to live with other people, didn't it?

He was glad the divorce hadn't been his mom's fault. Why had he believed his grandfather, anyway? Was it because of all those presents—and the promises Grandfather Neville had made? He'd hate it if Mom were to find out that he'd believed those lies about her—maybe he didn't have to tell her. He was pretty sure Lance wouldn't tell. Maybe he should tell her himself. It was always best to be honest. For one thing, when you told people lies, you had to have a good memory so you didn't give yourself away by accident.

Well, he'd think about that later. Right now, he wished Lance would hurry. The house had been quiet for a long time—what was he waiting for, anyway? Maybe—maybe he'd been caught. If so, then they'd never get off the island and he'd never see Mom and Dad again—

There was a scratching sound at the door, so faint that if Tad hadn't been listening so hard, he wouldn't have heard the key turning in the lock. Then the door was opening, and he saw a figure silhouetted against the hall light. When he recognized Lance, he let out a long relieved sigh. Lance heard the sound and put a warning finger to his lips.

Silently, Tad slid out of bed. He had kept on his rubber-soled shoes, too, so all he had to do was take off his pajamas and push a couple of extra pillows and blankets under the covers as Lance had told him to do, making it look as if he was still sleeping there.

Their trip down the hall toward the service stairs in the rear of the house was scary. Every creak of the floorboards seemed to echo through the dark. And going down the stairs was even worse. Tad vacillated between wishing the wind would blow harder so it would cover up any sounds they made and being glad it was quiet, because then he would hear if anyone tried to sneak up on them from behind.

They had almost reached the bottom of the stairs when Lance's hand on his arm stopped him. Tad could feel the tenseness of his father's body as they listened to men's voices coming from the kitchen. Under the kitchen door, a thin sliver of light showed, and from the racket, Tad knew it must be more than two men. He caught a few words and realized they were telling each other jokes—the kind he wasn't supposed to listen to. Under his breath, Lance said, "Dammit!" and then motioned for Tad to sit down on a step and wait.

The voices seemed to go on for hours. The men got louder and louder, laughing a lot, and Tad wondered if they were drinking whiskey and maybe getting drunk. He shivered, feeling cold. What if someone came through the door right now and found them sitting here in the dark? He wanted to crowd up close to Lance, but he didn't, because he was getting too old to act like a scared kid. Even so, he felt better when Lance put his arm around his shoulder, and after a while, his thoughts got hazy, and he dozed; his chin dropped down to his chest.

When Lance shook him gently, he came awake with a start. When he started to ask a question, Lance put a warning hand over his mouth. Only then did he realize that the voices had stopped, that the light under the door was gone. The men must have returned to their cabins for the night. But there were still the night guards to look out for—and the island was so small that it would be hard to avoid running into them.

The door creaked alarmingly as Lance eased it open. Moonlight flooded the kitchen through the windows. Tad stopped breathing until Lance finally made a beckoning gesture. Following closely on his father's heels, Tad crossed the kitchen, skirting the big table in the center where Cooky and the guards ate their meals, then went out through the back door, closing it carefully behind them.

The rear courtyard was filled with a silvery gray light. Every tree and bush stood out starkly. In the moonlight, Lance's shadowed face looked years older, very grim, and Tad felt an uneasiness that quickly blossomed into fear.

What if Lance was playing some kind of trick on him? Maybe he wanted Grandfather Neville's money all for himself, and it was a lie that he intended to take him back to his mother? Once they were under the water in their scuba gear, Lance could do anything he wanted to him and nobody would ever know. If Lance took his mask away and held him there until he drowned, they would just figure he'd been fooling around on the seawall and had fallen in. And then Lance would inherit all that money. . . .

"Come on, kid." Lance's whisper held impatience. "Time to make a dash for it."

Tad didn't answer—and he didn't move, either. His muscles tense, ready for flight, he stared at his father. He wanted desperately to believe him, but he was afraid, too.

"Scared, kid?" Lance said.

Tad hesitated, then decided on a half-truth. "Not too much. Just a little nervous."

Lance laughed softly. "You'll be okay. You've got guts."

He turned and started away, heading for the path that led to the lagoon, moving as quietly as a tiger—or maybe a leopard, Tad thought. Trying to imitate him, he followed closely on Lance's heels. He tried not to notice how dark the shadows under the trees were, or how the grass on the side of the path moved in the night breeze. The wind quickened, playing catch with his hair and blowing it into his eyes. As he brushed it away, the skin at the back of his neck crawled. He felt as if a thousand eyes were watching him.

But he went on anyway, and no one challenged them. No one stepped out of the darkness to stop them as they moved through the shadows under the grove of pines behind the house, feeling their way along the path because they didn't dare use Lance's flashlight.

When they reached the bathhouse, where Lance had left the scuba gear, he risked switching on his flashlight long enough so that they could see to put on their wet suits and weighted belts. Lance checked Tad's gear, then hoisted one of the tanks of oxygen onto his shoulder. It felt heavy and very cold, even through his rubberized wet suit, and he wondered if he would be able to move through the water for such a long distance, carrying so much weight.

Lance tied a rope around Tad's chest, then looped the other end around his own waist.

"I'm giving you enough rope so it won't be too restrictive," he said in a low voice. "I'll be using the underwater torch, so you can follow the beam, but just in case, the rope is a precaution. I don't expect any trouble, but if something should happen, don't do anything stupid. Slip out of the loop and swim like hell for shore. Neville won't be rough on you. Just tell him I forced you to go along with me. He'll believe you. He can't conceive of anyone being crazy enough to turn down all his money."

Traveling single file, they moved along the edge of the seawall. Following Lance's example, Tad bent over into a crouching position so he wouldn't be silhouetted against the sky.

Earlier, Lance had said that the best access to the place where his friend's boat was moored was through the lagoon, since it wasn't constantly patrolled, the way the beach had been since Tad's arrival. Unfortunately, the sea end of the lagoon was sealed off by heavy steel netting, so they would have to travel the entire length of the seawall to reach open water—and this was where they would be most vulnerable.

At the junction of the seawall and the netting, they stopped to put on their flippers. The only sound now was the wash of water against the seawall. Usually, it was a soothing sound, but tonight it seemed ominous to Tad— like someone whispering threats just out of earshot.

Even inside his wet suit he felt cold, and he wondered if the wind had suddenly changed and was coming from the north now. The water of the bay looked as black and thick as oil; the thought of going into it scared him.

Lance seemed to sense his fear, because he reached out and squeezed his shoulder. "Hang in there, son. Another half hour or so and we'll be in the boat and then—it's home free."

It was the first time he'd called Tad *son*; the novelty of it kept Tad quiet as he watched Lance don his mask, check his gear swiftly, and then slip into the water without another word.

When the rope tightened around Tad's chest, he took a deep breath and followed his father, trying not to make a splash. The water, closing over his head, gave him a trapped feeling, and he felt a moment's panic, a desire to climb back up on the seawall.

Suddenly disgusted with himself, he resolved to stop behaving like a baby. After all, he was with Lance, who was a—what had he called himself once?—a super-sportsman as well as a super-stud? Lance knew everything about scuba diving. He wouldn't let anything happen to his own kid.

The rope tugged against Tad's chest, and he pushed upward from the bottom where he'd been crouching, using his arms to gain his balance. As he followed Lance, he moved awkwardly, because he still wasn't used to the encumbrance of the scuba gear. Ahead of him, Lance's torch cast a triangular beam through the inky water, while overhead, he saw a small oval-shaped glow that he knew must be the moon.

A shiver ran along his back as he realized that with the moon shining on the water, anything—even something as small as a head—that broke the surface would be clearly visible to anyone standing on shore. What if he lost his mask and had to surface? Would Cotton or one of the other guards see him and take a shot at him?

It seemed strange now that he'd been so fascinated by their guns. Grandfather Neville had told him that the guns were just "window dressing," something to scare off picnickers who sometimes tried to land on the island. But he'd seen the guards shooting at bottles out behind the powerhouse, and he knew the guns shot real bullets.

The trapped feeling came back, almost overwhelming him, and he hurried his stroke, wanting to be closer to Lance. Against the light of the torch, Lance's body moved easily, without any wasted movement.

Tad felt a pang of jealousy. Even though Lance had called him a natural athlete, he knew in his heart that he'd never be in the same class as his father. Lance always won at anything he did—racing cars and tennis and mountain climbing. And although he hadn't said anything, Tad had sensed his impatience those times when he'd been showing him the right way to smash the tennis ball when he served, especially when he didn't get it right the first time.

On the other hand, Miles, who was pretty good at tennis himself, didn't seem to care how long it took Tad to catch on—or if he won or lost as long as he enjoyed the game and acted like a good sport about it. Did that mean that Lance was better than Miles—or just the opposite?

Something brushed against his arm. From the corner of his eye, he caught a movement in the water. He started violently as a large black shape slid past him and into the darkness. What was that a floating log or did sharks come this far north? No, he wouldn't think about *that* now.

He fixed his eyes on the torch beam, reassured by Lance's methodical and obviously unconcerned progress through the water. He tried to think about something pleasant, like getting home and having Mom make a big fuss over him. She would probably cry, but he wouldn't mind that, not this time. Miles would thump him on the

shoulder and say something like "Good show, Tad," and
Grandma Jessica would bawl him out and then she'd slip
him some money on the side so he could play the games at
the arcade and treat his friends to Big Macs and onion
rings.

Only maybe he wouldn't take her money this time.
Maybe he would tell her to give it to his mother to help out
with the bills. Yeah, that's just what he'd do—but not all
of it. No, he'd keep a little of it for himself. . . . And the
kids—they'd be all bug-eyed when he told them about
getting kidnapped and how his father had rescued him.

Up ahead, Lance stopped, so abruptly that Tad bumped
into him from behind. Lance caught Tad's arm, steadying
him, then motioned upward. Tad nodded, his heart
pounding. Had they reached the boat already? Or was
something wrong? He looked upward, but all he could see
was the shifting glow of the moon.

A couple of minutes later he surfaced next to Lance. "I
heard the hum of a motorboat through the water, but the
sound's gone now," Lance said, his voice low. "It's
possible we've already been missed and they have a boat
out looking for us. If so, it's moved around to the dock
side of the island. So we'd better get on with it. It could
get sticky if they spot us before we reach Corky's launch—or
if the motor won't start."

"You think they'll catch us?" Tad whispered.

"No, I don't—or I wouldn't have started this thing. But
just in case we don't make it all the way, I want you to lie
like hell. Tell Neville I tricked you into coming along and
I'll back you up."

"But what will he do to you, Poppa?"

His father didn't answer for a moment. Tad squinted his
eyes. Was Lance smiling—or was that a trick of the
moonlight?

"Not to worry, son," Lance said easily. "He'd just

keep me here until you're off the island, then toss me out on my arse. Or he might even take me along to Aristos. Either way, I'll be okay.''

He motioned for Tad to put his mask back on. After one last long look toward the island, he slipped under the water again and Tad, with more than a few doubts, followed.

The next minutes seemed endless. Tad's throat felt dry and achy from the oxygen he was breathing, and the water farther out in the channel was much colder. The current here was stronger, too, and harder to move against. Even the light from Lance's underwater torch seemed dimmer, and he wondered if the battery was running down—or maybe it was just that the water was blacker here, so far from shore.

When they reached the buoy where the boat was anchored, Lance turned off the torch and pulled himself up, hand over hand, using the boat's anchor rope. Tad followed, fighting against the urge to rush toward the air. As soon as he broke water, even before he took off his mask, he heard the distant hum of a motorboat.

''It could be anyone, of course, but we have to assume it's one of the old man's launches,'' Lance said. ''As far as I can tell, there's only one boat moving around out there. Even if we've been missed, they haven't had time to make a thorough search of the house and island. If Neville really knew we'd left the island, he'd have both launches out looking for us, so we still have time—provided luck's on our side.''

Motioning for Tad to follow him, Lance slid agilely over the edge of the boat, hardly rocking it. Tad wasn't nearly as graceful; the boat rocked wildly as he hoisted himself aboard. He fell onto a padded seat as Lance untied the anchor rope and cast it adrift, not taking the time to pull it on board.

Lance bent forward to peer into the space in front of the

wheel. "The motor hasn't been ripped off—which is a break for us. Now, if it's still working—"

When he tried to turn the motor over, it coughed once, then died. He cursed under his breath, then tried again. This time, it roared into life, shaking the boat, and Tad let out a long breath of relief.

Lance turned his head to grin at him and made a sign, his fingers shaped into a V, before he turned back to the wheel. Tad eased out of the tank straps and laid his mask on the seat beside him, but he kept on his flippers. He sniffed the odor of fish, brine, and bilge water happily; it seemed to hold the promise that he'd soon be home. When he found himself wishing he had a Snickers bar, he made a face. It seemed so dumb, being hungry at a time like this.

Although the wind whipped sharply against his face now, the boat seemed to be moving sluggishly. Why were they going so slow? Was Lance afraid of attracting attention if he went real fast, or was something wrong with the motor? Several times the motor made a coughing noise. Tad found himself leaning forward every time it made the sound, as if somehow this would help the boat move through the water faster.

He looked back at the V-shaped wake behind the boat; the water gleamed like silver, and when he thought how cold, how deep, it must be out here in the middle of the bay, the skin on his arms crawled.

Shivering, he huddled on the seat, wishing he had a blanket, wishing Lance would hurry, wishing he hadn't—no, not that. Because no matter how scary this was, he was still glad to be away from the island, to be away from Grandfather Neville with his dusty voice, his frosty eyes.

He felt a rush of gratitude, of pride, as he looked at Lance. If his father noticed the cold, it didn't show. But Lance's face, when he turned to look back, was watchful, and Tad realized that they still weren't out of danger.

I'm scared, he wanted to tell Lance. *After all, I'm just a kid, and I'm real scared.*

A strange thought came to him then. If that were Miles up there at the wheel, he would say the words out loud and not feel ashamed of being afraid—so why didn't he want to say them to Lance?

He heard a pulsating, throbbing sound then, even above the roar of their own motor. Quickly, he twisted his head around and saw another boat coming toward them, moving very fast. He started to shout a warning, then realized it wasn't necessary, because it was obvious that Lance had already seen the other boat. He cursed once, then increased their speed. Ahead of them was only darkness—no, wasn't that a light? Was it another boat—or was it land?

Tad popped both hands over his mouth to hold back a scream as the boat behind them roared closer. Against the sky, he saw the outline of two men. One was pointing his finger toward them—why did he bother? Surely, by now, the other man must know they were there.

He heard a popping sound; then a high-pitched whine like a mosquito buzzing passed his ear, but it wasn't until Lance fell sideways, crashing against the opposite side of the boat, that he understood what it meant. The man was shooting a gun at them—and a bullet had hit Lance.

Tad's throat hurt, and he realized he was sobbing out loud. He made himself stop, made himself move forward, even though his body was so stiff and clumsy with fear that he nearly fell as he climbed into the front seat. He slid down on the floor beside the steering wheel shaft and bent over Lance. Was he dead? His eyes were closed and—no, he was moving, trying to get up.

Lance groaned, then sank back down again. Tad stopped breathing so he could hear better when he realized Lance was saying something.

". . . Can't move . . . arm . . . bullet in shoulder . . .

cracked . . . side . . . boat . . . have . . . steer for me, kid
. . . grab wheel. . . .''

He closed his eyes again, and his breathing sounded so
queer that Tad wanted to put his hands over his ears to
shut it out. When Lance went on, his voice was so faint
that Tad had to bend closer to hear what he was saying.

". . . Wind knocked out . . . okay . . . few minutes
. . . up to you . . . still not licked . . . hold it steady . . .
don't let the boat turn . . . flip at this speed . . . head for
lights . . . run boat on sand . . . pray no rocks. . . .''

His head rolled sideways. Tad clutched at his arm.
"Wake up, Poppa! Please wake up. I'm scared—I don't
know what to do next—''

But there was no answer, and as Tad huddled next to his
father's limp body, he knew that he was all alone, that
whatever happened next was up to him.

Chapter 16

Christy was lifting a bag of groceries out of the car when she heard the phone ringing inside the house. She dumped the bag back on the seat and ran toward the front porch. As she dug in her purse for her key, she reflected that at one time she would have let the phone ring until she was ready to answer it, knowing that if it were important, the caller would call again, that if it wasn't, so much the better. These days, she couldn't take that chance.

The call could be so many things. It could be Miles, reminding her that he'd be tutoring after his summer-school class and would be home an hour later than usual. Or it could be Jessica, calling to ask if she could bring anything this evening when she came for dinner, or someone from work with a question about the latest miracle software package the company was touting. Maybe it was a friend, inquiring if Christy had heard any news and if there was anything she could do to help. Christy still got a few of those calls—and they were always welcome because they said someone cared. Or maybe it was Lucille Dubois, inviting her to come to the next meeting of the parents of missing children group.

It could be Detective Lombard, calling to report that she was still working on the case, still checking out every lead, no matter how remote. Her calls were like small pebbles shining in a stream of rushing water, something that in themselves meant nothing and couldn't stop the relentless flow of the water but that somehow added dimension to the whole. Otherwise, each day would seem exactly like the one before, and eventually, Christy was convinced, she would soon lose all sense of time.

There was always the possibility that it could be another crank call, usually a young voice asking if he or she could speak to Tadpole or Froggy, with lots of giggling going on in the background. By now, these calls no longer surprised Christy, although she'd never gotten used to the knowledge that there were people in the world who drew pleasure out of being cruel. She even had worked out a system to handle them. Her voice calm, she simply gave them Detective Lombard's number and hung up. And then she took the phone off the hook for half an hour or so.

But it was none of these possibilities that made her drop the bag of groceries and run. No, it was hope, the hope she lived with every minute of every day—hope that *this* time it would be the call she yearned for, the news that Tad had been found, alive and well, and was coming home.

She picked up the phone; when she heard Detective Lombard's voice, her body tensed with fear.

"Gena Lombard here. No news here. Just calling to find out how things are going with you, Christy. I thought I'd better let you know that business in Detroit checked out just as we expected, since the boy was reported to be at least thirteen, possibly a year or so older.''

"Business in Detroit? I don't understand—''

There was a brief silence. "I see your husband didn't tell you about it. Well, that's all for the best.''

The reserve in her voice alerted Christy to the reason why Miles hadn't passed along this information to her. A dead child—someone else's tragedy. Some other parents' pain. . . .

She closed her eyes, the pity running strong and deep inside her. "I'm sorry," she said finally. "I hope they find the parents. It's best that they know.''

But I don't want to know. If Tad is dead, I want to keep on hoping, even if it's for the rest of my life. . . .

She realized Detective Lombard was talking, asking if there had been any more crank calls. She answered sensibly, then asked a question about Gena's children, who were staying with their grandparents for the summer, and after another minute or two of general conversation, the policewoman hung up.

Christy sat there, still holding the dead phone, deep in thought. Already Gena Lombard's calls came less frequently. In time, would they stop altogether? And when that happened, would she be the one who called Gena, carefully calculating just how often she could call without becoming a pest and still often enough so that she wouldn't go out of her mind, not knowing if there was something, however small, that she could build hope on?

Well, she was grateful that Gena cared enough to call at least once a day. After all, she had other cases, all more immediate and pressing. According to Mrs. Dubois, missing-child cases were an embarrassment to the police, which was why so often they simply swept them under the rug. Even to the most hardened policeman, a missing child case was painful, so often unsolvable.

Sighing, Christy hung up the phone and went to get her groceries out of the car. Jessica would be here soon and she'd decided to fix something special tonight, one of her mother's favorites—Hungarian goulash. It was high time they got back to normal, because if things seemed normal on the surface, maybe some of it would rub off and she could forget—she winced, knowing how impossible that was. No, she couldn't forget Tad, nor did she want to. As long as she kept making promises to God, bargaining for his return, then she was doing something positive to help Tad.

But God, how come You're so slow? Why don't You hurry up and send him back to Miles and me?

She was adding crushed gingersnaps to the goulash when she heard Jessica's car turning into the driveway. She dusted the crumbs from her fingers and then went to open the front door for her mother, unconsciously smiling as she watched Jessica get out of the car.

Jessica was wearing a spring suit in muted shades of violet and lilac, and she looked impeccably groomed, as imperturbable as always. At one time, Christy would have been fooled, turned off by what she would have regarded as her mother's complete self-absorption. Now, when she walked to the edge of the porch to greet Jessica, to kiss her smooth cheek, there was genuine warmth in her voice because she knew that beneath her mother's unyielding façade, Jessica's fears matched her own.

She's tough, she thought as she had so many times Jessica never let down, not for a moment. At one time, this had irritated her and she'd longed to see her mother with her hair mussed, her lipstick bitten off. But no more. Not since she'd finally come to understand her. Jessica was a constant, a note of stability in a world that seemed so insane at times. It was only by maintaining conventions and rigid standards that Jessica kept herself going—and if she was a little hard to take at times and if her goals in life were different from Christy's, still she'd been a rock to depend upon during the horrors of the preceding weeks.

I've changed, Christy thought. *I'll never be so intolerant of people again after all this is over.*

And wasn't it strange that she had come to appreciate Jessica during this, the most terrible time in her life? Her marriage, too, had taken on a new dimension since Tad's disappearance. She had been warned that marriages often came apart during times of intense stress—but she and Miles had been lucky. Yes, in this one thing, they had been lucky.

"Something smelled delicious. That wouldn't be goulash, would it?" Jessica said briskly.

"It would. With noodles. Loaded with calories."

"Lovely—even though I'll have to diet like mad for the rest of the week."

Jessica tasted the goulash and advised Christy to add more paprika. She offered to help make the salad, something she wouldn't have done a month earlier, and Christy sat her down at the chopping board with a paring knife and a stack of salad vegetables. She put water on to boil for the noodles and then got out her rolling pin and began crushing crackers to add to the buttered noodles at the last moment. She and Jessica talked companionably—about Christy's job, about a new hairdresser Jessica was trying, about everything and anything except Tad.

"Miles late again tonight?" Jessica asked.

"He's tutoring a private student. He should be along any minute—"

Christy broke off as she heard Miles's quick step on the front porch steps; her heart jumped with relief, and she rose quickly and went out into the hall. This was something else she'd learned these past few weeks—not to take for granted such ordinary things as one's husband coming home at the end of the day.

Miles was opening the front door when she reached the hall. He tossed his briefcase on the old oak refectory table and came toward her with a quick, eager step. He kissed her, not a perfunctory lip-brushing, but a real kiss, deep and possessive, as if he too had learned new lessons about not taking anything for granted. Afterward, she leaned against him, drawing comfort from the familiar tweedy odor of his jacket, the warmth of his lean body—

"You okay?" he asked as he always did.

"Okay. It was busy at work today, though. A problem with the new payroll program from Tasco Electronics. Several glitches have turned up, and it looks like it needs more work before it can be distributed—"

Still talking, they went into the kitchen. Jessica's welcoming smile for Miles was wintery, as always, but he didn't seem to notice, also as usual. He bent and kissed her cheek, then dropped into a kitchen chair with a long sigh.

"Bad day?" Jessica asked, raising one of her perfectly arched eyebrows.

"Rotten. Collins Newton called an emergency budget meeting, and since I was at hand, I had to attend. It turned into a real hassle. Administrators with funding problems aren't my favorite people to share a lunch hour with, especially when it's so blasted muggy and hot in the faculty lunchroom. On top of that, I think my students all have late, late spring fever. One of the boys, a jock who's taking summer classes so he can graduate next year, fell asleep during a quiz this morning—"

They ate in the dining room as they always did when Jessica came. Christy had set the table before she'd left for work, and the crystal and silver gleamed; the tablecloth was immaculate, although wrinkled, because she hadn't had time to press it. But she had found time to pick a few early roses for a centerpiece.

Although the amenities had been for Jessica, she had to admit that there was something comforting in going through the motions of normal living. It didn't ease the pain, but it did give the illusion of normalcy—and that was all she had these days. Illusions—and hope.

Jessica, too, was making an effort. She praised the goulash more than it deserved and declared the wine superior, although it was an ordinary California mountain Burgundy. She even asked Miles questions about his work as if she really were interested.

Again, Christy felt a stirring of pride. *The Ames women are tough*, she thought. Then: *How much more toughness are we going to need in the future?*

Her appetite left her suddenly, and she found it hard to force down the remainder of the food on her plate. After dinner, Miles started to help her clear the table and even Jessica offered her services, but Christy sent them both off to the living room to watch the news on TV.

She lingered over the dishes, wanting to work her way through the sudden cloud of depression. By the time she joined Jessica and Miles, the news was over and they were deeply engrossed in a game of cribbage. For a while she watched, then picked up a book and tried to lose herself in it. She didn't succeed, but it helped. At least the book formed a shield that she could hide behind while she fought against the crushing fear, the ugly images that seemed to hang over her like a malignant cloud.

At eleven o'clock they watched the news again; then Jessica, pleading fatigue, went off to the guest room, leaving the two of them alone.

For a while, they sat drinking coffee and watching Johnny Carson. There was no reason to go to bed early. Tomorrow was Saturday—they could sleep as late as they wanted and Christy knew that Miles would want to make love when they went upstairs.

Well, she was willing. Not eager, but willing. Not since the night when she'd discovered that she was in love with Miles had she again been able to completely lose herself in sex. She wanted it to happen, wanted the blessed forgetfulness, but somehow it had eluded her.

Well, at least she was willing again, able to take comfort in the physical closeness between them. And Miles didn't seem to notice that it wasn't the same. For this, she was grateful. Maybe it was enough just to love Miles, to know he loved her. Someday, when this terrible time in their lives was just a memory, she would once more be a totally responsive woman, but like her eating, lovemaking had become a mechanical thing, useful for easing tension rather than something joyous and uninhibited and all-consuming.

When they went up to their room, she was the one who instigated their lovemaking, knowing it would please—and reassure—Miles. Although her body found release, the act of love couldn't seem to reach her heart, but she drew satisfaction from knowing that she'd given pleasure to Miles. Afterward, when he kissed her the special way that said he was grateful, that he loved her, she kissed him back, and he went to sleep with his arms around her.

Christy lay awake as she did every night now unless she took a sleeping pill, staring into the dark, her ears straining, waiting for the phone to ring, knowing that even if she slept, she would awaken just before dawn—that terrible time that her mother called the "wolf hour" when all the demons of the mind were abroad and every possibility, no matter how horrible, had substance.

She finally fell asleep, and it was the doorbell, not the phone, that awakened her. Someone was holding a finger on the button, not letting up for a moment, and the sound shrilled along her nerves, setting them jangling.

Groggily, she reached out to awaken Miles, only to find that he was already sitting up in bed. He snapped on the lamp then began pulling on his robe, but he didn't speak. She took in his gray face, the anxiety in his eyes, and her own heart clamored in her ears.

Oh, God, it's bad news!

By the time she had put on her own robe, Miles was hurrying out the door. Christy followed him—along the hall, down the stairs. Both of them had forgotten Jessica, who slept with earplugs and an eye mask; it would be a while before they remembered she was sleeping in the guest room and went to awaken her.

Miles paused for a split-second before he flung open the front door, and she wondered in some deep recess of her mind if he was preparing himself for bad news. When she saw that no one was there, Christy felt a quick anger, thinking that someone was playing another trick on them.

Then, in the moonlight, she saw a pale oval, and she realized it was a face—a small, anxious face. She knew then that Tad had come home, and even in the midst of her joy, a small section of her mind wondered what on earth he was wearing that would cover him in black from neck to foot.

For a moment, Tad stood there staring at them, as if he wasn't sure of his welcome, and then he was in Christy's arms, and she was rocking him back and forth. Miles put his arms around the two of them, and whether Christy laughed or cried or did both during those first delirious moments, she never could remember afterward. All that mattered was that Tad was safe, that he'd finally found his way home.

Then Tad was pulling away, talking excitedly, pointing toward the driveway. For the first time, she noticed a car, standing with its doors open, the glow from its domelight streaming out across the front lawn.

"Poppa's hurt—the man says he needs help getting him out of the car. I wanted to go to a hospital, but Poppa said no, that he'd made himself a promise to bring me back to you, Mom. But there's something wrong with his arm—a bullet hit him. There's blood all over his wet suit."

He must have seen her face change because he shook his head. "No, he didn't do it. Honest, he didn't! It was Grandfather Neville—Poppa got me off the island, but then the guards followed us in another motor boat and one of them shot him. He passed out and I steered our boat onto the sand near some fishermen who had a bonfire. Then Poppa came to and he asked one of the men to drive us home—but he's passed out again, I think. Or at least he's got his eyes closed."

Christy pushed angry suspicions to the back of her mind and followed Tad and Miles to the car. A middle-aged man wearing a plaid windbreaker and rubber boots was standing beside the open door, looking into the back seat.

"He's lost a lot of blood," he said. "I wanted to take him to a hospital, but he kept saying he had to get the kid home. I don't know what this is all about, but—"

"We'll take over from here," Miles broke in. "If you'll help me get him into the house, I'll call one of our neighbors who's a doctor."

Christy gasped aloud when she saw Lance. His face had a yellowish, waxy look, and she was sure that he was unconscious—until he opened his eyes and gave her a wan version of his usual smile.

"I promised Tad I'd bring him home to you, Christy-girl," he said, then closed his eyes again.

The two men carried Lance into the house and upstairs to the cot they kept in the sewing room while Christy went to awaken Jessica. Her mother, when she realized Tad was safe, had a rare—and brief—attack of hysterics and then helped Christy put Tad to bed. He fell asleep almost the moment his head touched the pillow, but even in his sleep he held onto Christy's hand as if he were afraid someone would take him away again.

When she finally went out into the hall, the middle-aged man was still waiting there. Looking embarrassed, he mumbled something about Lance's promising him a hundred dollars for the use of his car. Without hesitation, Christy emptied out her wallet and Miles's, then thanked him for his trouble and told him that if he had to get his car upholstery cleaned to send her the bill.

She returned to the sewing room to find that Dr. Moore, the neighbor Miles had summoned, had already put a bandage on Lance's arm. He stood up and beckoned to Miles and Christy to follow him out into the hall.

"The—whatever it was that punctured his arm went through the flesh, missing the bone," he told them. "I've cleaned the wound out and given him antibiotics—I'll leave you some pain pills to give him so he can get some sleep tonight. His other shoulder is badly bruised, but I'm sure the bone isn't broken. He'll be sore as hell for a while, but a couple of days in bed and he'll be okay. I'll check in on him tomorrow."

"Then you don't think we have to take him to a hospital, Dr. Moore?" Christy asked.

"There isn't anything more they can do for him. And if you do, he'll have to account for—for whatever it was that caused that wound in his arm. He tells me that he fell on an iron spike while climbing over a fence, and as far as I'm concerned, he's telling the truth. You've been through so much—well, it's up to you, of course."

Christy nodded her understanding of the doctor's not-so-subtle message. There had been enough publicity; if Lance had helped his son escape from his grandfather's estate, and if she wanted to let sleeping dogs lie—he was giving her an out.

"If you're sure he won't be in any danger, we'll skip the hospital," Miles said, and she knew that he, too, had caught their neighbor's message.

"A good rest is what he needs." Dr. Moore's face relaxed into a smile as he looked at Christy, and she remembered that his wife had been one of the people who had called often during the past month. "Glad you got your son back, folks. I know it's been hell—but thank God it turned out okay."

"Thank God," Christy echoed.

She returned to Tad's room, leaving Miles to show their neighbor out. Then, for a long time, she stood in the doorway to the sewing room, watching Lance. He was lying on his back, his bandaged arm propped up on a pillow, his eyes closed, and for a man who had been through so much, he looked indecently cheerful—and, she was sure, very pleased with himself.

Lancelot Winthrop, super-hero. . . .

But there was no sting in the thought. Lance had brought Tad home, and now something had happened to all the hate that had been stored up inside her. As if the past few minutes had been a purge, the bitterness was gone, and all she felt was gratitude. Impulsively, she walked over to the bed and bent to kiss his cheek. "Thank you for bringing Tad home," she said softly.

Lance grinned up at her, but something—a sizing up? a calculation?—was stirring in the blue depths of his eyes now. What was the true story behind his heroics? Obviously, something had piqued his conscience enough for him to risk so much to bring Tad home. Had Tad, his son, gotten through to him? But Lance was Lance. It wouldn't last. Inevitably he would go back to his old ways—and why was she so indifferent to whatever scheme was being concocted in his devious mind right now?

I don't care what he does from now on. He can reform or go to hell—but I hope he does it somewhere else, preferably in Europe, with an ocean between us.

There was a sound behind her. When she turned, she saw Miles standing in the doorway. His face was pale and his eyes—she had never seen so much anger in Miles's eyes before. He came across the room and put a possessive arm around her as he glared down at Lance.

"This isn't going any further," he said coldly. "You're no good for Christy, Winthrop. She's mine now—you've forfeited all right to her. We're grateful for what you've done—but don't get any ideas about moving in on her again."

Christy didn't know whether to laugh or cry. Miles had seen her kiss Lance and he was jealous—and it was all so ridiculous! And yet—and yet, it was rather nice, too, come to think of it—not that she intended to let it go any further.

She opened her mouth to tell Miles that the kiss had been prompted by gratitude, but Lance beat her to it. "Hey, fellow—you should know your own wife better than that! She wouldn't have me on a gold platter."

Miles looked at her. "Is that how it is, Christy?"

"That's how it is." But she said it absently, because an idea, a realization, was growing in her mind.

"You were right about one thing, Miles," she added, forgetting they had an audience. "Lance *was* the spoiler in our marriage. It was my hate for him, my bitterness, that was coming between us, making me doubt my own judgment. When I married you, I kept telling myself that what I felt was something else—sex, affection, a need for stability, everything except what it really was. And even after I finally realized that I was in love with you, something held me back. I was afraid to let go, afraid of making another mistake. But that's all over now. I don't hate Lance anymore—and that makes all the difference.''

Miles was silent, staring into her eyes as if there was something there he'd never hoped to see.

''You'd better kiss her before I get up and do it for you,'' Lance said.

Miles did just that—a long kiss that put everything right in Christy's world, a promise of what was to come—and this time, she knew, she would be more than willing.

She realized Lance was watching them, his smile a little crooked.

''What will you do now, Lance?'' she said. ''Neville will be furious with you for upsetting his plans.''

''Oh, I have a few plans of my own. While you're still in a grateful mood, you might consider doing me a favor.''

''A favor?''

''I know your first instinct is to call the police and file kidnapping charges against Neville, but—well, if you don't want a big legal hassle and a lot of publicity, why don't you let it drop? You might also consider letting the old man give the kid a few gadgets now and then—provided he agrees to abide by your terms.''

Christy opened her mouth to reject his suggestion, but Miles laid his hand on her arm, stopping her.

''And what do you expect to get out of all this?'' Miles asked.

''Would you believe it's because I feel a little sorry for the old boy?''

''No,'' Christy said bluntly. ''But maybe you think you can convince Neville that you talked us into a few concessions?''

Lance grinned up at her. ''Would I do that?''

''You would.'' Christy discovered that she wasn't angry. Lance was the product of his background, his upbringing.

And in spite of that, he had come through for his son—and for her.

"If we let Neville into Tad's life," she said, "there's always the danger that he might be influenced by the material things his grandfather can offer him. Neville's kind of wealth can be very seductive—as you know so well."

"The kid's got more sense than I had at his age. He saw right through the old man. After all, he turned his back on all that booty and returned home the first chance he got, didn't he?"

Although his eyes were guileless, Christy, who knew him so well, stared at him with suspicion. He gave her one of his incongruously sweet smiles, and she shrugged. She knew her son—and the truth probably wasn't as simple as Lance wanted her to believe. But the fact that he would lie about it softened her—or maybe he really was telling the truth and she had a too-suspicious nature.

She glanced at Miles and found him watching Lance as if he were some strange sea creature who had just washed up on the shore.

"What do you think, Miles?" she asked.

"Let's play it by ear. If we don't press charges, Winthrop may have enough sense to stay away, which would solve that problem. And I don't think Tad would be corrupted if he saw his father once in a while—provided he wants to."

A strange expression crossed Lance's face. "You'd agree to that?"

"Why not? You earned the right tonight."

The two men locked stares, assessing each other, and Christy knew they had forgotten her for the moment. When Lance nodded slowly, she let her breath out in a long sigh. Did she really want Tad to see Lance again? What about his eventual disillusionment—or maybe her son was wiser than she had once been. Maybe he wouldn't be hurt when Lance disappointed him, which he inevitably would.

"I won't make a pest out of myself, but—yeah, I'd like to see Tad from time to time," Lance said.

"What will you do now?" Christy asked.

"Oh, I have a scheme up my sleeve. The old man thinks Tad is his last hope to be a grandfather, but I might have a surprise for him there." He looked so pleased with himself that she had to smile.

"You really are a—"

"Opportunist?"

"*Rat* was the word that came to mind."

"Yeah. Well, I majored in business at Harvard, not scruples. And I'm not my father's boy for nothing. And no apologies for that."

For a moment, he was silent and when he spoke again, his voice had lost its tinge of irony. "You did a good job with the kid. He's going to be okay, provided you sit on him now and then. He's got a lot of me in him—and a lot of Neville, too."

"Miles can handle it," she said with confidence.

"And you. You're a strong woman. I hope this business didn't cost you too much. I didn't tell Tad the whole truth—or at least, I shaded it a little as I am wont to do. I did go to the island to talk Neville into returning Tad, but when the old man waved a carrot in the form of a fat lifetime annuity in my face, I went over to the enemy without a whimper until—"

"Until what?"

He shrugged, looking glum. "Maybe I've got a streak of self-destruction in me."

"Or maybe Tad got under your skin?"

"Something like that—but a lot more complicated. Could be I just couldn't resist the opportunity to pay Neville back for some things he's done to me in the past. Sort of my way of thumbing my nose at the old bastard.''

''Well, whatever the reason, you brought Tad back to us.'' A thought came to her. ''What if Neville hasn't given up? How can we protect Tad from the same thing happening again?''

''I don't think you have to worry. Neville knows now that there's not a chance in the world that Tad would cooperate.''

''Tad would never turn his back on us, no matter what Neville offered him,'' she said, and, despite herself, it sounded like a question.

Again, Lance smiled at her. ''Your motherly instincts are right. Tad didn't believe Neville's lies about you for a single minute.''

Satisfied, Christy turned to Miles. ''I think we'd better let Lance get some rest now,'' she said.

Miles put his arm around her shoulders to lead her from the room, to their own bedroom, to the small private world that sustained her, nurtured her. At the door, she looked back at the man who had treated her so cruelly—and to whom she owed everything good that had come into her life. ''Thank you, Lance,'' she said, and there was the ring of sincerity in her voice.

Epilogue

It had been Jessica's idea to have the picnic; that was the first surprise. The second was when she offered to bring the potato salad.

"You've got enough to do without all that extra work," she'd said, and then she'd added that she just might try that elegant crab-and-potato recipe one of her friends had given her.

"I'm a little doubtful about the crab part," Christy confessed to Miles. She was putting the last touches on the picnic lunch, and Miles was helping, peeling hard-boiled eggs. "I don't think she really understands about botulism. But I figured I'd better keep my reservations to myself. A month ago it wouldn't have occurred to Jessica to make the offer."

"Well, she's mellowing out," Miles said. "She actually complimented me on the job I was doing with her grandson. Who knows? In time, she may even mellow out enough to stop giving you advice.''

"That'll be the day," Christy said. "I guess we're all mellowing out. Would you believe that I actually let Tad talk me into an advance on his allowance so he could treat that rich friend of his to the water slide yesterday afternoon? Seems Cappy's father is stingy about allowances, and Cappy was flat broke.''

"And would you believe that he hit me, too—and that I fell for that same sad story?''

They looked at each other and began laughing. Somewhere along the line, Christy's laugh changed into a sob and then she was clinging to Miles, wiping her wet face against his sports shirt.

"Oh, Miles, I'm so grateful! I'm so very, very grateful that we have him back. But I just can't help thinking of all the people who aren't so lucky, who are still waiting, maybe for the rest of their lives.''

"Uh-huh. And knowing you, you're probably thinking about doing something about it. I caught the tail end of that conversation you had on the phone this morning with the Dubois woman—what exactly was it that you said you'd be glad to do?''

"Just help a little with the information bulletins for the parents of missing children's group,'' she confessed. "I do have access to a Xerox machine at work—it only means two or three hours a week. And if it helps one couple find their child—''

"Good for you. I may volunteer to help out myself. Maybe they could use someone who's got a way with words—''

"Who's got a way with words?'' It was Jessica. She came into the kitchen, not seeming to notice their stunned silence. She was wearing jeans, obviously new, a T-shirt, and a huge Mexican straw hat, and she looked cross and hot and thoroughly out of sorts.

Christy was afraid to look at Miles. If the bastard laughed, she would lose control and then they'd both be in trouble. But no, he looked properly sober, just as if he saw Jessica in jeans and a T-shirt that said A-NUMBER-ONE GRANNY every day of his life. He kissed his mother-in-law's powdered cheek, took the covered dish out of her hands, and set it on the table.

"It looks like one of those 'that'll be the day' days," he murmured to Christy as he passed her on his way back to the sink and his hard-boiled eggs.

Unable to resist, Christy uncovered the dish and regarded its contents curiously. Although the lumpy concoction inside must have started out as potatoes, it could have been anything now—anything with tiny streaks of pink in it.

"It looks delicious," she said before she replaced the cover and carefully tucked the dish in the refrigerator behind a row of milk cartons. With luck, everybody would forget it was there until they reached the picnic grounds and began unpacking the food.

"Delicious," Miles echoed, his voice hollow.

"Well, it does *taste* all right," Jessica said a little defensively. "But it doesn't look like what Elaine served at her bridge luncheon. I wonder if she left one of the ingredients out? It would be just like her." She nibbled on a piece of celery, her eyes pensive. "I do hope there aren't any ants where we're going. And caterpillars. I hate the loathsome things."

"No ants. No caterpillars. It's a promise," Miles assured her.

"Well . . . of course, I realize a person has to be a good sport about inconveniences on a picnic."

"And you are that, Jessica," Miles said promptly.

"I try to be. God knows these past few weeks have been—difficult. I don't know what Christy and I would've done without you, Miles." She hesitated, then added hurriedly, "I know I haven't always appreciated you in the past, but it wasn't personal. It was just that—well, I was so concerned about Christy and Tad's future. About their security, you understand. Christy has always been such a—a thoroughbred, and she deserves the best. And, of course, Tad is just like her. An Ames, through and through. Good breeding always shows, you know."

"I wonder why I feel I should whinny just about now," Christy said, giggling.

"Well, it's good you can still joke," Jessica said. "When I think of what that horrible man put us through—I still think you should've had him arrested. To let him off scot-free was just too good for him. Not that I didn't have my say when I was interviewed by that newspaper reporter," she added with obvious satisfaction.

"Oh, you did that, Jessica." Miles exchanged glances with Christy. "I'm sure Neville's ears must still be burning."

"Well, he deserved it. And it was only fair that he reimburse you two for the money you spent on detective fees. You should have taken that settlement he offered—it was just conscience money, you know."

"We don't need his money. Just as long as he leaves us alone in the future." Christy discovered her nerves were tightening, and she added quickly, "Where are the boys? It's time we got started."

As if her words were a signal, there was a clatter of feet at the door, and Tad, followed by his shadow, Cappy, came bustling into the kitchen. Cappy was several inches taller than Tad; he had carrot-red hair and a cocky smile as he surveyed the kitchen with interested eyes.

"When are we leaving?" Tad said. "Cappy's getting hungry—"

"Oh, he is, is he? Then I'll just give Cappy something to chew on to keep him from starving to death." Christy handed Tad's friend an apple from the picnic basket.

"Hey, don't I get one, too?" Tad said.

"Oh? I didn't realize you were hungry. I thought it was only Cappy."

"Aw, Mom—" Tad said.

"Man, she's got your number, Tadpole," Cappy snickered.

"Don't call me Tadpole," Tad said, but he grinned sheepishly and caught the apple Christy tossed him. "Can we take something to the car?"

"You may indeed," Miles said. "Those thermos bottles go—and those blankets, too."

"And don't forget the insect spray," Jessica said. "And suntan oil—you know how delicate my skin is."

Privately, Christy doubted that even one ray of sun could penetrate the shade under Jessica's enormous hat, but she nodded and went upstairs to get the spray and suntan oil from the bathroom. By the time she had returned, the kitchen was empty except for Miles, who was gathering up the last of the folding chairs.

"Don't worry," he said sotto voce. "She didn't remember the crab-and-potato salad."

Christy giggled. "It looks to be one hell of a day," she said.

Miles put his arms around her. "They all are, Christy. They all are."

She leaned against him, liking the feel of his wiry body, the uniqueness that was Miles. "We're two lucky people," he added. "How did we get so damned lucky, Christy?"

"Good breeding always shows, you know. I'm not sure about you, but—" She gave a nonchalant shrug.

He gave her a slap on the rear. "And you, my friend, are getting to be a regular little cut-up. You're mellowing out—just like your Mom."

"I don't take things quite so seriously," she conceded. "When you've been through the storm—well, how can you ever take little irritants seriously again?"

"Been through the storm—and weathered it like the thoroughbred your mother says you are," he said huskily. "God, you don't know how it feels, having my Christy back again. I missed you—almost as much as I missed Tad."

"And it's even better now, isn't it?" She met his eyes, and what she saw there made her blush.

"If you don't stop looking at me like that, the picnic is really going to get off to a late start," he said, nuzzling her throat.

She pushed him away. "Shoo! Go pack the car. It'll take an engineer to get everybody and all our gear into the Pinto. I notice Jessica didn't volunteer her Chrysler."

"What—and have an ant crawl on it? Never!"

Christy laughed, gave him another push, and then went to check the doors and windows. She was passing the phone, on her way through the kitchen, when it rang. She hesitated, tempted not to answer it. There had been so many calls in the two weeks since Tad's return—reporters and well-wishers, friends and neighbors—and some conspicuous by their absence.

Miles had explained that—about how those people were probably ashamed of having lost faith or something. But in her heart, there was a small cold spot that she doubted would ever thaw completely. Still—she had learned something about the goodness of people, too. She wasn't going to let a few rotten apples spoil that.

The phone rang again, and with a sigh, she picked it up and said a noncommittal "Yes?" into the mouthpiece.

"Christy of the cool, unrevealing voice. You're the one constant in an inconstant world, aren't you?" an amused—and familiar—voice said.

"And so are you, Lance," she said evenly. "If you changed, it would be the millennium for sure."

"Oh, but you're wrong there. I'm a reformed character. Would you believe that I'm back in the old man's graces?"

"I never doubted that you'd find a way. What did you do?"

"I'm just a repentant young man who sees the error of his ways and wants to be a big tycoon like Daddy. It was the love of a good son that turned me around. Right now I'm working as a slavey in one of the august offices of Neville's banking firm." He paused, then added thoughtfully, "Of course, I don't know how long I can hack it. In a couple of months, it'll be ski time in Aspen. You know my weaknesses—cold snow and hot women."

"How did you manage it? What lies did you tell Neville to get off the hook?"

"Would I lie to him?"

"You would. I'm sure you did."

"Oh, you cut me to the quick—but you're right, of course. I told him that I was in good with you since I'd let Tad talk me into taking him home. He figures that in time I might still swing some kind of compromise so he can see Tad from time to time—and get his chance to corrupt the kid with all his goodies—or, as Neville calls them, his carrots."

"That will never happen, Lance," she warned.

"*You* know it and *I* know it, but Neville doesn't. He lives by the premise that every man—and woman—has his price. Well, I'm a gambler. I'm gambling that I can string him along until he finally passes on into that great corporation in the sky."

"You really are a bastard, Lance."

"I know," he said cheerfully. "But aside from that, I'm really not a bad sort."

"Yes, you are," she said, "You're bad." But despite herself there was a hint of laughter in her voice.

Lance must have caught it, because he said coaxingly, "And you aren't going to get stuffy about me seeing the kid sometimes? Like I said, I won't make a pest out of myself."

She hesitated, then told him, "We're still thinking about it."

"Trust the kid, Christy." Lance's voice was suddenly serious. "He's got a lot of you in him—he won't be seduced by me any more than he was by Neville's promises."

"You don't have to cover up for him, Lance. I know he bought his grandfather's lies about Miles and me. He told me all about it."

"He did, huh? Well, that proves my point. He's more you than me. Now, I never admit anything. You can't get hanged for what you don't admit."

"Uh-huh. Well, I'd like to chat with you, but we're going on a picnic, and everybody is waiting for me in the car."

"Too bad. I was hoping to talk to Miles."

"Miles? Why would you want to do that?"

"Hey, I like the guy. A little stuffy—but an okay fellow."

"Uh-huh. Well, he's busy. And so am I—so good-bye, Lance."

"Okay—see you around."

After she hung up, she stood there for a while, thinking about the conversation. Lance was up to something, and she was sure she knew what it was. He hadn't given up hope of bringing about some kind of compromise from which he would reap the reward. And since she was proving difficult, he intended to work on Miles.

So why wasn't she angry? And why the devil was she

smiling? Lance was the same bastard he'd always been. He hadn't changed—but she had. The hate was gone—and with it had gone her distrust of men, even of Tad. In the future she would be easier on him, a more relaxed mother—

"You ready to go, Christy?" Miles was standing in the doorway, looking impatient.

She turned to smile at him. "I'm on my way. And it's about time, too. I've wasted enough time already."

About the Author

Irma Walker, the daughter of a professional musician, was born in Cincinnati, Ohio. After she married her childhood sweetheart, George St. Clair Walker, an Air Force careerman, they lived in fourteen states, including Hawaii, and have traveled extensively in the Far East. Their only child, Sharon, was born in the Philippines. Miss Walker often draws on her travels and her experiences as an Air Force wife for background for her novels.

Irma Walker was first published in 1964. Her nineteen books to date range from mysteries and romantic suspense to contemporary novels such as HER DECISION (which was excerpted in GOOD HOUSEKEEPING) and THE NEXT STEP. Miss Walker now lives with her husband in Petaluma, near Northern California's redwood empire and wine country. Their daughter is married, and they have a grandson.

Ballantine brings you more...
Romantic Novels for Today from,

LOVE & LIFE